MW00635438

THE SECRETS WE KEEP

NIKKI LEE TAYLOR

Magpie Creative Media

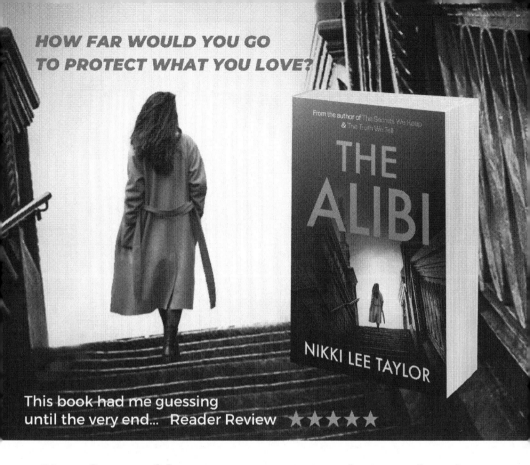

How far would you go to protect what you love?

He's handsome, charming, and the city's beloved Mayor. He's also a cheating husband. But is he a killer?

When a surfer discovers the gruesome remains of council staffer Lauren Ellis in sand dunes just meters from Lord Mayor Andrew Ashley's beach-side home, rumours of his close relationship with the victim quickly begin to circulate.

Andrew's secret affair with local newspaper reporter Elle Nolan is proof he can be an unfaithful husband – but is he also guilty of murder?

As the search for answers continues, Andrew refuses to tell police where he was the night of Lauren's death.

When Andrew reaches out to Elle from police lock-up begging her to provide an alibi for the night in question, she quickly realises that instead of just reporting the story, she's about to become irrevocably entangled in it.

A thought-provoking and page-turning thriller from the author of domestic thriller series The Secrets We Keep and The Truth We Tell that will make you question – how far would I go to save what I love?

Get your FREE BOOK at nikkileetaylor.com

Published by Magpie Creative Media

ISBN: 978-0-6484406-1-1

nikkileetaylor.com.au

What Readers Are Saying

"If you want to add this to your To Be Read List, you certainly can because this nail-biting thriller gets you and at the same time makes you emotional. There is a beautiful pain this book leaves behind, and I certainly couldn't figure out the cover till the end and that is also something that I was not expecting... NOT AT ALL."

★ ★ ★ ★ ★

"This is one intense, twisted, addictive, complex, jaw-dropping novel! Not only is this a very well-written book with wonderfully interesting characters, but the suspense builds at just the right pace as the story unfolds."

★ ★ ★ ★ ★

"This novel had quite a few twists and turns and the twists are so juicy that I couldn't stop reading."

★ ★ ★ ★ ★

"The book touches on so many sources of pain addressing each with intelligence, empathy, and humanity. It is a true thriller in women's fiction."

★ ★ ★ ★ ★

'The Secrets We Keep was by far the best book I have read this year. Many twists and turns throughout kept me looking forward to my reading time each day. The ending was fantastic."

★ ★ ★ ★ ★

"The suspense never ends and parts of this book rip your heart right out of your chest. It is so hard to read through the tears but you have to because this book grabs you and pulls you in!! That quality is rare in a book!"

★ ★ ★ ★ ★

"I loved this book so much!! The depths of the twists in here will leave you speechless. It's a huge work of great storytelling."

★ ★ ★ ★ ★

THE SECRETS WE KEEP

BOOK ONE

For my mother Glennis Craig, who has spent every day teaching me what a mother's love should feel like...

Foreword

According to research, in Australia 18 per cent of women and 4.7 per cent of men report having suffered sexual abuse before the age of 15. International analysis suggests the rates are even higher, reaching 19.7 per cent for girls and 7.9 per cent for boys. Even more alarming is a survey carried out in 2016 by the Australian Bureau of Statistics which reported only 10 – 15 per cent of Australian cases included a stranger as the perpetrator. These are horrific statistics.

While this kind of abuse is not a major theme of The Secrets We Keep, it does play a role in highlighting the importance of shining a light on child abuse.

All characters and events are fictional in The Secrets We Keep, and as the author I have paid careful mind to tackle this subject with the most delicate of care and consideration. There are no graphic abuse scenes in this book, however I do hope the references make you, as the reader, uncomfortable enough to realise this is an ongoing problem and one that should not remain behind closed doors.

While ever we shy away from things that make us uncomfortable, evil will continue to find its way through the cracks. We must be brave, and we must be vigilant, and most of all, we must always stand up for those in need of a plain-clothed hero.

If this book raises issues for you, please contact your nearest mental health provider. **In Australia call Beyond Blue on 1300 223 636 or Lifeline on 13 11 14.**

Preface

When something breaks, when it shatters, sharp edges are always left behind. That's how it was with me. I saw myself as a broken window, fraught with shards sharp enough to make the hardest of hearts bleed. I cut people, not because I meant to but because I was broken.

It had been that way for as long as I could remember. Only pieces existed. Pieces that whispered and pieces that shouted. Pieces that sought solace and pieces that screamed bloody murder. Pieces that ached, pieces that longed, and pieces that drifted on the breeze, quiet and gentle like ghosts in the dark.

People had tried to repair me. They wanted to round out my razor-sharp edges, but it never really worked. I was angry. I was hurt. I was a person without hope. I lived in the dark, surrounded by invisible walls too high to climb.

As a mother, I always saw myself as wanting. I never could figure out how things went so wrong. All I could do was live with the outcome, the fallout of my failures.

On the day it happened I hadn't seen it coming. I had no idea that what started out as a simple conversation would end the way it did, with a secret so dangerous it threatened to destroy us all.

Chapter One

SOPHIE

The blinds are drawn because I need them to be. There are days the light is welcome, but not today. Today, I need the darkness. It's the best way I know to pull them in close, here in the dark in the empty spaces where they no longer exist and yet still take up every particle of air.

My life. My love. My family. James and Josh. My husband and son, stolen while I was sleeping, peacefully unaware at that very moment the entire world was shattering around me.

It's the small things that hurt the most. An unexpected letter with his name on it. A television commercial for Linvilla Orchards – where we picked peaches every July, just the two of us at first and then with Josh. His familiar scent trailing behind a stranger, its ghostly arms wrapping around my lungs and squeezing. And worst of all, the sudden ring of a child's laughter breaking the silence and tearing my heart into a thousand tiny pieces.

I stroke the fur on Miss Molly's golden head and close my eyes. "I'm sorry," I whisper, even though dogs don't understand apologies. "It's this day, it's…"

I let the words trail off, unable to say out loud that five years ago my husband and son took their last breath trapped in a car wreck and I hadn't been there. Unable to say that while they were dying, I lay peacefully in bed, useless and selfish, taking an afternoon nap. It hadn't even woken me. I hadn't sat up, my instincts kicking into overdrive. I hadn't experienced so much as a bad dream.

At the time friends told me I should try to forgive myself, that it wasn't my fault. They brought soup and sent messages. They held me and promised things would get better. They stood on my stoop and reminded me, *"There's nothing you could have done."*

Therapists call my depression and anxiety a form of post-traumatic stress disorder. Survivor's guilt they say, although that's not the official term. Apparently, it's natural for parents who outlive their children to experience a sense of guilt, but I have struggled to believe there is anything natural about it. Could there be anything more unnatural than for a mother to bury her six-year-old son?

Then there were the people who told me to have faith. I've never been a religious person, but I have stood alone on a rainy afternoon and heard the hollow thump of dirt shoveled onto a tiny white casket. I've heard the mournful cry of a loon as people, not knowing what else to say, turned and made the sad walk back to their cars. I have stood as day turned to night staring at two holes in the ground hoping my husband and son wouldn't be cold on the first night away from their beds. Away from me.

Having faith would mean believing James and Josh were taken for a reason, that there was some divinity to their absence. But there is not. There is only pain and empty spaces.

I get up from the couch and pull the curtains further across but no matter how dark I make the room there are always slivers of light that keep me in the place I don't want to be. Slivers that never let me bury the one question I still have no answer for.

How do I ever find the strength to step into the light when they are forever lost in the dark?

Chapter Two

MADELYN-MAY

Thirty floors below, people are scattered across Washington Square Park like colorful confetti. They're gathered around the fountain, its splashing water hypnotizing them away to some place they'd rather be. How many of them know the leafy space was once a Potter's Field? That right under their noses lie thousands of discarded bodies, the remains of soldiers from the American Revolution, victims of yellow fever, slaves and criminals, all scattered across the park, their secrets buried along with them.

"Madelyn May?"

"What is it, Sarah?" I ask without turning around, my mind still buried in the past.

"I have a candidate for the video producer role. You'll like her."

I roll my eyes. "I'll *like* her?"

"Yes," Sarah nods. "She's a mom herself and -"

"No. No mothers." I turn in time to catch Sarah swallowing hard. Her forehead is creased and confusion rests heavy on her brow. She's been my assistant for three months and I can already tell she isn't going to work out. She's emotional, soft, and tries too hard. "You signed a confidentiality clause when you started here," I remind her, slipping my feet back into new-season Guccis, "so I will explain this to you once and once only. I do not hire mothers. Is that clear?"

"Yes, Madelyn-May. I understand."

"But do you?"

Sarah is stuck. From the strained look on her face, it's clear she has no idea what I'm trying to tell her or what the correct response might be. She is a people pleaser. I knew that when I hired her, but I'm still not sure if she is smart enough to please me.

"Our key messaging, my brand, is based around the notion that here at *Love, Mommy* we love mommies more than anything else in the world. And we do, Sarah, we love mommies. Do you know why we love mommies so much?"

"Sure," she nods, "they're just like you."

I grin at her attempt to placate me. "No, Sarah, we love mommies because they are our core customer. They are who make this business, my business, a success."

"Of course," she nods, her eyes dropping. "My mistake."

"There are two kinds of mothers out there, Sarah. The ones who are thoughtful and loving and will do anything for their families and the mothers who are weak, confused, and in desperate need of direction. Our content caters to both types of women, but neither can work here because either their priorities are elsewhere or they won't handle the pressure. Do you see?"

"I do, Madelyn-May."

"I personally create the core content base for our subscribers, our evangelists. Outside of that, I need smart, hard-working, loyal staff, who want this company to succeed as much as I do. I saw that in you, Sarah, so don't let me down. I don't have time to replace you right now. Not with everything that's going on."

As she turns and scurries out of my office, I glance back to the email message filling my screen.

How long can you hide the truth?

I found it in my inbox this morning amid a scrolling list of messages about blog content, speaking tours, and social media. The sender's name was unfamiliar, and the subject line was empty.

Over the years there have been hundreds of nasty emails and letters from women who either didn't agree with something I wrote, were jealous of my success, or were just plain crazy. But this one is different. There's something sinister about its simplicity, something that makes the hair on the back of my neck stand up.

I press the intercom on my desk. "Sarah, get IT on the line for me please."

After a brief conversation with a techie named Brad, it's clear the best they can do is provide a location the email was sent from. It's not what I wanted but it might be enough to determine whether the email was sent from a crazy person - or worse.

I close my eyes and rub slow circles across my temples. Anything to calm my mind. Today is becoming one of the rare occasions I imagine leaving early, sneaking up the drive of our Chestnut Hill home, kicking off my shoes, and falling onto the cool crisp sheets of our California King. It's unusual for me to leave the office before six pm, but right now the stillness of an empty house with no rambling footsteps on the stairs feels pretty inviting.

"Madelyn-May…"

Sarah's voice cuts through the intercom and I leap in my seat. "Jesus Christ… Sarah, what is it?"

"It's Brad from IT again. Should I put him through?"

The phone buzzes and I scoop up the receiver. "Do you have more information?"

"The ISP of the computer shows the email was sent from a terminal at DigiMads but that's about all I can tell you."

"DigiMads?"

"Oh, my bad, Ma'am. It's a communal workspace down by Samson Street. Digital nomads and online influencers use the space for publishing online content to social media management platforms and travel blogs, stuff like that. It's like a community office full of hot desks if that makes more sense. My mate Jethro runs an online-"

"Did you say Samson Street? As in, here in Philly?"

"Yes, Ma'am."

I clear my throat. "You're telling me the email was sent from someone right here in Center City?"

"Yes, Ma'am."

"And you're certain?"

"As far as I can tell."

I fall back into my seat and tug at the stray ends of my hair; a nervous gesture I thought I trained myself out of fifteen years ago. "And there's no way it could have been re-routed or something?"

"I couldn't say for sure, but it doesn't look that way."

My eyes fall over the angry scar on my wrist. "There's absolutely no way in your opinion the email could have come from somewhere in say, California?"

I think back to the place I grew up and wonder if my own history can remain buried, silent and still like the bodies in the park below. Or if someone is about to go digging up the past.

"Not that I can see, Ma'am, no."

"Alright thank you. Oh, and Brad?"

"Yes, Ma'am?"

"This conversation didn't happen. Is that clear?"

"Course, Ma'am. I understand."

"Good. And for God's sake stop calling me Ma'am."

Chapter Three

SOPHIE

When the knocking fails to wake me, Miss Molly takes it upon herself to rouse me from a dream state I would like to have stayed in, preferably forever. Before I can even open my eyes, her wet nose is up against my cheek.

"Okay, I'm awake..."

More knocking, and another excited bark from Miss Molly.

"It bothers me how excited you get to see him," I scold her gently. "You know that, right?"

Unperturbed, Miss Molly runs in circles, her tail wagging so hard that her entire body becomes an obscure U-shape.

"You're going to hurt yourself," I grin. "Settle down."

With no time to find a brush, I pull my messy chestnut hair into a ponytail and consider leaving him out on the stoop while I clean my teeth. But he's seen me at my worst and sometimes it gets a lot uglier than this, so instead, I turn and follow Miss Molly downstairs. "I'm coming, hold on..."

By the time I get to the final step, Miss Molly is pawing at the door. "Now that's just embarrassing," I tell her with a smile. "Didn't anyone ever teach you about playing hard-to-get?"

I unbolt the latch and the rich aroma of coffee brings a smile to my face. "Almond milk mocha?"

He nods and as usual, I cave. "Alright, come inside."

Today his suit is royal blue accompanied by the same lavender tie he wore on my last day in the office. A day that feels like a million years ago. Bastian. My light in an otherwise darkened world.

Miss Molly throws herself at him. Her front feet reach his thighs and strands of her golden hair immediately attach to his perfect pant legs.

"Molly, get down," I tell her. "We've talked about this. Sorry..."

"Aww, it's alright, isn't it Miss Molly?" he smiles, playfully rubbing her head. "At least someone is happy to see me." He hands me the cup and strolls easily toward the kitchen window. "Your back lawn need doing yet?"

"Bastian..."

"What?" he shrugs. "I'm just asking. It's summer. Grass grows fast."

"I know, but I can do it myself."

"I can't remember the last time I even saw you go out there."

And there it is. That tone. That judgmental, sympathetic, degrading tone that screams *you're an unstable, incapable, good-for-nothing waste of space who can't mow her own grass.*

"Don't do that," I tell him. "I can mow my own lawn, and I sat out there yesterday if you must know."

He nods, knowing better than to challenge me. "Okay, I'll believe you. Come here..."

"Bastian..."

"Sophie, come here and stop being such a pain in the ass."

Knowing he'll win me over eventually, I shuffle toward him. My gray sweatpants hang loose and there is still sleep in my eyes. "Why do you come here and do this?"

"You know why." He gently tucks a wayward strand of hair behind my ear. "Tell me you know why."

I want to look away, to tear my eyes from his, but as usual, they pull me in. "Fine, I know why."

"Then let me help you."

I sigh, and gently trace the olive skin of his cheek. "Fine, you can mow my grass."

"I thought of you last night," he says. "Anniversaries must be hard on you."

I pull away, the moment between us instantly broken. Yesterday marked five years since the accident and another man mentioning anything to do with my husband and son still feels like a betrayal.

"Did you get through the night okay?" he tries again. "I'm just asking, Soph. It doesn't have to mean anything."

"I know, but it's hard for me. I still feel like..."

"...you're betraying him?"

I flop onto the couch and pull my knees to my chest. "It's like when I'm with you there's a part of me that's still in relationship mode. It helps to keep me in the emotional place I was with him. But at the same time, I feel so guilty letting anyone else in. It feels I'm like betraying him, but then I wonder, if I close that part of me off completely will it be like he was never here at all?"

"Sophie—"

"I know how it sounds, Bastian, and I don't expect you to listen to all my problems. I don't even know why you keep coming over to be honest."

"I hope that's not how you think I feel?"

I throw up my hands. "But surely it can't be worth it? I mean, look at me. I'm a mess. You can't be attracted to me. I'm ten pounds overweight because I only eat what can be delivered to my door. I haven't put on lipstick since, God, I don't know when, and most of the time my hair isn't even brushed. I cry half the time, I'm angry the rest, and in between—"

"And in between, you're still incredibly smart and beautiful, Soph," he says, "and you're doing your best. I'm not trying to be him – I need you to know that. For so many reasons, I would never do that."

Just outside the window, a tiny sparrow hops between the green leaves of a dogwood tree.

"And besides," he grins, sitting down beside me, "who said anything about coming to see you? The only reason I come over is to see Miss Molly. I thought you knew that?"

I manage something that almost sounds like a laugh. "Well, she likes seeing you that's for sure. But I feel like you're wasting your time with me, Bastian. I'm just... broken, or something."

"You're not. And besides, who am I to judge? We all have our issues, Sophie, Jesus." He runs a hand through his thick brown hair. "I'm hardly a great catch, but we found each other. That's what matters. Not every relationship has to have a label on it."

I take him in. Broad shoulders from his days playing full-back for the Tigers at Princeton. Slender, artistic fingers. Straight, determined nose. When we first met, he reminded me of a compass perpetually facing north. Unwavering and resilient. Then I came along. A magnetic field, misfiring and bound to pull him off course.

"Why are your eyes so blue, anyway?" I ask, changing the subject. "I thought all Italians had dark eyes?"

"Because, signora, my family is from Veneto in Northern Italy," he exclaims, mimicking an Italian accent and dramatically waving his hand. "My family comes from a small village outside Verona, home of the famed star-crossed lovers Romeo and Juliet."

"Oh God... why did I ask?"

He grins and pulls me into the dip beneath his shoulder. "But seriously, Soph, we should go there, just the two of us."

"That wouldn't go well."

"I mean it, Soph. There's Venice but there's also beautiful mountain ranges and medieval villages. It would do you good to get away."

"Bastian, I think it's time you went to work. You'll be late."

"It's not like the boss is going to fire me."

"Ever heard of leading by example?" I laugh. "Seriously, you should get going."

"Will you at least think about the trip?"

"No, that's ridiculous. First, I can barely make it to the market without having a full-blown panic attack. Second, I have Miss Molly. And third – well, let's not get started on third."

"Let me worry about third. I can make it work."

"No you can't, and if you did, you'd hate yourself. Now, thank you for the coffee and for checking in on me but you better get going."

He gets to his feet, his tall frame forcing me to stand on tippy toes to kiss him goodbye.

"I do appreciate the thought, though," I tell him. "Maybe in another life we could have wandered the streets of fair Verona holding hands and I would have loved that."

He nods and kisses me softly on the forehead. "Call if you need anything, alright?"

"I will."

"Promise?"

"Promise. Thanks again for the coffee."

He kisses me one last time on the cheek, and I know what's coming.

"I don't want to hassle you, Soph, but the Jackson manuscript is due today," he reminds me. "Think you'll get through editing it?"

"Yes, boss," I say with a grin.

"Don't call me that. You know I hate that."

"Well, technically..."

"Yeah, I know, but it's weird."

"Come back for dinner? Miss Molly said she'll order your favorite pizza. Quattro Stagioni from Napoli around the corner."

"I'd love to, Soph," he sighs, "but I can't tonight. Madelyn-May has some Women in Business event she's speaking at so I'm home with the kids."

"Of course," I nod, hating myself for having asked. "No problem."

"Sorry..."

"No need to be sorry. You're a great dad. You shouldn't have to apologize."

"I'm not apologizing for them, but for the Madelyn-May part." He drops his eyes and kicks at an invisible stone on the stoop. "She's just…"

"…your wife, Bastian. There's no need to apologize."

"I know, but still…"

"Miss Molly and I will be fine," I tell him. "And I'll email the manuscript through by two pm."

I close the door and when the sound of his footsteps disappear down the path, I turn and press my back against the wood. The situation is far from ideal, but somehow knowing we can never be together, that he can never fill the space James left behind, makes the guilt of needing him a little easier to bear.

After making toast and pulling on a clean sweater, I grab the manila folder that's been gathering dust on my desk and brace myself for what's to come. Even if I dedicate the entire day to working on the Jackson manuscript, I'll never get it done in time. At my feet, Miss Molly licks her lips and I slip her the last corner of toast. "You happy now? You've eaten my breakfast."

Content with her corner of jam-covered toast, Miss Molly pads over to the checkered dog bed beside my desk and flops down. A full day of editing someone else's work can get tiresome but at the same time, if it's good enough and the writer talented enough, it might transport me away from my own tear-jerking tale.

When the computer comes to life, I open the file marked 'Jackson Manuscript.' I'll make my notes and changes on this electronic version for the author to see, but I like to read the old-fashioned way - holding paper in my hands. Bastian makes fun of it, calling me prehistoric and analog, but the texture of the paper provides an authenticity that helps me lose myself in the story. It's a practice I try to implement throughout every aspect of my daily life. Ever since the accident, I have shunned the internet and any form of social media. As an editor, all my communications are provided via email, but that's my cut-off. The boundary of my safety zone. I know there are undeniable benefits and efficiencies that technology provides, like the way it allows people to reach out and see in, but it's just not for me.

"Alright, Miss Molly, we'll break for lunch at twelve-thirty. Sound good?"

I take her disinterest as a resounding yes and flip open the manila folder. According to Bastian, the author Geraldine Jackson is going to be the next Jodi Picoult and he's thrilled her agent chose his company Marozzi Publishing to represent her debut novel.

"What's it about?" I asked when he initially handed me the manuscript over some mediocre Chinese take-out.

"I actually think you'll enjoy this, Soph. It's about a mother's search for her missing son," he'd told me.

My fork clattered onto my plate, and I stared at him in disbelief. "You've got to be kidding? You know I can't deal with something like that."

But he'd been adamant. "It's not what you think. It might be hard for you in some ways, sure, but that's why you're the perfect person to edit it, Soph. No one has more perspective on this subject than you. It's going to hit the *Times Best Seller* list. I can feel it, and we need a Picoult in our stable. You can do this. I know you can."

The manuscript has been gathering dust ever since, mostly because I've been too afraid to open it.

"Okay, here we go, Miss Molly," I breathe. "Let's hope this little exercise doesn't end badly."

Chapter Four

SOPHIE

2003

*I*t was the first time I ever paid any attention to my mother's hands. Between trying to write my first novel, which of course was a spectacular failure, texting, dating, and cocktails at Rittenhouse Square, looking at the skin on my mother's hands had never been on the radar. But as we sat in the doctor's waiting room with its mint-colored walls and hushed tones, I noticed how her skin had taken on a translucent quality. Her veins were cobalt-blue, swimming beneath the skin like stinging tentacles of a Pacific man-o'-war.

"Did they give you any idea on the phone?" I asked. "Did he say anything about what they think it might be?"

But she shook her head. "They just said my tests were back, and I had to come in. Who knows what it is, but I hope they fix it fast. I'm sick of being sick."

I nodded gently and squeezed her hand, careful not to press too hard.

After the doctor asked us to take a seat in his consult room, he steepled his fingers and then folded them together into one bulbous strangle he used as a chin rest. "I'm afraid the news isn't good," he began. "The combined results of your pelvic exam, the transvaginal ultrasound we sent you for, and the CA125 blood test all indicate the presence of abnormalities within your ovarian region, Mrs Miller."

My mother leaned forward, and my body automatically moved with her. "What does that mean, abnormalities?" she asked.

"Mrs Miller, there's no easy way to say this so I'll just come out with it. The tests conclude you have ovarian cancer. We won't be able to confirm the severity until we can remove tissue samples from your pelvis and abdomen. We determine the stage of the condition using what's called the American Joint Committee on Cancer TNM staging system, which is a fancy way of describing a series of further tests. Through those tests we will be able to determine the size of the tumor and whether it has spread outside the ovaries or further through your body, such as to the lymph nodes or distant sites."

"Distant sites?"

"Areas such as the lungs or organs like the liver."

My mother's hands gripped the edge of his desk. "Is that likely?"

"We can't know for sure until we go through the staging process, and there's no use panicking in the meantime. The good thing is that we found it. Once we know more, we can determine the best course of treatment."

"Treatment," she repeated. "So, there's something we can do, it's not..."

"I think it's best if we wait until the results tell us what we're dealing with. Now..."

He continued talking about where my mother would need to go to have samples taken, and what would be involved but I didn't hear a word. My mother had cancer. Her hands were so pale...

"Miss Miller?"

"Huh?" I snapped back and looked at the doctor. In any other situation, I might have noticed he was no older than thirty-five with thick blonde hair and a delicate freckle by the side of his nose. But I didn't want to see. I didn't want to look at his face or remember his name. I wanted him to disappear, to stop existing. Then this might all go away.

"Ovarian cancer is known to be hereditary," he was saying. "So, it might be worth getting a check-up yourself, and even considering the option of freezing some eggs if children are a part of your plans for the future."

"Children?"

"Yes."

"I'm twenty."

"Well, you're never too young to consider these things," he said with a gentle smile. "With any luck, we'll have your mom here fighting fit and it would serve you well to be aware of the risks and take any precautions you can. Just my advice."

I nodded and reached for my mother's hand. Children were the last thing on my mind. I was still her child.

My mother asked me to spend the night since my brother was away and my father was experiencing what she liked to call, 'the blues.' In truth, he had been experiencing 'the blues' for the past eight years, the result of being dishonorably discharged from the United States Marine Corps after a lifetime of service. When morning came and he sobered up, she would need me for moral support. She knew he wouldn't take the news well. He didn't take anything very well, not since 'the incident.'

When I opened the door to my old bedroom, I expected to feel larger than life with its single bed, heart-shaped vanity, and lavender comforter. But down on the floor, with my back curled against the mattress, I felt small enough to crawl into the dark space under the bed like I did when I was five. In the dark, you could create your own world without the bright lights illuminating every missing piece, every imperfection, every crack. In the dark, flaws stayed hidden. No one had to know the truth. Under the bed, I could pretend whatever I liked. But out in the light, I was a twenty-year-old girl with the aching feeling her mother was going to die

Chapter Five

MADELYN-MAY

H er slender legs kick back and forth as summer air spirals in, catching her hair in invisible ribbons. Beside her, he shovels pasta from his plate into his mouth – fuel for a body that never stops growing.

My twins, Harry and Harlow, born right on my due date and in perfect health. Even my labor was easy compared to the horror stories of other women. The first contractions began at two pm, and by six-thirty pm, they were in our arms. Harlow came first, a soft bundle of pink skin wrapped in white swaddling. She had the brightest eyes and the loudest wail I'd ever heard. Her face was round and punctuated by the same cheeky dimple that had charmed me on my first date with Bastian. She was warm, sweet, and drenched in the scent of possibility - the kind that exists only on the skin of a newborn baby. To anyone else, she would have been a miracle but not to me. The nurses gushed and hovered over her, the baby they called the prettiest on the ward. It took some time, but I kissed her eventually, more of an apology than anything else because I knew they were wrong. She was not perfect. She was a living flaw. A personification of the pain and mistrust woven into my DNA. She had to be. A womb as fractured as mine could not have created anything else.

I watch her now, with filly legs she is yet to grow into and hair that reflects the light like glass. She's eleven years old and has Bastian's homemade spaghetti sauce splattered across her face and neck. Before my eyes, she digs a spoon into the sauce and flicks it at her brother, squealing in delight as his face freckles with red.

"Harlow!" Bastian cuts in from the other side of the kitchen. "Don't throw sauce at Harry. We've talked about this." The ladle balances in his hand and a tea towel is folded over his shoulder, the corners as neat as an origami swan.

"Daddy, but he wanted me to," she sings in a voice made of sugar and candy. "He likes it."

My husband rests his hands on his hips in a bid to look intimidating. "Harlow, that's not true. What did we say about telling lies?"

"But it's not a lie. He likes it. Look…"

Beside her Harry is poking out his tongue, twisting it at an almost inhuman angle trying to reach the sauce and making it difficult to argue.

"Harlow," Bastian sighs, looking to me for support, "I know this might be hard for you to understand, but we can't just act however we like. There are rules and one is that we don't throw food at each other, even if he does like it. Got it?"

She rolls her eyes and stabs her fork into the spaghetti with the violence of a Joe Pesci film.

"Harlow," I try, "there are other ways to make Harry laugh that isn't breaking the rules. You could make faces at him or do that thing you learned at school, you know when you pretend to walk down invisible stairs behind the bench?"

"Mom," she sighs, without looking up, "I haven't done that since I was like, eight. Why do you even bother?"

This time the stab reaches my heart. Have three years passed since the last time I saw her do that? Shaking it off, I gather myself and push out from the bench. "I have some work to do upstairs. Are you right to watch them?"

"How about we take the bikes down to the park?" Bastian counters. "It is the weekend, after all. You could come."

At the mention of bikes, Harry's head snaps up and his fork drops noisily onto the bench. "Can we, Mom?" He leaps off the stool, his weight shifting from one foot to the other, like a dog ready for its afternoon walk. "Can we?"

"Harry…"

"Come on, Mom, please. You never come with us."

"I'm sorry, buddy. I have a lot to get done for my meeting in the morning."

"Maybe you could write a story about riding bikes at the park?" he tries.

His pleading eyes immediately convince me that I'm broken. But instead of feeling compelled by his desperation, it annoys me that saying no will lead to that familiar itch of guilt. "I can't," I tell him flatly. "I have work to do. But Dad will take you, and Bastian, don't forget it's Sunday."

"Right, Madelyn-May," he replies. "Like I could."

My gaze lingers on his face, and I contemplate forcing a smile, but instead nod and look away. From Bastian's tone and the lusterless way he mutters my name, it's clear that once again I've let them down. Not that he'd ever say it. There's always so much left unsaid between us. These days every conversation is fraught with silent curses and unspoken accusations that hang in the air like storm clouds.

Taking the stairs two at a time, I wonder how something as simple as tone can convey so much. There were times when Bastian said my name in tones so hushed the inflection alone caused my heart to race. There have been times he's choked it out in pieces so fraught with laughter I thought we might both stop breathing. He has spoken it with such tenderness, such outrage, such passion, purity, and persuasion, that I would have followed any instruction that came after. But now my name is said in a tone so empty the letters echo off each other, repelling and colliding in the air.

Right now, he will be down there cleaning and cooing and making sure they have everything they need. Their backpacks will have water bottles. He'll take a small medical kit complete with Band-Aids, disinfectant, a bandage, and tweezers. He'll take three pieces of fruit - a banana, an apple, and a pear. Harry will want the banana, its disregarded skin to be packed away in a zip lock bag if no bin is nearby, and Harlow will devour the apple, tossing the core when no one is watching. To anyone else, it would appear almost scripted, but Bastian is just like that. He's organized, thoughtful, and prepared. I can only imagine it's the result of growing up in a loving, well-managed home where everyone got their favorite snack and no one ever went without.

In a few short hours, my community will be logging on to read the regular Sunday blog post on *Love, Mommy*. It's my weekend update, a recap of how I spent time with my family, what activities we enjoyed, and tips for when they bundle up their own children to carry out the same activity next week. There are the odd occasions I go out with Bastian and the twins and take pictures of them, but most weekends my photographer takes care of that. I take credit for the images to make it look like I was there, and when my subscribers ask why I'm not in the photos I always tell them the same thing - *I was just too focused on capturing the joy of my family.* Isn't that the trait of any devoted mother, after all – to stay in the background while her husband and children shine?

When Bastian and the children eventually tumble back into the house, I head downstairs completely unaware that we are about to get caught up in our first out loud argument of the year. And all because of a string of ducklings on the pond.

He's at the sink, busy rinsing their water bottles away and despite the awkwardness hanging between us when he left, I smile and touch him gently on the shoulder. "How was the park?"

"Interesting to say the least," he says. "Can I talk to you outside?"

I follow him out and he sits down on a cane seater by the pool. "There was a mother duck and a string of ducklings on the pond," he begins. "Cute as all hell, but it got Harry thinking. Eventually, he asked where babies come from."

"So, what did you tell him?" I ask as a tiny brown bird flits and hops from branch to branch in the tree beside us.

"Well, I considered going with egg because they were ducks and it's still the truth, even for human babies," he smiles. "But instead, I told him about the Guf."

"The Guf? What's that?"

"The Tree of Souls."

"Like in *Avatar*?"

"Not like in *Avatar*," he grins. "I mean the Jewish version."

"The Jewish version? I thought your family were Lutherans?"

"Well, that's a long and slippery slope. But according to Jewish scripture, the Chamber of Guf is like the Tree of Souls in the Garden of Eden."

"Okay... and this helps Harry how?"

"The Tree of Souls is supposed to be where all souls reside before descending to Earth. Each soul has its own purpose, its own role to fulfill. When a set of circumstances presents itself that will allow the soul to fulfill its destiny, like a bird it descends from the tree ready to be born in human form."

"Like a bird?" I think about how babies are really made and realize never once have I considered conception to be anything like the graceful flight of a bird. "Are you joking?"

"In fact," he continues, "sparrows are said to be the only living creatures able to see the soul as it descends from the Guf and onto the earthly plain."

"Sparrows?" I cast my eye back to where only moments ago the tiny bird was hopping from branch to branch, but it's gone. "And you actually believe that?"

Bastian is thoughtful for a moment. "I'd like to. It makes a lot of sense."

"How do you figure?"

"Well, it's like fate I suppose. The theory that everything happens for a reason." He stands up and nods to no one in particular. "When bad things happen, it allows us to fall back on the theory that it's all part of the journey we were meant to have, the one God chose for us. It's a lot better than thinking we experience things that are painful just by being in the wrong place at the wrong time. How could we ever make peace with an ideology that random? It would scare people."

"I hope you didn't tell him that?"

"I told him we are his parents by design. That his soul saw us and knew it was meant to be."

I rub at the scar on my wrist the way I always do when I'm nervous. "And he bought it?"

"Bought it? Why would I have to sell it?"

Memories of my own parents find their way in and I know without a doubt I would never have chosen them for myself – or anyone else. "Because there are some parents that no one would choose, Bastian. Not for any reason and not ever."

"You mean because yours died when you were young? That wasn't their fault, Madelyn-May, and maybe—"

"And maybe what?" I snap. "I wanted the experience of having no one love me for most of my life?"

He bites down on his lip, his way of not saying something he might regret later. "Madelyn-May," he begins calmly, "you never talk about your family, so I can't really comment can I? You never say anything about your childhood, so how would I know how you think or feel? It's like..."

"...like what?"

"It's like you were a ghost before I met you. You never talk about anything that happened in your life. I don't know a thing about you."

"My parents are dead." I fold my arms across my chest and stare back at him, my eyes daring him to argue. "There's nothing else to say."

"Fine, Madelyn-May, whatever..." he sighs. "But it's pretty hard to understand something if you won't tell me what it is."

If he screamed. If he shouted. If his family had been through even one scandal, there might be a chance he'd understand. If his shirts weren't pristine, and he didn't always have the right answer. If he cut corners, or dare I say it told a lie, then maybe I would consider letting my heels crack the eggshells we walk upon. But how could a man like Bastian ever understand a woman like me? I'm stained from the inside out.

"Bastian, I'm so tired of this," I sigh. "It's exhausting. Leave it be."

"Don't we always?" he huffs. "I don't have much choice."

There are times that I want to shout and cry and let him see the ugly version of who I am. The unloved, hideous girl who on a hot Californian night ran from her parents' trailer covered in sweat and shame and never looked back. There are times I feel exhausted from the repetition of asking myself over and over if he would still love me if I ever let the veil drop. But the things Bastian longs to know, the secrets that threaten to shout their way out of my heart, are things I can never tell him. He might think of me as a ghost, but he's wrong. I'm not some phantom floating out in the ether. My soul did not choose its parents and descend to Earth amid the sparrow's song. I fought my way here. I scratched and dug and clawed my way out of the ashes. I made myself into the wife he wanted me to be, and not a moment too soon because he is unequivocally the love of my life.

"I wish you would let me in," he tries one last time. "Tell me what it is that's haunting you."

"There's nothing to tell," I shrug, my secrets drifting back down into the dark. "I wish you would just accept that and leave the past where it belongs."

"Fine, Madelyn-May, have it your way. I'm sick of going around in circles."

I search his eyes for any glimmer of the love we once shared. But seeing none, I drop my head and turn away. As usual, he will go his way and I will go mine, both of us lost in a house so big it's all but impossible to find our way back to each other.

Chapter Six

MADELYN-MAY

1988

*T*he night was hot, even by Californian standards. A small electric fan balanced on a pile of old magazines by the door. My sisters had gone with Mommy and Daddy to a tailgate party, but I stayed home because of a pain in my tummy. I was stretched out on Mercy's bed, which was totally against the rules.

It was eight pm when the screen door of our trailer slammed. I knew because the big hand on my watch was pointing straight up and the little one was on the eight. Mommy had given me the watch last year for my seventh birthday. It had a green frog on the face and a grown-up leather strap. She had given one to Melody too because we were twins and shared the same birthday, but I liked mine better. Hers had a dog on it. I didn't like dogs because the brown one two trailers over pulled so hard against its chain whenever I walked by that its two front legs lifted from the ground like it wanted to eat me.

When I heard the fridge door open and close, I knew Daddy had come home by himself. If my sisters were back, they would have been shouting and arguing and Mommy would be yelling at them to pipe down. But all I heard was the popping of a beer can. It wasn't unusual for my daddy to drink a whole case of beer most days, and when he and Mommy shouted at each other he would always say it was better to be drunk than look at her twenty-four-seven with twenty-twenty vision. I didn't know what twenty-twenty vision meant, but it was no secret he would rather be drunk than look at Mommy. I never understood why because she won the 1979 Miss Sonoma Sexy Shorts and Swimwear pageant down at the local tavern. It was before any of us were born and she loved to remind everyone that if it hadn't been for us, she could have moved to Hollywood and been a star in all the movies. She said if we hadn't come along the way we did, she could have been an actor, maybe played a starring role in her favorite movie *Flowers in the Attic*. It made me feel bad when she said things like that because she was so pretty. Her dark hair almost reached the bottom of her T-shirt and her eyes sparkled like winter dew on the grass outside our trailer.

When Daddy's footsteps, one, two, three, came toward our room, I sat up. As he rounded the corner and loomed in our doorway, the stink of beer and cigarettes got all caught up in the fan and blew across my cotton nightie like a stain. "Hi, Daddy," I said.

He didn't answer and instead stood leaning on the door frame, the beer can hovering at his lips.

"Daddy? Are you okay?"

"The question is, pumpkin," he replied, "are you okay?"

I shrugged and touched my tummy. "I think so."

"Is my little girl becoming a woman? Is that what's got you all churned up in the tum?" He sat on the edge of Mercy's bed, semi-circles of sweat drawn beneath his armpits.

"I'm only eight," I reminded him.

"Well, sweetie, some girls become women earlier than others. Happened with your big sister Mercy." He leaned in close, his breath sour and old. "Did you know she got her first period when she was only ten-and-a-half? You didn't know that, did you?"

I shook my head and pulled my nightie down over my knees. It was pink and on the front was a unicorn with sparkles on its horn.

"It's true," he said. "One day just out of nowhere, bang, there it was."

"She told you?" It felt weird to think of Mercy telling Daddy she got her period. She was older than me and had always been the same way; angry. She had never hugged me, not once, and not Melody either, even when Melody broke her arm on the swings at the back of the trailer park. Mercy had just dragged Melody up off the ground by her other arm and pulled her along screaming until we found Mommy.

"Your big sister tells me everything, Madelyn-May," he said. "She used to anyways, before she turned into a pain-in-the-arse teenager. All she cares about now is letting boys... Well, that doesn't matter," he trailed off. "What matters is I still have you don't I, Madelyn-May? I still have my sweet girl."

I shifted around on the bed and glanced toward the door. "Is Mommy coming back soon?"

"Mommy? I thought you and I might spend some time together, just the two of us."

"But I feel a lot better now," I told him. "Maybe we could go meet them?"

From the way he looked at me, I couldn't tell if he was going to cry or raise his hand. He had never actually hit me before, but he'd threatened, usually when I wouldn't go to bed on time. Some nights, when he and Mommy were fighting I would hear her fall and the next morning she'd have a swollen eye or a purple welt along the side of her cheek. She always told us she'd been clumsy and fell. We were kids, but we weren't stupid.

"I just wanna spend some time with you, and all you can think about are your mom and sisters," he said. "Don't you love me, Madelyn-May? Don't you care about your dad?"

I felt guilty like a rock had sunk to the bottom of my belly. I was being mean. "Daddy, no, I didn't mean it like that."

But he shook his head and stood up. "You've always been my favorite, Madelyn-May. I try to hide it, so the others don't see, but I thought you knew. I thought you understood that I love you the most. Maybe that was a mistake."

"Daddy, no," I cried. "I'm sorry. I do understand."

He took a long mouthful of beer, crushed the can, and dropped it onto the old drawers beside our bunks. "Forget it. I'm going back to the party. You should stay here."

"No, please take me with you. I didn't mean it. I want to be your favorite. Please, I do."

I leaped from the bed and wrapped my arms tight around his leg. Mercy hated me and Mommy wished she could be in Hollywood instead of with us. I loved my twin sister Melody so much, she was my best friend, but it hurt that Mommy was always brushing her hair and letting her try different colors of lipstick. Whenever I asked to try on make-up or if I left a hairbrush on the couch beside her, she was always too busy or said my hair hadn't grown out as well as Melody's. She'd say there was no point brushing it because it would never be like my sister's. I wanted so badly to be somebody's favorite. I had to be because if I wasn't, why did I even exist?

"Please, Daddy," I tried again. "I want to be your favorite. Please..."

"You do, huh? Then think about what you say, Madelyn-May. Your words can hurt people. I know you're young, but you understand don't you, that you can't go around saying anything you like to people?"

I nodded obediently and let go of his jeans.

"I need to be sure you understand, otherwise you can't be my favorite girl."

"I do," I promised. "I understand."

The single mattress groaned as he sat back down. "Because if you're going to be my favorite girl, then we have to keep it a special secret. You can't go telling anyone because your sisters and your mother, they'll get jealous."

He traced his finger across the soft, pale skin of my leg. "They won't understand, and if your mom thinks I love you more than her she'll make me leave. Then there'll be no one to pay for the trailer, you understand? Everyone will be out on the street, and it will be all your fault."

My eyes dropped as his fingers slid further toward the edge of my nightie. "I do, but..."

"Madelyn-May," he sighed, "I should've known you'd be too young to understand. Your sister Melody, she's just like your mother. They look alike and they act alike. She's just as pretty as your mother was and she's more mature than you. Maybe I made a mistake coming to spend time with you instead of her. I even brought you a present, but I guess you don't want it."

"A present?" My eyes lit up, and for a moment I forgot about his hand on my leg. "What is it?"

"Forget it. You're too young to wear lipstick anyway. I'll give it to Melody."

"But we're the same age!"

"Well, technically she is older than you."

"Only by a minute and a half," I protested. "Please Daddy, please let me have the lipstick."

He grinned, and I saw he had chewing tobacco stuck in one tooth. "Okay, but you have to promise me two things. Can you do that?"

I got to my knees on the bed so my face would be the same height as his. "Anything, just please let me have it."

"Okay, first thing is you can't tell anyone I gave it to you. I'll keep it safe and you can wear it when no one else is around, alright?"

My shoulders dropped. I wanted so much to show Melody that I had a lipstick, but I didn't want to let him down, not when he was being so nice. "Okay, I guess. What else?"

"You have to let me put it on like Mom does with Melody. Do we have a deal?"

"But only girls know how to put on lipstick," I giggled. "You're not a girl."

"Well, that's the condition. What do you say? Will you let your dad have a go at putting lipstick on his favorite girl? You'll look so pretty, Madelyn-May. We might even take a photo. What do you think?"

He reached into the back pocket of his jeans and pulled out the lipstick. It had a shiny gold case and when he twisted it I saw that it was bright red.

"Now, Madelyn-May," he began, "this is a color for grown-ups, so when I put it on you have to act like a grown-up. Do you understand?"

"I could put on some of Mommy's high heels?" I suggested.

"No need for that. Just pucker up your lips like Mommy does in the mirror."

I puckered up and felt the lipstick slide across my lips, smooth and glossy. "How does it look?" I asked.

"You are even more beautiful than your mother when she was a girl," he smiled. "Let me get my camera. We need to take a photo."

While he went to get the camera, I jumped off the bed and stared at my reflection in the mirror. Could it be true? Was I really as pretty as Mommy?

"Alright, Madelyn-May," he announced as he came back into the room. "Jump back up on the bed so I can get a picture of how pretty you look.'

I posed for Daddy, first with my lips puckered like I was blowing a kiss to the air, and then with my hands on my hips. But when we were done, he looked at me and furrowed his brow.

"Something's not right," he mumbled. "Nope, I don't reckon these will be any good."

"No good? Why? What did I do wrong?" I hated the idea of letting him down, or that maybe I wasn't pretty enough.

"It's not you, Madelyn-May," he began, "I think it's..." he looked me over and nodded. "Yep, it's the nightie. The pink doesn't go with the red lipstick."

My mind raced as I thought about the small selection of clothes I had tucked into my drawer. "I have a red T-shirt," I beamed. "I'll get it."

"No, I think we need something else," he said, halting me mid-flight. "You know what would look so pretty, is if you had your hair out on your shoulders." He sat down next to me. "How about if we get rid of that kid's nightgown and I'll take photos with your hair spilling out over your shoulders like the models in the magazines Mercy reads."

"My nightie?" I glanced down and brushed at a crease that wasn't there.

"You'll be just like those beautiful models, Madelyn-May. Maybe we could send the pictures to one of those beauty magazines. You could be on the cover one day."

"I could?"

"Of course, you could. You're much prettier than all those girls. You just need to seem a bit older. A bit more mature."

I glanced at the stack of magazines holding up the fan. Was it true? Could I really be on the pages someday?

As I was daydreaming about becoming a model, he grabbed the bottom of my nightie and lifted it over my head, catching me off-guard.

"Alright, that's much better," he smiled. "Now kneel on the bed and put your head down but look up at me with your eyes."

I did as he asked, but it felt weird being on the bed in just my underpants. He hadn't seen me without a bathing suit or training bra since I was four years old, and Mommy always made sure I was covered up. She insisted I pull on my nightie or pajamas before I stepped out of the tiny bathroom. She wouldn't even let me run to our room wrapped up tight in a towel.

"Daddy, I kinda feel weird," I told him. "What if I just get a swimmer top? My shoulders will still be bare."

"You're doing great, Madelyn-May. You're a natural at this. Don't go ruining it. In fact, why don't you lie down and I'll take the photo from above like those pictures of models on the beach? It will be a lot easier for you if you just lay down and relax."

Some of the girls in my class at school already had boobs, but I had none. Last year after I came home from gym class crying, Mommy bought me a training bra, but I knew it was just to make me feel better. Mercy still made fun of me all the time, calling me pigeon tits and surfboard. I didn't know what pigeon tits meant, but I had a fairly good idea it meant having no boobs. But as I lay on the bed, I had never felt so self-conscious of my bare chest. "Maybe that's enough, now?" I said. "I'm not really...."

The camera dropped to his side. "...you're not really what?"

I shrugged and buried my face into the pillows. "I feel weird."

"Madelyn-May, you're doing so great. Don't you want to be in all the magazines someday? That would show your sisters. They'd be so jealous."

I thought about Melody's face if I was ever on the cover of Teen Vogue, or better still, her favorite magazine, Vibrant. She would be so jealous. We were twins, but we didn't look exactly the same. She was prettier. Everyone knew that, including me. "Alright, maybe just one more."

He hovered above me at different angles, clicking the camera this way and that until he was done. "That's not too bad," he said. "Hmm..."

"What is it? Did I do something wrong?"

"No, you're doing so great, but I think maybe..." He paused and rubbed at his chin. "...no, never mind, that's too grown-up for you."

"What is?" I sat up and looked at him, my ebony hair spilling out over my chest.

"Well, it's just... your underwear looks kinda old. If it wasn't for that, wow, Madelyn-May, you would be just like those models. I mean exactly like them."

"My underwear?" The word hung in the air between us.

"The red lipstick is a little too old for you anyway," he said eventually. "I probably shouldn't have given it to you."

Thoughts of letting him down, and of him taking the lipstick away were unbearable. "Maybe just one picture," I said, butterflies beating their wings against the inside of my ribs.

"Here, let me..."

His fingers curled around the elastic of my underpants. As he slipped them over my knees, I closed my eyes. "Daddy..."

"What?" he snapped, his breath heavy. "What is it?"

"My tummy... I think I feel sick again."

"No, you're just excited," he smiled. "And you know what, Madelyn-May? That's okay. It's natural." He leaned in and kissed me softly on the forehead, the way Mommy did when I had a fever. "You're doing great."

I forced a smile and lay back down, my hand resting protectively across my privates.

"Perfect. You look so pretty." He clicked a few more pictures, then ran his hand softly up the inside of my leg. "We just need to..." He moved my leg a little to the right and carefully placed my arm back behind my head. "...that's it."

The night air fell across my privates and more than anything I just wanted to put my nightie back on. I felt bare and there was a gritty lump inside my throat like a curse word that hadn't been shouted. He knelt at the foot of the bed and took pictures, then stood up and took more from above.

"Can we finish now?" I asked.

"Not without your reward for being such an amazing model."

"I get a reward?"

"Of course. All good models get a reward, and since you can't keep the lipstick I have something extra special for you. But Madelyn-May, once I give it to you it means you're all grown up. Do you understand?"

I nodded and glanced longingly at the unicorn's face all bunched up on the floor.

"Close your eyes," he said.

"Is it a surprise?"

"Sure. Now, close your eyes and keep still for me."

I waited for the sound of his footsteps going to get my surprise, but instead, he curled his fingers around my ankles. My eyes flung open and I tried to sit up, but he gripped my ankles tighter, holding me in place.

"I said, keep still," he growled. "Are you going to be grown up, or are you going to act like a baby?"

I swallowed hard as he parted my ankles. "Daddy, don't..."

"Quiet!"

"No, I want Mommy!"

"She's busy with your sisters."

"But I want Mommy. Now!'

"I said quiet, Madelyn-May, and I fucking mean quiet! Now lay down, keep still, and be quiet. We don't have much time left."

Not knowing what else to do, I did as I was told. He moved in closer and I squeezed my eyes closed as tight as I could. I wanted him to love me. I wanted someone, anyone to love me.

And then he did. Just like he'd loved my big sister Mercy until she got her first period when she was ten and a half.

Chapter Seven

SOPHIE

A t six-thirty pm, I close the manuscript, take off my glasses, and throw an empty tissue box into the wastepaper basket.

"Jerk," I say under my breath, causing Miss Molly to look at me with as much concern as a dog can muster. "It's okay. It's not you," I tell her. "It's Bastian. I hate to say it, but he was right. Jackson is a genius, but this story line is killing me."

My eyes burn, and the soft skin at the base of my lashes feels raw from having constantly dabbed at it with tissues. If Bastian knew the truth, he would never have given me the manuscript. It's too close to home. Every turn of the page is a paper cut - a hundred tiny slices across my heart.

For the most part, there are no secrets between Bastian and me – that's the beauty of having an affair. You can be yourself and it doesn't matter if you don't cook dinner or devote your Saturdays to cleaning the house. It doesn't matter if you hate his friends or share your secrets - the ones you're too ashamed to tell anyone else. It doesn't matter, because with an affair a different set of parameters is at play. You will never be his wife and he will never be your husband. No consideration is given to whether you will be responsible with money, if you will be monogamous, or look the part at his work function. All that matters are the moments you manage to steal, spent in private, that come completely without judgment. But despite all of that, there is still one truth I keep hidden in the dark and this manuscript is daring to bring it into the light.

Outside, a flash of lightning illuminates the sky and I pull down the blinds. Miss Molly is close on my heels. She hates storms and it isn't unusual for her to try and climb onto my lap, despite her size, the moment thunder rolls overhead. "You're okay, Miss Molly," I assure her. "It's just a storm."

Unconvinced, she stays close by my side and leaps onto the couch the moment I sit down. "Let's have a look at the weather report, then I'll get your dinner. How does that sound?"

As soon as I turn on the television, a Severe Storm Warning alert flashes across the screen. The entire East Coast is about to be thrashed by a storm front moving in across the Atlantic.

"Okay, dinner, toilet, then we're on lock down. You got it?" I tell Miss Molly. "No messing around, that storm front looks serious."

After Miss Molly eats, I stand guard outside while she pees, gauging how long we have by the inky tones of the sky. "Alright, come on that's it, I'm locking us in for the night."

As she trots up the stairs and into the house, an icy wind unusual for the summer months whips around my neck and tugs at my hair. Something is coming.

On the counter, my phone lights up with a text from Bastian.

Bastian: *This storm coming in looks pretty bad. Stay safe you two x*

I smile and hit reply.

Sophie: *Will do. You too x*

It feels nice to have someone who cares. A port in the storm.

I put down the phone and consider what to order for my dinner. The kitchen drawer is so full of menus that it almost requires one foot against the cupboard for leverage to yank it open. There's Chinese, pizza, Thai, and fried chicken, but all the options come with a side of guilt that some poor bastard will have to battle a storm just to deliver my food. Instead, I quickly change back into jeans, an old Penn sweater, and pair of runners. This probably isn't the best idea I've ever had, but if I'm quick I can run the two blocks to Joe's store, grab a frozen pizza and be back in time. It will save someone from getting drenched and I can also grab a tub of chocolate fudge brownie ice cream.

"Miss Molly, you have to stay here, alright?" I tell her. "I won't be long."

But as I hurry toward the front door, Miss Molly decides she's having none of it. She barks, cries, and turns herself in circles panicking at the thought of being left alone in a storm.

"It's only thunder, Miss Molly. You'll be okay, I promise. I'll be back before the storm hits. You have my word."

As I close the door, I turn to reassure her one last time but to my surprise, she rushes right by me and out onto the stoop. "Miss Molly, no! Stop right there."

THE SECRETS WE KEEP

I grab at her collar, but my fingers miss their mark, and she dashes out onto the street. Terrified she could be hit by a car, I immediately race after her. "Molly, stop!" But the wind blows my voice away and she disappears into the dark.

Overhead thunder crashes and suddenly the entire street falls still. The wind holds its breath and I gasp.

"Oh no... Miss Molly, come here right now. We have to get back inside. It's coming!"

But it's already too late. The sky opens and driving rain blows in from the east, tattooing my skin as it soaks me to the core. Trees sway in the blustering wind, their summer leaves surrendering to the storm.

"Miss Molly!" I call again, my tears mixing with rain. "Where are you?"

My runners slap against the wet pavement as cars speed by, spraying water from their wheels.

I turn right at the next block, hoping she might be following our usual afternoon walking route. "Miss Molly!" I scream again, my voice breaking. "Miss Molly!"

The storm swallows my words as I run aimlessly through the streets, hair plastered to my face and my feet squelching inside rain-soaked sneakers. Drowning in fear and fatigue, I try my best to keep going but my legs burn despite the cold. Outside the sushi bar where Bastian and I sometimes steal a Monday lunch, I bend forward, hands on knees, and try to catch my breath.

"Miss Molly, please!" I shout, spluttering and gasping. "Where are you?"

Has she come this way or am I heading in the wrong direction? Maybe she ran left on North 26th toward the coffee place, or maybe she kept going straight? Unable to decide which direction to take, I push at my wet hair and step out into the street where a blaring car horn stops me in my tracks. The headlights are blinding as I shield my eyes and stumble back.

"No, no, no," I gasp, as streetlights swim and mix with the rain. "Not now. This can't happen right now."

I try to steady myself, but my heart races faster and faster. My breath is sharp and shallow. My hands tremble. Pins and needles sting their way from my fingertips toward the insides of my elbows. Since the accident, panic attacks have been sabotaging my life. They are all-consuming and despite suffering them for five years, every time they hit I'm convinced this is the time I'm going to die. Too scared to move, I sink to the ground and my vision narrows. The lights on Aspen Street blur into a sickening kaleidoscope of swirling colors.

"Miss Molly," I whisper. "Please, where are you?"

"Are you alright?" A man's voice cuts through the dark and I try to steady myself. "Do you need help?"

"My dog," I manage, as rain drips from my chin. "She ran away, and I'm... I'm having an anxiety attack, I think, or...." I count to three and look up hoping to see him clearly enough to communicate.

"Do you need me to call anyone? Do you need an ambulance?"

"No, no ambulance," I mumble. The last time I called 911, a responder reminded me that anxiety was not a medical emergency and that I should try to breathe through it and calm myself.

"Someone else then?" He glances down at the gold band on my ring finger. "Your husband?" He has messy hair that's probably blonde when it's dry and sympathetic eyes. "There must be someone I can call for you."

I think of Bastian at home, warm and dry, probably cooking dinner for his kids. He'll want to help but won't know how.

"No, there's no one."

"Why don't you come inside and we'll get you dried off?" he suggests. "That might be a good place to start?"

"No, I have to find Miss Molly," I tell him. "She's scared of storms and she's out here somewhere. Thank you for coming out in the rain. I appreciate it, but I have to find her."

Talking to him has interrupted my spiraling anxiety and the fog is lifting from my mind. I get to my feet and hurry back toward home. When I reach Joe's store, I burst inside the crashing bell over the door signaling my arrival.

"Jesus Christ, Sophie!" Joe exclaims when he sees me. "What the hell are you doing out in this weather?"

Joe is an overweight, fifty-something divorcee with cheeks that are permanently blushed – the result of too many beers. He has known James and me since 2008 when we moved into our brownstone, and with no fridge had come looking for food.

"I've lost Miss Molly," I cry, water dripping all over his floor. "She ran off in the storm and I can't find her anywhere. Have you seen her? Has she come past here?"

Joe wipes his meaty hands on an old navy-blue apron and makes his way out from behind the counter. He counted the days with us until Josh was born and brought food to my house every day for a month when they died.

"Shit, Soph," he says, folding an arm around my shoulders, "I haven't seen her come by, but I can help look."

"Don't be silly. It's pouring out there and I'm already ruining your floor. It's okay, just call me if you see her, please." Without saying goodbye, I turn and hurry back out into the storm, the wind instantly whipping hair across my eyes.

I imagine Miss Molly cowering in the dark, confused and alone. I see images of her running blindly across busy roads searching for me. I envision her lying on the street broken and bloodied and not understanding why I'm not there. She is a dog, but I am still her mom and that's what moms do – they fix the things that are broken. Toys, zippers, hearts, and even dreams if they can. But I have failed. I can't find her. I couldn't get to him in time. The paramedics worked on Josh for fifteen minutes before they had to call it. Fifteen long minutes of my baby wondering where his mommy was and why she wasn't there to fix him. It had taken twelve hours of labor for Josh to open his eyes and only fifteen minutes for them to close. They had been the most important fifteen minutes of his life and I wasn't there. Instead, he had spent his last moments with strangers, scared, alone, and confused.

"Goddamn it!" I scream, my voice cutting through the storm. "Miss Molly, get back here right now or I swear to God..."

My heart is breaking and my clothes are soaking. I call her name one last time and when she still doesn't appear, I consider throwing myself down on the ground and never getting up. But when a finger of lightning illuminates the rain-soaked street suddenly I see her. Miss Molly, cowering beneath an evergreen three houses from the corner.

"Don't move!" I shout, but my feet are already sprinting toward her before the words come out. "Stay right there! I'm coming."

As I crawl under the hedge, wet branches scratch and sting the side of my face. "I'm here," I tell her. "I'm here and I'm taking you home." I close my fingers around her collar and finally let out a breath. "I've got you, Miss Molly. I made it in time."

Chapter Eight

SOPHIE

2003

*W*e were too late. My mother's cancer was Stage IIIC, meaning it had already spread to both ovaries and to the lymph nodes in her abdomen. According to her staging results, the mass was larger than two centimeters in diameter. In other words, it was bad.

Doctors at the Philadelphia Center for Cancer Research had given her a five-year survival chance of thirty-nine percent. To me, it was a sixty-one percent chance she was going to die before I reached the age of twenty-five. A sixty-one percent chance she would never see me get married or be a grandmother to my children.

When the results came back, the first thing they did was perform a hysterectomy and bilateral salpingo-oophorectomy – the removal of both ovaries and fallopian tubes. It was called debunking, and they hoped it would remove as much of the original tumor as possible. Afterward, she would need to undergo six cycles of combination chemotherapy using an intravenous tube and two different drugs – carboplatin and bevacizumab.

From the moment she was diagnosed with Stage IIIC, our life as a family changed forever. My brother David, a Marine Corps Logistics Specialist stationed in Afghanistan, video-called in every other day instead of once a fortnight. My father, who was usually passed out with a beer in his hand by seven-thirty pm stopped drinking, and we all began speaking a foreign language. Instead of saying, "How was your day?" we said things like, "What was the result of the last CA-125 tumor marker?" When making a shopping list, instead of asking if Mom needed milk I asked if she needed paclitaxel, pazopanib, niraparib, olaparib, or any of the other myriad of drugs they had her taking. When we used the full medical words, they usually sounded more like Klingon than English – words like micrometastases and columnar epithelium. But most of the time, instead of saying entire words we spoke in acronyms. "What does it say on the SEER (Surveillance, Epidemiology and End Results) website?" We talked about literature provided by NCI (the National Cancer Institute). There was also HDC (High-Dose Chemotherapy), and of course, the acronym causing the most heartache of all: VA (Veteran's Affairs).

For twenty-five years, my father had been a serving member of the United States Marine Corps. He was a Lieutenant Colonel Battalion Commander, serving eight tours of Iraq, two in Afghanistan, and one on the Horn of Africa. He was a good man who believed in serving his country and protecting his fellow man. Camaraderie and teamwork ranked high on his personal mission statement, and so on a sweltering night in Iraq when humidity had swallowed the air and flies stuck to skin like leeches, the sound of a woman screaming had triggered his moral code. When he came upon two corporals standing guard outside the colonel's quarters, he demanded to know what was going on inside. What happened next would not only change the course of his life forever, but nine years later cause his only daughter to make a choice that could never be undone.

Chapter Nine

LACY

You ever heard the one about why leg amputees are the most courageous people on earth? Because whatever the situation, they never get cold feet. *Ba-dum-bum-ching.*

When you're an amputee, a sense of humor helps a lot. Unfortunately, the not-so-funny part about losing a limb is something they call phantom pain, which to me is a whole lot of bullshit. There's nothing even remotely 'phantom' about cramps that feel like your nerves and muscles are twisting around bone, or the strange ache of something that is no longer a part of you.

I could tell you that losing my left leg has given me a whole new perspective on life, or that once I got accustomed to my prosthetic I ran the County Marathon and became a hero to female amputees everywhere. But that would also be a load of bullshit. Adversity or not, you are who you are, and let's face it, I was never going to be anyone's role model. In fact, in the years since my operation, no one has ever seen my stump. It is ugly and repulsive and reminds me of a potato that someone left too long in the pantry. But as gross as that might sound, it's the empty space beneath it that bothers me most. The vacant space that will mock me for the rest of my life – a constant reminder of what I've lost.

My phone lights up with an email alert and I snatch it up. There's only so much that Netflix and painkillers can do to keep you entertained, and there's only so long you can sit with your potato elevated on a cushion before shit starts going sideways in your head.

Her email is short and to the point. It has no emotion and there's no way to know what she's thinking. The one thing I do know is that she has no idea who I am. Then again, that doesn't surprise me. No one deserves to be beautiful, smart, and have the kind of luck that's fallen into Madelyn-May's lap. Everyone has their shortcomings and given her perfect face and blessed life, I think it's fair to assume that the elevator doesn't go all the way to the top if you catch my drift. How she ever managed to build an empire like *Love, Mommy*, I'll never know. Then again, good things always happen to lucky people.

I read it over again:

> *I know this email was sent from DigiMads here in the city. My team can
> trace your identity. If you contact me again I'll call the police.*

If she knew who sent the email, there would be no mention of calling the police. Made-lyn-May is a lot of things, more than I gave her credit for - beautiful, successful, and like I said, lucky as four rabbit feet still attached to the rabbit – but there's one word that defines her most, something that dwarfs all the rest. Guilty. And when you're guilty of doing something as despicable as what she did, trust me, you're never ever calling the police.

The other thing is, I'm not stupid. I did my homework on how all that IT, ISP, XYZ stuff works with emails and tracing a sender is not as easy as you might think. Fair enough, those IT geeks in her office figured out where I sent the email from like I knew they would, but all that tells her is that I was at an internet café frequented by hundreds of people every day. It's also no coincidence that I chose a place without security cameras. There's no way she can ever find out who I am from that email.

Like I said, I did my homework.

What she also doesn't know is that I've followed her home three times in the past week. Now if it were me, I'd always be watching, waiting for the day someone came around digging in the dirt and holding my secrets up to the light. But not her. That's the thing about being a narcissist – you never can see past your own reflection.

I scan her response one last time and resist the temptation to write something back. Instead, I swipe over to the texting app, type a quick message, then hit send.

She took the bait.

For all her success, Madelyn-May is the kind of woman you want to pull in close and squeeze the life out of. She is conceited, entitled, and everything that's wrong with the world. Driving her Audi and watching the world go by through tinted Tiffany sunglasses. She has no right. Not after what she did. Someone needs to remind her of that and so slowly, slowly I will squeeze, tighter and tighter, until her insides bleed and her rose-tinted world turns black.

Chapter Ten

SOPHIE

"I can't believe he gave you this bottle of wine and we're drinking it," Samara grins, as we clink glasses. "Do you have any idea how much this is worth?"

Bastian had given me the bottle of San Filippo Brunello Di Montalcino Le Lucere about a month ago and proceeded to laugh out loud as I tried to pronounce the name. When I asked the occasion, he simply said, '*you*', and kissed my forehead. At the time, the bottle had evoked visions of him and me, glasses in hand, tangled up on the couch, the patter of rain on the roof. But the content of the manuscript, coupled with my adventure out in the storm with Miss Molly, seems like a good enough reason to open some great wine and share it with someone I love. And tonight, that someone is Samara.

We met on a Monday morning during my first year at Penn. She was sitting at the desk next to mine, perched on the edge of her chair like a fledgling bird contemplating its first flight. She was new to school, and to Philly, and I quickly took her under my wing. For the remainder of the class, we giggled over a length of toilet paper stuck to the professor's shoe like a discarded veil and I knew we would be friends for life. Later that night, over a cask of wine, I learned she had transferred to Penn mid-semester after a failed engagement. But his loss turned out to be my gain, because as she relaxed into our daily routine I found that Samara was sarcastic, funny, and to my delight, she loved the Phillies despite having grown up in Louisiana. Over the years we have laughed, cried, fought, and made up. Despite the contrast of our skin, she is my sister and twenty years of ups and downs, of wins and losses, have been enough to create the type of bond that lasts forever. Blood has never been required to bind Samara and me. Life has done that for us.

She takes another sip and rests her glass on the table. "You sure he won't be mad we're drinking his fancy wine?"

"No," I smile. "Bastian's not like that. He probably just gave it to me to be nice."

She grins and looks at me with a face I know all too well. It's question time.

"He must have serious feelings for you, Soph. How does that sit with you?"

There's a part of me that considers trying to brush the question off, but Samara will never let that fly so instead, I think of the vaguest answer possible. "He makes a good living, so $300 for a bottle of wine is not like $300 to me. It's probably not a big deal to him."

"Come on, Soph, you know what I mean," she pushes. "Are you okay with it, you know, given everything?"

There are no words to explain how I feel about Bastian or how I want him to feel about me. It's complicated and it's confusing. He's the key that unlocks the shackles of being left behind, a firefly against the night sky. Without him, there's only darkness.

"Soph?"

"Yes and no," I say eventually. "I mean, in some ways, I have to say no I'm not okay with it. There can never be another James that's a given, right? But, at the same time..."

"...but at the same time?"

"Bastian feels like a nightlight in the dark. Sometimes just knowing he's there helps me find my way."

She lifts her glass but keeps her eyes trained on me. "Do you love him?"

"Samara..."

"It's just a question, Soph. Do you love him?"

Instead of answering, I nervously rearrange items on the coffee table. "I can't—"

"Because it's okay if you do," she says. "You have to move on sometime. It's allowed."

"No, it's not. It's never okay to move on from them," I tell her. "Move forward maybe, but never on. That sounds like I'm letting them go like they're something I could forget."

"You know what I mean."

"I'm not ready."

Samara sighs and sits back against the couch. It's the sign I've been hoping for, the one that says she's about to let it go. "I want you to know that no one would hold it against you if you did," she says. "Especially me. It's been five years."

I nod and drink the rest of my wine. I will never completely move on from James and Josh. They were my family. It would be like trying to untangle God's knot.

"So, what are you working on right now?" I ask, eager to move the conversation away from Bastian. "Anything interesting?"

Hearing about Samara's work always makes me smile. For the past few years, she's been an Associate Professor of History and African-American Studies at Penn. Her last paper, '*The Ties That Bind: A History of the Forten Sisters and How They Influenced Philadelphian*

Abolition' received critical acclaim among her peers for its insight into the country's first bi-racial organization formed by female abolitionists in 1833. It was my greatest honor to serve as her editor on the project. I also learned a lot about African-American history.

"I'm actually working on my first book," she beams. "It's based on my paper, and... I'm hoping you'll be my editor?"

"You're serious?"

"Of course!"

"Oh my God Samara, that's incredible – and yes of course I will," I tell her. "Can I ask what it's about?"

She sets down her glass and it's immediately clear to me, even if she needs both hands to explain it, there's a good chance it will hit the best-seller list at least in its category. I make a mental note to mention it to Bastian.

As she tells me about her book, I picture the Nineteenth Century Forten sisters, Margaretta, Harriet, Sarah, and their mother Charlotte, working together to establish Philadelphia's first female Anti-Slavery Society. A mother and her three daughters sharing a bond so strong that it forever changed the course of Philadelphian history.

"It's so interesting, Soph, honestly," she gushes. "Margaretta, in particular. You know she was a teacher and eventually opened her own school? That's in addition to her work within the family to support women's rights and abolition."

"Wow," I exclaim, pouring another glass. "You thinking of opening your own school?"

"Very funny. I just love the poetry of a mother and her daughters contributing to our city's legacy even if it was a rocky road to get there. Philly has such a male-dominated history, Soph, you know that, even down to being known as the City of Brotherly Love. It's always been about kings and presidents and politicians, all men. But I feel like I've found a kindred spirit in her. What must it have been like, Soph, to grow up with a mother like that? Someone who inspired you to help change the world?"

I think back to the loss of my own mother and how it felt to suddenly be out in the universe all alone. Samara had grown up in the foster care system, never knowing her real parents. It was hard to figure out which might have hurt more.

"You did fine," I tell her. "You're an amazing mother and an incredible person. You don't have to change the world to be a successful parent. Your daughter is one of the coolest kids I know."

She smiles warmly and touches the simple gold band on her finger. "Yeah I know, but a lot of that is Gerard."

"A lot of that is you."

Samara has a relationship with her husband that most women would envy. They met in our final year of college when I had a bout of appendicitis that forced her to rush me to the campus clinic. Gerard, older than us, was in his final year of residency at Milton, a hospital on University Drive. He was reliable, committed, and unwavering. He was also handsome, athletic, and smart as a tack. She loved his passion for medicine and the bond he had with where he grew up. He had been adamant about specializing in reproductive medicine and remaining close to his family. She had been smart enough to see his stability as a strength, and together they never wavered.

"He's a good man, my Gerard," she grins. "I'm lucky."

"Well, I'm glad you brought him into our lives. You have no idea how much he helped me through that whole egg-freezing procedure, or should I call it torture, all those years ago. After Mom got sick, it was the last thing I wanted to go through, but it was such a relief to have him there by my side the entire way. I don't think I would have got through it with anyone else."

I force a smile - a bid to cover up what I'm really thinking. If she knew just how much Gerard had helped me, what he really did, he and I might both lose her from our lives forever.

"You still with me, Soph?" she asks. "Looks like you drifted off somewhere. Is there something on your mind?"

"Nope, I'm good." *I wish I could tell you, but I can't.*

"You can tell me anything. You know that, right?"

"I know." *Not this.* "It's nothing, just the shit that goes around in my head," I tell her. "Maybe enough wine for tonight, though."

Samara nods and uses her phone to order an Uber. Early gym class in the morning.

We hug at the door, and I feel genuinely grateful to have her in my life. She's like a sister and I hate keeping things from her. Perhaps one day I can tell her everything. I want to, long to even, but there are other people involved, people who would be hurt. Perhaps someday I can come clean, but for now my secrets will have to stay just that - secret.

Chapter Eleven

SOPHIE

2004

*W*hen we were kids, my brother and I were convinced our father had a lie detector built into his heart that went off whenever we tried to keep a secret. I don't think either of us ever got away with a single mistruth. "Accountability is the key to success," he would tell us when we got caught out. "If you want to make it in this world, you have to be accountable for your actions. It's the only way to improve."

That night in the Iraqi desert, when the very same lie detector triggered in his heart, my father pushed past the corporals standing guard and marched right into the colonel's quarters. Cowering in the corner was a naked woman, bruised and beaten, trying desperately to cover herself with her hands. He would find out later that she was the widow of a local soldier killed in action, and mother to three young daughters. But at the time he walked in, she was a woman being held against her will, and to my father, the how or why made no difference. Disregarding rank, he immediately reported the colonel for raping and imprisoning the woman.

After the case was preferred back in the States, an informal investigation was held. The corporals claimed to have seen my father drinking. The colonel, who was third-generation Marine Corps, swore on his service of God and the United States Marine Corp that he had been asleep the entire time. My father was swiftly court-martialed and an Article 32 Proceedings was scheduled. At the colonel's request, a jury trial was waived and my father's fate fell into the hands of a military judge. He was dishonorably discharged in less than an hour.

Despite our best attempts, which sometimes consisted of yelling and cursing, and at other times pleading and crying, the Department of Veteran's Affairs refused to pay for my mother's treatment. Spousal medical care, including oncology, was traditionally covered by the VA but the circumstances around his discharge meant we were denied. My father blamed himself.

In the year since she was diagnosed, my mother's condition deteriorated significantly. The cancer had not responded to chemo and within three months of her bilateral salpingo-oophorectomy to remove the original mass, it returned with a vengeance. Within eight months, it spread *to her spleen, liver, and intestines. Within ten months she was diagnosed with Stage IV or what they call the final mesothelioma stage. It was terminal. They gave her a year.*

With the bill for her treatment already over $185,000, my parents' savings were gone and my father had taken a second mortgage. Her oncologist advised that the best thing to do was in-home palliative care. We agreed. The only problem was that we had no money left.

When my father went to the store, I video-called my brother David to see if he had any ideas on what to do next.

"It's Mom," I told him when his face filled the screen. "I don't know what to do."

David had a thick neck, and his jaw, my dad used to say, was made for breaking fists. He also had a habit of leaning in so close during our video chats that his face looked like it was coming through the screen. "Is it money?" he asked.

"Yeah," I nodded. "As in, we have none."

"Right." He nodded, and for the first time in two years fell back in his chair, allowing me to see his entire torso.

"You look good," I managed. "Everything alright over there?"

"It's as expected I s'pose. I mean, it's messed up, but it's Afghanistan, so..."

I nodded and rubbed at my right temple. "Any ideas about Mom?"

"How much do we need?"

"How long is a piece of string? I mean, she needs palliative care so she can stay at home for as long as possible before she goes into hospice. But it's about $100 per day and the VA is still saying no because of Dad. We can't use private medical because they didn't have oncology care as part of their premium."

"Well, why not," he snapped.

"Because, David, she's forty-eight. Jesus, it's not like you think you're going to get terminal cancer that young."

"I know. Sorry, Soph, I didn't mean it like that. I hate being stuck over here with all that's going on at home. I mean, what if..."

"You'll be back in time, don't think like that," I told him. "She might have ages yet. You don't know."

"So, how much for now? Just to get us out of trouble."

"I don't know. Like, around $17,000. That would cover probably six months of palliative care. After that, we can re-assess whether she needs to be in hospice."

He groaned and ran a hand through his hair. In the background, men and women dressed in camos buzzed back and forth. "Shit, Soph, I just don't have that kind of money."

My last hope was dashed. "Me either. So, what do we do?"

He swore and trained his eyes on something in the distance. A tactic so as not to cry in front of his little sister.

"David, you should know that Dad is—"

"I can imagine."

"No, you can't," I said. "It's worse than that."

"How bad?"

"Bad. And it's not just that. He's back on the drink and—"

A voice boomed in the background, calling my brother to the comms room. "Shit, Soph, I gotta run. I'll call back when I can."

And just like that, he was gone.

My brother's military health cover didn't lend itself to parental medical care. My father's medical cover and pension had been canceled as part of the Marine Corps findings, as had any benefits for my mother. Results of BRCA1 and BRCA2 genetic testing I had done on the advice of my mother's oncologist had identified a gene fault. It meant there was a thirty-to-sixty percent chance I would develop breast cancer and a twenty percent chance of developing ovarian cancer. In other words, there was every chance that if I waited too long then children might not be on the cards. That made me a twenty-one-year-old student who had decided to spend her only savings, a grand total of $8,000, on having thirteen eggs harvested and cryogenically frozen. That choice plagued me most when I looked at my mother, knowing how much she needed care that now none of us could provide.

My parents' house was a two-story cottage on Horseshoe Road in Schwenksville, Pennsylvania, with a magnolia tree in the front garden and the shape of our hands forever imprinted in the concrete of the garage floor.

In the sunroom, my mother had fallen asleep. I leaned on the door frame and watched her breathing slowly in and out, sunlight warming her face. Moments like these made it easy to pretend we were still a normal family, that my mother wasn't dying, and that my father, who was in perfect health, hadn't already become a ghost.

The silence was broken when he came in from the store, a brown paper bag of groceries balanced in the crook of his arm and his fingers clutched around the neck of another bottle of scotch.

"Did you pick up Mom's medication?" I asked.

The paper bag dropped onto the counter, a glass bottle of milk rolling out and smashing on the tiles. "Jesus, Dad," I hissed. "Mom's sleeping."

"Christ…" he sighed and looked down at the mess. "I'll go back and get another one."

"Forget it. I'll go to the corner store. Did you get Mom's tablets?"

"Yeah, I got 'em. You talk to your brother?"

He might be drunk, but he would still know if I lied. "I did. David said he doesn't have the money either."

"Damned if I know what to do then."

"Dad, you can't talk like that. We can't just say 'to hell with it.' It's Mom's life."

"You think I don't know that?" He took a glass from the top cupboard and cracked open the bottle of Scotch.

"It's not even one pm."

"Does it matter?"

His body was so limp that I couldn't tell if he was already drunk or if even his bones had surrendered trying to hold him up. "You drove home like this?" I asked. "Where were you, at the pub again?"

He drained the glass in one mouthful and slammed it down on the counter. "Well, the upside is that if I close my eyes, I can't tell the difference between you and your mother. You both sound the damned same."

Tears burned and I bit my lip. "Okay, Dad, have it your way. I'll find the money for Mom. Just forget it."

"Sure, kid. Whatever you say."

I swallowed the lump in my throat and stared at him. "You believed in being accountable once. It's all you ever drummed into our heads. What happened to you?"

But he just shrugged and turned away. "Life happened, I guess. Gets us all eventually. You'll see."

Chapter Twelve

MADELYN-MAY

When a week passes with no more threatening emails, I begin to relax. Clearly, the sender was just another crazy who has since got themselves caught up in whatever the next crazy thing is that crazy people do.

In the living room, Bastian and the twins are sprawled out across the carpet watching a movie. Harlow's wrist rests gently on the lip of the popcorn bowl, and Harry's legs are spread out like a wishbone. They are the perfect family. Every mother's dream. But once again, I find myself hovering in the doorway like an uninvited guest.

For the past week, I have been a bad person, a cold mother, and a distant wife. Instead of coming right home after work, I spend hours driving around without calling or checking in. Lost in the past, and with my demons hitching a ride, dark streets and unknown neighborhoods call to me. Caring little for my family, I answer. Anything to avoid going home.

The first few nights, Bastian waited up frantic over where I'd been. But by the fourth consecutive night, when I returned the house was silent and still, the warm kitchen light turned out. It hasn't been my intention to make his life difficult. It was that damned email, pulling me back to the one place I have tried so desperately to escape. Right now, staying in motion feels like the only way to keep my mind from imploding. Like if I dare to sit still, the past might finally catch up with me.

"You want to watch with us?" Harry turns and asks, his face glowing with the promise of second chances.

"Sure, if I'm allowed?" I glance at Bastian.

"Oh, I don't know," he says in mock protest. "What do you think, kids? Is Mom allowed?"

I'm grateful he never holds a grudge. If I am the distance, Bastian is always the bridge. But to my surprise, Harlow shakes her head. "No, I don't want her to watch. The movie is just for us."

"Harlow," Bastian gently scolds, "that's not very nice."

"Well, she's not very nice either." Harlow gets to her feet and stares at me, her arms folded defiantly across her chest.

Beside her, Bastian bites his lip and looks away. I can't be sure whether it's to stop himself from scolding her or to hide the first hint of a smile. I know he wouldn't find it funny, but there's every chance he might think it's deserved.

"Well, how about I come over and be nice now?" I try. "Would you let me watch with you guys?"

Her face softens, and I can see she wants to concede. But what she does next is like a knife in my heart. Instead of answering for herself, she looks to Bastian. It's such a tiny gesture, innocent and void of any harsh words or temper tantrums. There's no cursing or name-calling, just a look, but it speaks volumes. She needs his approval to allow me in. *Is it safe?* Without uttering a word, that's what she's asking: *Dad, is it safe?* The honest answer, and the one that fills my husband's eyes, is that *No, she is not safe – but I am.* He's their loving parent, while I am a shadow that haunts them. But Bastian simply smiles and rests his forehead against hers. It's as beautiful as it is painful. He whispers something in her ear and she reluctantly nods.

"Go on then," he encourages her.

"You can watch with us," she tells me, her eyes cast downward. "I suppose."

He always has my back when it comes to the kids, although I strongly suspect it's more for their benefit than mine. I mouth him a thank you and he shrugs and turns back to the television. I'm in. For now.

We've been watching the movie for about thirty minutes when the gate intercom buzzes. It's unusual for anyone to turn up at our property unannounced, as I always have packages delivered to the office. Looking for an explanation, I turn to Bastian. "Are you expecting someone?"

But he shakes his head. "No, not me."

I stare at him for a minute, just to be sure, then get to my feet and look at the camera screen.

The chubby face of a delivery man looks back. "Package."

"For?"

He looks down at the screen of his device. "Madelyn-May Marozzi."

I pause and try to gather my thoughts. "What is it?"

"Look like I got X-ray vision to you, lady?" he snaps into the camera. "It's a package."

"And I have to sign for it?"

"What's going on?" Bastian calls from the living room. "Who is it?"

"It's a delivery,"' I call back. "It must have been addressed here by mistake. I'll take care of it."

My finger hovers over the gate release, visions of the email returning to haunt me. "Who is the sender?"

"Oh, come on, lady," the driver whines. "It's only my business who it's to, and far as I can tell, that's you."

"Well, it's certainly *my* business," I tell him, "and I'm not buzzing you or anyone else, into my property unless you tell me the name of the sender."

"Fine," he sighs, "you win. The sender is Mom and Bub Baby Wear. That good enough for you?"

I press the button and watch through the window as the delivery man's ample shape bobs up and down, closer and closer, until he is full-size and standing on my porch.

"All good?" Bastian calls.

I sign the delivery man's device and try to look apologetic. "You have to be sure these days."

He rolls his eyes and hands me the box. "Whatever you say, lady."

I close the door behind him and remember to answer Bastian. "Everything's fine. I'll just run this up to my office."

No one has ever sent a work package to our home. Had I refused the delivery, Bastian would have asked questions, the kind I couldn't answer – but something isn't right about the box. I can feel it in the twist of my gut.

Upstairs I take a deep breath, stretch my shoulders, and begin cutting off the tape. At first, all I can see inside is packaging but as I dig deeper, I brush the corner of a small box made of cardboard. The moment I see it, my breath catches and the room spins. A book of matches. Without thinking, I immediately throw it onto the floor, anything to get some distance. There's no note, no message, but the matches say all they need to. Someone knows about the fire.

"Everything okay up here?" Bastian pokes his head around the door.

At the sound of his voice, I leap in my seat. "Jesus, you scared me."

The book of matches lying in the middle of the floor catches his eye, and he leans over to pick them up.

"No, don't touch them!" I shout. "Leave them!"

"What the hell, Madelyn-May?" He pulls away as though his fingers have already been burned. "Why would you leave a box of matches lying around where the kids can get them?"

"I'll pick them up," I tell him. "Just leave them where they are."

He steps back but stares at me in confusion. "You're not making any sense. What the hell is going on? Why are there matches in the middle of the floor?"

If his fingers close around those matches, the two worlds I have spent my life trying to keep apart will collide. That life. Those secrets. He's so much better than all of that and I don't want him anywhere near my hotbed of lies. "I need a minute," I tell him. "Okay? I know you must think I'm being crazy and strange, but please, Bastian. I. just. need. a. minute. Alright?"

"You know what?" he says, disappointment heavy in his eyes. "It's not alright. I've been running this ship alone for what *feels* like forever, but for at least the past week while you just disappear. For a tiny moment downstairs, when you came to watch that movie with us I thought maybe, just maybe, you were coming around. But now this." He throws up his arms. "I don't know what's going on with you, Madelyn-May, but I've had enough."

"I know, but—"

"No, you don't know," he snaps. "But you will."

"What's that supposed to mean?"

"It means now it's my turn to disappear for a while."

"What? You wouldn't—"

"I need a break. For a while, it's your turn to take care of the twins. You are their mother, after all."

I stare in silence as he turns and walks toward the door. "I'll be back when I'm ready," he says over his shoulder. "Until then, at least try to look after them."

Downstairs the front door closes with a thud and Harlow starts to cry. A voice in my head tells me I should go to her, but my body refuses to move. Instead, I sit at my desk and stare vacantly at the matchbook lying on the floor. *How do they know?*

At some point, the crying must have stopped because the house is silent when Harry sneaks his chubby face around the corner.

"Mom, Harlow's saying she's hungry. You want me to go ahead and heat something up for her?"

"I'm sorry, buddy," I manage. "I'll come down now."

"Thanks, Mom."

He's growing so fast. It feels like just yesterday he couldn't tie his own shoelaces. "Don't thank me, honey. I'm your mom, I'm supposed to take care of you."

"Yeah," he shrugs, "but we know that's Dad's job."

I stare back at him, words failing me.

"I didn't mean..." he stammers. "...I just meant—"

"It's okay, buddy. Daddy loves taking care of you, but you know what? So, do I. So, let's go make some dinner, huh?"

"Can you make hotdogs?"

"Let's not get crazy," I grin. "How about I order a pizza?"

On the way out of the room, I scoop up the book of matches and tuck them inside my desk drawer. I am not a child anymore. I'm an adult, and tonight I need to think about people other than myself. For now, the matches and whoever sent them will have to wait.

Chapter Thirteen

MADELYN-MAY

1993

*O*n the day of my thirteenth birthday, I became a teenager and a woman all at once. Seeing that bright red stain on my underwear was the happiest moment of my life. It was over. He would never touch me again. Unlike Mercy, who was lucky enough to get her first period when she was ten-and-a-half, my body had refused to allow me the same escape. When my blessed period finally came, I had been Daddy's 'little girl' for five years.

On the day it happened, I decided not to change my underwear. I thought maybe if I left the soiled ones on, even though it was totally gross, he would know not to touch me down there anymore. He said himself that he'd stopped visiting Mercy after she got her first period, so if he curled his fingers around my underwear and found blood, I'd be safe.

But that day Mom wanted to do a wash, and when I took off my underwear, she shrieked out loud. "You got your first period! Oh, Madelyn-May, that's so great. Good girl."

It was the first time I ever saw her genuinely smile, and the first time she ever told me I was a good girl. I wanted so badly to take credit for the accomplishment, but it had kinda happened all on its own.

"You hear that, Bobby-Ray?" Mom shouted out. "Madelyn-May got her first period."

"Did she just..." he mumbled between swigs of beer. "Well, ain't that somethin'."

"It is something, you big dope. Now if you're not going to fix the closet at least go pick up those tools off the bedroom floor. And quit being so damned lazy. That isn't where they go and you know it."

I was too happy to have my special day ruined by their bickering, and I knew the start of an argument when I heard one. So, for the rest of the afternoon, I wandered around the trailer park waving happily at other kids and enjoying the sun on my face. Eventually, I walked over and plonked myself down on the swings where Melody was pushing herself back and forth, higher and higher, until she was slicing through the sky.

"Stop it, Melody – you're going to hurt yourself!" I called out, but she wouldn't look at me. She just kept pushing higher and higher, her face frozen in place.

"Melody stop, please..."

As I watched her soaring high into the blue, it was like an invisible hand was driving her forward, pushing her harder and higher. "Melody, you're going too high!"

But she only leaned back and pushed harder into the swing, propelling herself forward.

"Melody..." I called again. "What's wrong?"

Eventually, she ran out of puff and the rusty chains softened, the swing lulling to a stop.

"Melody—"

"Don't! Alright? Just... don't."

"What's wrong? Why are you so upset?"

"Your periods came?" she asked.

"Yeah, finally," I smiled. "Yours too?"

When she shook her head, the rock in my stomach told me exactly what was wrong. "I'm sorry, Melody, I thought—"

"You thought what, Madelyn-May?" her face snapped around, sharp and angry, "that you were his only special girl? Well you're not, and why would you be? You're not special, obviously."

I swallowed hard and told myself she was only being mean because of him. "I don't like it either," I tried. "I hate it."

She didn't answer, and instead dug the toe of her sneaker into the dirt.

"I'm sure you'll get yours too," I said. "I mean, you have to, right? We're twins."

A soft breeze picked up the loose strands of hair around her face, then dropped them. "Don't know. Guess he'll only be coming to see me now you got yours."

"I'm sorry," I whispered. "I didn't mean to." I touched my hand to my stomach, the twisting cramps no longer feeling so miraculous. "I could maybe..."

"You could maybe what?"

But I just shrugged and stared at the ground. "I don't know."

It felt like forever that we sat there, the two of us contemplating a horror no child should ever have to face. "We could kill him," I said with a grin, hoping to break the tension.

But Melody didn't meet my gaze or return my smirk. Instead, she stared straight ahead and whispered, "Yeah, we could."

Chapter Fourteen

SOPHIE

A few days after the accident I had been drifting, far away inside the ethereal space that lingers between slumber and awareness. Lost in a place where just for a moment, my brain had forgotten they were gone. Then I opened my eyes.

It hit with such intensity that I gasped and clutched at my throat. The room spun and my entire body froze. A hundred invisible fingers pulled at my skin trying to yank me up from the bed. Caught inside a dazzling confusion of wanting to die and being desperate to survive, the room warped. I clawed at my chest. I sucked in air, too fast and too shallow. I hyperventilated, the tingles like electricity along my arms. It lasted less than half an hour but felt like an eternity. When it was over, my knees were jelly and my hands felt like they belonged to somebody else.

When it happened again the next night, and the one after that, I called a doctor to the house. He told me it was a panic attack, a normal and natural reaction to grief. He said contacting a counselor and talking it through would help. Unfortunately, on my way to the first appointment I got no further than three blocks down the road before another attack took hold, so debilitating that I had to pull over. When I tried to get out, my balance faltered causing me to trip and hit my head on the gutter. At the hospital, a duty doctor in blue scrubs administered a local anesthetic and three stitches. She also advised that keeping sedatives on hand during the initial stages of my *'situation'* might be a good idea. I thanked her and tucked the prescription inside my jeans pocket. But by then I no longer cared. I took the pills, and then some more, and hoped they would cure me or kill me. Either would suffice. When they did neither, I accepted my fate of working from home, buying basic groceries from Joe's, and eating out at the corner sushi bar but only when Bastian could come with me.

Small miracles and little wonders formed the fabric of my day-to-day life. A perfect spiderweb in the back garden. The tapping of rain on my window. Tiny birds hopping from branch to branch and onto the feeder I hung on the tree outside. In the past five years, I have never ventured further from home than I can cover on an afternoon walk, except for when I adopted Miss Molly from the shelter over in Fishtown. On our walks, I'm grateful she never lets on to the fact we pass the house at least four times, and I'm always amazed at how she finds new smells to sniff on every lap. Our world remains minuscule because my anxiety is monumental.

It feels weak to admit, but I hate being alone in times like this. To be frightened of your own body is a unique form of fear that most people will never understand. Every tingle, pain, pinch, and palpitation sparks a flow of terror through my nervous system. Each pulse alerts another part of my body to danger. It's fight or flight, but when your enemy dwells within it's difficult to throw up your fists ready for battle. Outrunning yourself is also an impossible task. So, what do you do? Put simply, you implode. I know most of the sensations are nothing more than natural shifts of my body, the way an old house moves on its footings after too much wear and tear. Even houses that weather the greatest of storms can suddenly begin to sprout cracks and leaks. They appear out of nowhere, tiny at first, then quickly become catastrophic divides that threaten to tear a home in two.

As I sit alone, terrified of every rise and fall of my chest, I think of Bastian and wonder if this is happening to him as well. Is he also watching his life split in two? His wife on one side, he on the other, and his children stretched across the divide, their tiny fingers desperately linked and trying to hold on. He speaks so little of his home life that it's been easy for me to push the idea of her all the way to the back. If I were honest, in my mind I've almost created a world where she doesn't exist at all. Sometimes I wonder if that makes me a bad person or if I can go with the excuse that the marriage is his responsibility and not mine. I could tell myself that if it weren't for me, he'd be cheating on her with someone else, but deep down I don't believe that's true. In my heart, I know if I wasn't in his life, Bastian would be a faithful but empty husband, doing all he can to be a great—but almost single—father.

According to the doctors, long, deep breaths, in through the nose and out through the mouth are the key to calming an anxious mind. But outside the light is slipping away and being alone at night does nothing to help my sense of unease. I pad over to the kitchen and take out my bottle of pills. In the past year, I have trialed a rainbow of different anti-depressants but found they all escalated my anxiety to an unbearable level. I've never managed to get through the standard two-week period before they 'kick in' and start doing whatever it is they're supposed to do. Instead, a single bottle of Diazepam sits on my shelf. I use them when I need to, which unfortunately seems to be most days.

Aside from the medication, there is one other thing that calms me on nights like these. With Miss Molly on my heels, I climb the stairs and pause outside his bedroom door. It's only on the worst of days that I contemplate turning the handle and going inside. If it were to become a habit, I fear I would end up living my entire life in a room that time forgot, my knuckles white around the door frame should anyone ever try to pull me out.

I crack the door and gingerly peek inside as though there's a chance I might still catch him, shoulders hunched over a coloring book, his tongue twisted in concentration. But as always, the room is empty and only the framed image of his smiling face stares back at me.

After Josh died, it was therapist number three who told me it would be beneficial to pack his things away and turn the room into a space that didn't tug at my heart. But the two times I tried to fold his clothes into a box, I ended up down on the floor in the fetal position, sobbing and gasping until the night sky swallowed the sun.

Miss Molly is so close that I can feel her fur against my leg. She senses my mood and understands what sadness feels like. Love is not something afforded only to humans. It is universal, and I know without a doubt that Miss Molly has felt loss. When I found her a year ago, she had been in her own darkness, alone and without a family.

The trip over to Fishtown Animal Shelter had not been without its hiccups. If I hadn't been so determined, Miss Molly and I would never have met. At the time it had taken ten milligrams of diazepam and a lot of internal dialogue to turn the key of my Mini. Throughout the entire trip, my speedometer never broke thirty. The chorus of horns behind me louder than the 1776 choral of the Liberty Bell marking the Declaration of Independence. Still, it was the first time I had driven in over a year, so it seemed fitting a celebration of self-governance should ring out from the brownstone-lined streets of Fairmount.

When I eventually reached the shelter and stepped inside, the corridors were so dark I could barely see a foot in front of me. I squinted and lifted my forearm across my nose to try and block out the smell, but it did little to stop the biting stench of urine. A lanky kid in gray overalls told me that they had all kinds of dogs at the shelter, but that *none of them were real good*," whatever that was supposed to mean. He shoved his shoulder against a heavy wire gate and I followed blindly to a brick shelter filled with cages. Inside, dappled sunlight filtered in and I could finally start to see. In the first cage, half-hidden in shadow was a dog the color of butter and sunshine, cowering down, her hip bones protruding like question marks. When I asked her name, the boy told me in no uncertain terms there were no names in the shelter, only serial numbers. A wet patch had formed on the ground beneath her nose and in the corner was a pile of feces. Without moving, she looked over at me and the ache of her loneliness reached my heart.

When I paid her adoption fee and bundled her into the back of my car, I realized she was a lot bigger in my tiny backseat than she seemed in the cage. I wasn't sure if bringing a dog into my already messed-up life was the right thing to do, but instead of worrying about it, I turned and said, "Maybe we can save each other, hey Miss Molly? What do you say?" It was the first time she lifted her head and looked at me. The name stuck.

Miss Molly surprised me on our first night together, when right after dinner she went to the open back door and looked at me expectantly. After glancing back one more time just to be sure, she took the stairs down onto the grass and I caught myself instinctively leaning against the door frame to watch over her. She sniffed the ground and crouched to relieve herself, then surprised me a second time by walking gently over to the couch and laying down where my feet would go. She had been part of a family once - that was obvious. Somewhere in her mind, the memory of eating, of going outside, of relaxing at her family's feet remained, and I wondered what had happened so that she ended up terrified and alone in a dirty cage at the animal shelter. What had been her car crash?

I lift the teddy bear up to my face and breathe in Josh's scent. Powder, cinnamon, and daydreams. A childish bouquet so pungent I can almost feel him wriggle in my arms.

Beside me, Miss Molly lifts her head and nudges my hand - her way of pulling me back. Taking the cue, I rest my hand across her back. As our breathing falls into rhythm, slow and steady, I wonder again where I would be if it wasn't for her. Since the day I found her, Miss Molly has learned to embrace her new life. She is a calm, quiet, and loving dog, who somehow understands that while she has become whole, I remain in pieces.

Chapter Fifteen

SOPHIE

2004

*O*ur lives were falling to pieces. For as long as I could remember, Mom had been our full-time cheerleader, encouraging my brother and I's wild ideas and picking us up when we fell. Now she needed our help and I had no idea what to do. Without the money for a palliative care nurse, she would have no choice other than to depend on us. We wanted to be there, and we wanted to do all we could, but what the hell did we know about end-of-life care? Dad was drunk more often than not, my brother was in the middle of a war zone, and I could barely stop crying. My mother was a strong, independent, and proud woman. She had spent her life teaching grade school to gaggles of loud and ill-prepared seven-year-olds, all who cared more about which of their classmates had just farted than anything she ever had to say. But her patience was as wide as the horizon, her kindness brighter than the sun. She remembered all their names long after they graduated prep school and I could still recall her greeting a former student, Scott Hansen, by name despite the fact he was working as a bank teller and she hadn't seen him since he switched schools in the eighth grade. Now she needed someone to assist her, to help her navigate the unimaginable with dignity and self-respect. What she didn't need was to feel like a burden and without a professional carer that's exactly what would happen. If my mother spent her last days feeling like anything other than our north star, we would all lose our way, forever lost in the shadow of our failure.

The walk from my classroom at Penn had taken a little over half an hour, but Love Park was my favorite place in the city to go and think. Its bright red sculpture, the letter O in LOVE famously tipped on a precarious slant, reminded me how easily we could lose our balance when it came to matters of the heart. I never knew for certain if that's what the artist had intended or if I was always coming at love from the wrong angle, but either way, something about looking at that sculpture made me feel less alone.

I found a bench and pulled my knees up to my chest. All around me, fuzzy gray squirrels raced from one tree to the next and back again, their bushy tails and animated faces a welcome *distraction. Where could a student with nothing of value to her name, and no skills worth a damn, come up with $17,000, I wondered.*

As I sat and pondered, people came and went. They ate sandwiches, played with dogs, read books, and stared in vague wonder at the clouds above. I wondered if any of these people, even one, was going through anything as painful as me. Better still, could any of them tell me what the hell I should do?

It was that thought that filled my mind when I saw her. Two benches away, she sat hunched over, her dark hair falling around her face like a weeping willow. She was staring intently at a couple swinging a small child as they walked, their fingers interlocked like three shapes in a paper chain. As I watched, it was hard to decipher the look in her eyes. Was it sadness? No. Frustration? Not quite. Was it jealousy? Closer, but still no. And then it hit me. Helplessness. The very same emotion I saw in my own eyes every time I looked in a mirror. Welcoming the distraction, I wondered about her story. Was she having an affair with the man? Or maybe it was with the woman? Was she a long-lost sister? Had she lost a child of her own? What could have her so tied up in knots over two parents and a child in the park? Then, to my surprise, she turned and looked right at me. Caught off-guard I forced a smile, the kind that purses your lips but doesn't reach your eyes. The kind that says, 'I get it – but don't know what to say.' She blinked slowly, took one last look at the couple, then got to her feet. I scolded myself for staring. It had made her uncomfortable. But instead of leaving, she came right over.

"You were looking at me." It wasn't a question.

"I was, and I'm so sorry," I mumbled. "I was... looking for a distraction I guess."

She nodded and motioned to the space beside me. Even though there was more than enough room for her sparrow-like frame, I made the obligatory sliding motion and she sat down.

"Do you think they're happy?" she asked, looking over at the family.

I followed her gaze and thought for a moment. "I think everyone is happy sometimes."

"Are you?"

"I was... before."

She nodded and folded her hands carefully into her lap. Her fingers were long and slender, almost elegant, except for the jagged edges of her nails. "Can I ask what happened?"

I couldn't say why I answered, but I did. "My mother is dying. I have no money for her care. I feel like..."

"...a failure," she finished.

"Yeah, pretty much. And you?"

"My husband wants children."

"And you don't?"

She slid her gold wedding band slowly up toward her knuckle, then back again. *"It doesn't matter whether I want to or not. I can't."*

"There's options," I offered.

"Not to him."

She looked a little older than me, and I found it ironic that had it not been for the doctor's advice I may have found myself in the same situation later down the track. *"And your husband, he can't accept the idea of you guys not having kids?"*

She rubbed her wedding ring back and forth like Aladdin, and I wondered if she was hoping a genie would pop out and magically fix all our problems. I held my breath and watched in the hope it might work.

"He doesn't know, and I can't find the words to tell him that I can't fall pregnant," she said. *"Having a baby is all he cares about."*

"I'm sure that's not true."

"You don't know him." She paused. *"And your mother? There's no hope?"*

I shook my head and gazed out over the park. *"Not for recovery, no. I want to take care of her until it's time. She's always taken care of me, and my brother too. I just… don't know how to give that back to her."*

"Can I ask what condition she has?"

"Cancer. It started in her cervix and then spread. We tried every treatment possible, but all we can do now is keep her comfortable and provide end-of-life care – if we could afford it, that is."

"That's tough."

"Tell me about it," I threw up my hands. *"The irony is, the doctor convinced me to use all my savings to freeze my eggs because it's a hereditary condition. We'd been hoping for a miracle, you know? Then this happens and I have no money left for her care."* Tears stung at my eyes. I had no idea why I was telling a woman I had never met before my most private thoughts, and yet the words just tumbled from my lips.

"How much do you need for her care?"

I shrugged and pushed at my hair. *"Too much."*

"Ballpark?"

"$20,000, give or take." I rested my forehead in my hands and rubbed at my temples. It felt good to get everything off my chest to a stranger, but hearing the words out loud made it sound preposterous. I would never be able to raise $20,000. It was impossible.

"I have money."

I thought I imagined hearing it. But then she said it again.

"I have money, and what I'm about to say might sound crazy, but I believe that things happen for a reason."

My first thought was that she was right, it did sound crazy. "What are you talking about?"

"I have money, enough for what you need. Maybe we could help each other?"

"Help each other how?"

She took a deep breath and surprised me by reaching for my hand. "I could buy some of your eggs. If we kept it a secret my husband would never have to know."

"What?" I instantly pulled my hand from hers. "You've got to be joking?"

"Think about it," she said. "I buy your eggs for $20,000. I tell my husband I want to try IVF, but we use your eggs instead. He'd never have to know."

"No!" I exclaimed, moving further down the bench. "That's crazy, and it's lying. Just tell him the truth and use an egg donor. It's still his baby. I couldn't..."

"No, he would never allow that."

"But I don't understand."

"You don't have to understand," she said. "All you need to know is that you can pay for your mother's care, and the child my husband and I have will be loved. He or she will never want for a thing. You have my word."

I stared at her, my mind reeling. "That's... no, I couldn't."

She was desperate. I could see it in her eyes, but what she was suggesting sounded insane.

"Tell me something," she said. "Why did you come to this park?"

"Huh?"

"This park," she repeated. "Why did you choose here as a place to come and think?"

"I don't know, I guess I like the sculpture."

"Yes. Because it makes you think about what love can do. The way it can turn everything on its side."

I looked at her closely. "I suppose you could say that."

"Don't you see? There are no coincidences. Sometimes things just happen for a reason." She smiled and held out her hand. "I'm sorry. All this, and I haven't even introduced myself. I'm Jane."

I didn't take her hand. Instead, I got to my feet and threaded my bag over my arm. "Well, Jane, I don't know much about fate and all of that, but what I do know is the idea you're suggesting is... I mean... how would it even work? There'd be paperwork and appointments for you and your husband. There's no possible way you could keep something like that a secret."

She reached into her bag and pulled out a scrap of paper. "I'm going to write my cell phone number down. If you change your mind, call and then hang up after the first ring. Wait fifteen minutes and call back. Just in case he's there. It will give me time to move to another room."

Despite the circumstances, I laughed out loud. "This is not some spy movie. This is real life, Jane. You can't do these things in real life. It just doesn't work like that."

"But what if it could?" she asked. "Just think about it."

Despite my reservations, I took the number and folded it into my jeans pocket. "I'm not going to call."

"Just think about it. That's all I ask."

I shrugged and turned to leave. "I hope you work things out with your husband. I'm honestly sorry for what you're going through."

"You too," she smiled. "I'm sure your mother is a wonderful woman."

I knew her smile was genuine, but would a sane person offer to buy a stranger's eggs? And in a park, no less?

On the walk back to Penn, I forced myself to think of anything other than the conversation with Jane. But no matter how I tried to distract myself, her words kept spinning around in my mind. It was impossible... But what if? And then my phone rang.

"Dad? What is it?"

"Come home, Sophie, right now. It's your mother."

Chapter Sixteen

LACY

I drop what's left of my cigarette out the hotel window and hop back to the couch. Doctors say I shouldn't be smoking, but I say *what the hell*. Cancer wasn't responsible for taking my leg. In fact, I can't remember ever being sick a day in my life. Goes to show you, if life's out to get you, it's going to get you. So why shouldn't I smoke? Besides, it helps me think. And I have a lot to think about.

I would've enjoyed nothing more than seeing her face when she opened that parcel and saw the box of matches. And the timing – had it been on point? Was he there when she opened it? Were the kids? I'd love to say that tormenting her like this is enough for me, but the truth is that it's more frustrating than anything else. There's no payoff, no satisfaction. I don't get to see the strain on her face, the fear in her eyes. I need more. And more will come. I just have to be patient. Trouble is, patience has never been my strong point.

When they first fitted my prosthetic, I expected it to work right away. I figured if amputees could run marathons and compete in the Paralympics, then walking to the store shouldn't be all that hard. But I was dead wrong. Amputation above the knee is the most difficult to get used to. It requires rehabilitation therapy, occupational therapy, and physiotherapy. Not to mention sweating, pain, frustration, and most of all, my own impatience.

And it wasn't just the walking. It was everything. One minute you're an attractive woman clinging tight and waiting for your moment, the next you have a battered stump where your leg used to be. The worst part is when you're faced with the realization that from this moment on, the only glances you'll ever attract are born of morbid curiosity and pity—sometimes both— and it makes you start to wonder, *where to from here?*

School was never my thing and when I was signed by a local modeling agency at fourteen, I never went back – fat lot of good that ever did me, though. Turns out, a pretty face doesn't always open doors. Sometimes it closes them, usually around one am, when a cute boy with ripped jeans and a belt chain says, *"I love you,"* followed by, *"We don't need a condom, I can pull out in time."*

After they took my leg, I went to therapy and considered trying to accept the things I cannot change. I read books and watched documentaries about Aimee Mullins, who had both her legs amputated when she was one year old and went on to become a Paralympian. She was also named one of *People*'s 50 Most Beautiful People, but like I said, I was never going to be anybody's role model. So, when acceptance failed I decided on something that felt a little closer to home. Revenge.

If someone takes everything from you—your children, your freedom, even your mobility—what are you supposed to do? Just sit back and take it? Not me. Until now, she has never cared about what she did to us – but she will. It's taken twenty-two years to find her and had she not tried to big-note herself, creating that website or whatever it is, I probably never would have. She's built a fantasy world about who she is, and all those sheep buy into it. But not for much longer. I'm here now and when I'm done, when it all comes out, the story of Madelyn-May will be completely re-written forever.

Chapter Seventeen

MADELYN-MAY

1995

R omance stories with girls who needed saving were always my favorite kinds of
books, mostly because I liked the happy endings. Melody and I were fifteen, and
almost all the girls we knew who lived in the trailer park had already lost their virginity
– mostly to boys in the trailer park in clumsy spurts of intimacy that never lasted longer
than the time it took to zip back up. I couldn't say for sure about Melody, but despite all
the humping and grinding going on around us, no one had ever touched me like that.
Other than him.

In the books, all the girls and women lived happily ever after. No matter how bad their
situation was, there was always a prince or a cowboy, or dare I say it, a knight in shining
armor to kick down the door and defeat their captor. That's why, on the day someone
actually did burst through the door of our trailer and turn my life upside-down, I never
dreamed it would be a fifteen-year-old girl.

On the afternoon it happened, I'd been tucked up in bed and surrounded by books for
at least a week. It was the sickest I'd ever been. I had a fever, snotty nose, and cough so
full of phlegm it even sounded green. But I was in no hurry to get better. Whenever I was
sick, he left me alone and I got to stay home all day without the noise and annoyance of
everyone else.

When I heard Melody come back from school early, I put my book down and dabbed
at my clammy forehead. She must have caught my bug. The room we shared was tiny. It
was bound to happen sooner or later. I pulled back the sheets and folded my legs over the
side of the bed, thinking the least I could do was go and apologize. But before I got to the
door, she burst in and grabbed at my arm.

"Ouch, you're hurting me," I told her when she wouldn't let go. "What are you doing?
Quit it."

Her usually shiny hair was a mess and her eyes were wild. "Hurry, we don't have much
time," she whispered frantically. "I need to explain everything before he gets back."

"What are you going on about? Before who gets back?" I asked. Then to my horror, she climbed onto Mercy's bed and crossed her legs.

"That's not going to be okay," I warned her. "You know we're not supposed to be up there."

"So what? You know as well as I do, she's not coming back."

Our older sister had been gone for almost a month. According to Mom, she was shacked up five trailers over with "that loser kid who looked a bit like the guy from The Walking Dead, and not the hot one, the other one." Since I'd never been much into the whole zombie apocalypse thing, I had no idea who she meant or which loser my sister was shacked-up with. In the trailer park, you could close your eyes and point, and chances were you'd be looking at a loser.

"Still..." I glanced nervously at the half-moon creases rippling out from Melody's bottom. "If she knew—"

"Focus, Madelyn-May. Screw Mercy. All that matters is that I finally know what we have to do. I have a plan."

I pulled my focus up to her eyes and a knot formed in my stomach. "A plan for what?"

Her bony shoulders hunched forward and black hair fell in feathers around her neck like a raven. "For taking care of Daddy."

Melody had always been the good one. Her hair was longer, her skin shone brighter, she was smarter, funnier, prettier, and according to Mom, simply better than me. She had even beaten me at being born, coming out seconds earlier and making a grand entrance of it. But as I watched her sitting there on the bed, something had changed. There was an itch about her, something that squirmed behind her eyes.

"Melody, are you okay? Do you have a fever? If you've caught my cold—"

"For fuck's sake, Madelyn-May!" she snapped. "Would you pay attention? I don't have your damned cold."

"Well, whatever it is, spit it out already. You're starting to creep me out."

She pushed her hands, now bunched into fists, into the pale skin of her thighs and leaned forward. "We can end this, Madelyn-May, tonight. For good."

"End what?"

She stood up, and despite the way she was carrying on, all I could think about was straightening out the wrinkles in the quilt.

"What do you think I mean, Madelyn-May? Him. We can end him and all his filthy, disgusting visits to our room. Don't you want that? Don't you want it to stop?"

She was staring right at me, but no matter how hard I stared back, I was certain the girl who had been my sister for the past fifteen years no longer lived behind those eyes. "You mean..?" I stepped back, tripping on an old magazine.

"Think about it, Madelyn-May. We can do this. You and me. Don't you just want it to be over?"

My mouth was so dry that when I tried to swallow, my tongue got stuck to the back of my throat. "Melody, you can't be serious. We can't... I mean... we couldn't. What about Mom?"

"What about Mom?" she mimicked. "Mom's not stupid, you get that right? She knows what he does to us."

"No she doesn't," I protested. "She wouldn't let him."

"Wouldn't she?" Melody planted her hands on the emerging curves of her hips. "What is she without him, huh? Come on, Madelyn-May, deep down you know it's true. Mom doesn't care about us. You should know that better than anyone."

"But she's Mom."

"No, she's a middle-aged woman with nowhere to go, and no cash, who isn't pretty enough anymore to find someone else. That's who Mom is. I know it, she knows it, and Daddy knows it. The only one who doesn't know it, Madelyn-May, is you."

"Why are you being like this all of a sudden? What's making you act so crazy?"

She twisted and contorted her face until her features were unrecognizable. She was so full of hate. It was like the pain had changed her into someone else.

I thought back to what we learned in school, about how animals could adapt to their surroundings. How they changed in order to survive. Fish evolved to be amphibians, amphibians evolved into dinosaurs, and from there came birds and mammals, and other creatures. It had been difficult to imagine, reading it from a science book, but as I stared at her the words leaped off the page and knitted together to form the new shape of my sister.

"Are you seriously asking why I'm acting this way? You of all people?"

We were still teenagers, but at that moment, I realized the rape, abuse, and betrayal we had been subjected to for the past seven years had triggered an evolutionary process in my sister. The pain had woven itself into her DNA. She wasn't the Melody she once was. The girl standing in front of me had become someone—or something—else entirely. "Melody, I understand," I began. "I promise I do, but we can't—"

"Has he been to see you since you got your period?" Her knuckles were white and her eyes were wet.

"What?"

"You heard me. Has he come to see you?"

"He has, but—"

"Exactly. He was supposed to stop after we got our periods. That's what you told me. That's what happened with Mercy, right? He stopped after she started bleeding."

"Well, that's what he said."

"What he said," Melody scoffed. "Well, why hasn't it stopped then, huh? He's a rapist and a liar. Why do you think Mercy isn't here anymore? Wake up, Madelyn-May. This is never going to stop. Not ever – unless we stop it."

"I can't, Melody. I can't do... what you're saying." I moved toward the door, but she cut me off.

"How can you be okay with what he's done to us? And to Mercy."

"I'm not okay with it," I told her, choking back tears. "But what you're saying is... we just can't."

"Why can't we?"

"Because..."

"Because why? He's killing us, Madelyn-May. They both are, he and Mom and you know what? They don't give a shit."

My mind was reeling. I had a fever. I couldn't think straight. "I don't..."

"We have to."

"I don't feel well. I can't think..."

"Pull yourself together, Madelyn-May, there's no time for your 'I'm sick shit'." She dug into her pocket and pulled out a handful of skinny white pills. "Here, look..."

"What's that?"

"Xanax."

"You're going to OD him?"

"No, there's not enough for that."

"Then what?"

"We're going to drug him. Then when he's out, we suffocate him with a pillow. I need you to help me hold it down over his face. He won't feel a thing and then we'll be free, Madelyn-May, finally. Mom too."

"Who would pay rent on the trailer?" I hated myself for even asking.

But my sister had it all figured out. "He has a life insurance policy. I overheard them talking about it one night. Mom made him take it after that time he fell and hit his head, remember?"

I thought back to that afternoon. He fell because Mercy had all she could take and kicked him so hard in the chest that he lost his balance and fell back, hitting his head on the corner of our dresser. I glanced over at the fractured wood. "He really wouldn't feel anything? And we could just live here in peace with Mom?"

I didn't know if it was the fever taking hold, the primal look in my sister's eyes, or that cracked wood on the corner of the dresser, but somehow the plan was starting to make sense.

"Not a thing."

"What if he wakes up?"

"He won't," *she assured me.* "I have enough to make sure he stays down."

I leaned in and inspected the pills. "Where did you even get those?"

"Doesn't matter. Are you in?"

His damp brow moving back and forth over my face. The guttural sounds. His nicotine-stained fingers pressing into my arm. Maybe he did deserve to die.

"But why now?" *I asked.* "What's changed?"

She stepped back and her hand came to rest across her stomach. "Because Madelyn-May, that fucking bastard made me pregnant."

Chapter Eighteen

SOPHIE

2004

*B*y the time I got back to the house, Mom was already in an ambulance. The tumors had caused urine to build up in her kidneys and they were losing function.

As I followed the ambulance to the hospital, a million thoughts collided in my mind. Would she require dialysis? How much would that cost? Could we do it at home, or would she have to sit in a treatment center for hours every week?

When I arrived, they directed me to the waiting room. I folded myself into a seat, surrounded by an eclectic mix of patients and the people who loved them. After what felt like an eternity, Mom's oncologist came out and asked that I follow him into a small, white-walled room.

"Your mother is stable, but she'll require dialysis until we reach end-of-life," he said. "I'm recommending hemodialysis, a process which uses a machine to remove waste products and water from the blood, just as functioning kidneys would do. She can have these treatments performed at home, and that's our recommendation if it's financially viable for you. Patients usually require treatment three times per week for about four hours. That kind of routine can become exhaustive and will have an impact on patients who are at your mother's stage of cancer."

I nodded and rubbed at my temple. "But she's okay for now? I mean, she's not..."

"She's stable."

"And the treatment you mentioned, the hemo..."

"...hemodialysis."

"How much does it cost?"

He hesitated, and I held my breath. "Annual treatment can run in the area of $70,000 minus any healthcare benefits she may qualify for."

"$70,000?"

"It's unlikely your mother will maintain life for more than six months, Sophie. Maybe less. You should prepare yourself for that."

I searched my mind. What preparations were there for life without the one person who had cheered on all my accomplishments? Even before I could walk, she had been by my side to celebrate every milestone, from my first mouthful of solid food to sleeping an entire night in my crib. I knew because she had documented everything in my baby book. "And she needs this right now?"

"She does."

"Can I see her?"

When I eventually called my father, the exhaustion in his voice stopped me from telling him the cost of her dialysis treatment. I had one parent being taken against her will. My fear was watching the other one follow, a victim of utter defeat. Six months of dialysis treatment and end-of-life care meant I had to come up with $50,000. If I didn't, the alternative was unimaginable. At the time, Jane's proposal in the park had seemed insane but I suddenly found myself wondering - would she pay $60,000 to use my frozen eggs? It was three times the amount we had discussed. I'd need the additional $10,000 to make my plan work, and I quickly reminded myself this was not about morals. It was about necessity – for her, and for me.

I called the number Jane gave me, let the phone ring once, then hung up as she'd instructed, wondering every moment what the hell I thought I was doing. But inevitably a voice kept whispering back, saying, 'what you must'. When I called back the second time, fifteen minutes later, she answered in a voice brimming with hope and disbelief.

"You actually called."

"Yes. But there's been a development," I told her. "Things have changed."

"Alright," she said. "Tell me."

"I think I know how we can do this without your husband ever finding out. But the thing is, my situation has changed. I need $60,000." I held my breath as the line fell silent. "Jane? Are you there?"

"I'm here," she said, eventually. "When can I give you the money?"

She insisted on paying in cash. On my way to meet her at the same park bench where our lives collided, I was overcome with a mix of excitement and apprehension. I had no clue if my idea would work.

"I didn't know if you'd show," she said as I sat down on the bench. "I'm glad you did."

I stared straight ahead, unable to look her in the eye. "My mother has gone into renal failure. She needs weekly dialysis, as well as end-of-life care. There's no other way we could ever afford the treatment she needs."

THE SECRETS WE KEEP71

Jane nodded and stared at the same imaginary spot in the distance. "What will you tell your family about the money?"

"I have no idea," I told her honestly. "The main thing is that my mother will get the care she needs. She will be out of pain and at home for as long as possible. After that, she can leave us peacefully without ever having felt like a burden. Right now, that's all I care about."

She nodded again and nudged a tote bag along the bench. "There's $30,000 inside. I'll give you the rest once the doctor begins the process. You understand, right? I need to be sure."

"Of course. I'll speak with the doctor and let you know when it's all organized," I said. "In the meantime, you should talk to your husband. Won't it seem strange that suddenly you want to do this?"

But she shook her head. "He's been wanting—no, hounding me, actually—to do this for the past eighteen months. I've been making excuses because I knew I could never fall pregnant with IVF alone. If he ever found out I couldn't give him kids of our own..."

I nodded and wondered what kind of man would be willing to leave the woman he loved instead of considering egg donation or adoption.

"You're saving our marriage," she continued. "I want you to know that, Sophie. There's no way I can ever really thank you for this."

"I don't think I could have ever found a way to give my mother what she needs if it hadn't been for you. I know I was skeptical at first, and truth be told, I'm not at all comfortable with what we're doing, but it's a lot better than the alternative."

"Remember, there are no coincidences," she smiled. "You and I will be forever linked now, Sophie. I'll always believe this was meant to be."

After a beat, I threaded the tote over my shoulder and made my way out of the park. What we were doing was wrong and yet there were so many ways to justify it, at least to myself.

Lying to a man about the very DNA of his children was unforgivable, but what kind of man would cast aside his wife as punishment for having unviable ovaries?

Taking money, far more than was legally or morally acceptable, for my frozen eggs was reprehensible, but if I didn't my mother would suffer horrendously every day until she died.

Living with the knowledge that one of my eggs would be used to conceive a child I would never know was heart-wrenching, but what kind of child was I if I could save my mother from a painful death and chose not to?

And yet, what I was about to do – asking my best friend's husband to keep a secret like this was the worst thing a friend could do. But there was no other way to make this work.

As I walked through the park, I wondered about the math of coincidence. Statistically speaking, what were the chances of Jane being there on that very day at that very time? I wondered whether fate was stronger than morality and whether the purity of good intention was tarnished if it required keeping a secret as big as this one.

The bag was heavy and by the time I got to the car my shoulder ached. So did my head and my heart. This wasn't me. I didn't do things like this. I was a good girl, a soldier's daughter. My father had taught us to be accountable for our actions, so if this all went to shit, I knew there was only one thing I could do - put my hand up and ask for mercy. After all, mercy lived at the heart of all this. It was the one thing I was trying to give my mother, the woman who had loved me all my life. I would just have to hope that in a worst-case scenario, I might be afforded the same thing.

Chapter Nineteen

MADELYN-MAY

1995

*M*y eyes immediately fell over my sister's stomach.

"You're pregnant? But we're fifteen. I don't... I mean, I didn't that was - "

"Six weeks," she huffed.

"Six weeks..."

"Forget that for now, it doesn't matter," she spat. "What matters is we get that son-of-a-bitch. Tonight. Alright? We have to. He has to pay for what he's done to us."

"But what will you do? With the baby, I mean?" I caught myself staring at her stomach again, and quickly pulled my eyes back to hers.

"Don't know," she shrugged. "Find someone to get rid of it I s'pose."

"Melody—"

"I'm doing this tonight, Madelyn-May. You can either help me or not, but I'm doing it."

It struck me how hard her eyes had become, like two shields ready to reflect anything that might come her way.

"Are you in or not?"

Unable to say yes out loud I nodded instead, a wave of guilt instantly flooding over me.

"Alright, here's what we have to do."

As she explained her plan, it was clear Melody had thought out every detail, and I wondered how long she'd been planning all of this.

"Are you going to be okay with helping hold down the pillow?" she asked. "Like, you're not going to freak out on me are you?"

The door to our parents' room was only a few steps away. I looked over and imagined Daddy's body lying in there cold and quiet and dead.

"Madelyn-May?"

"Okay, alright," I agreed. "I'll help hold the pillow. I won't freak out."

"Alright, so when he comes in, I'll make his drink and you distract him. Now, come and help me crush the pills. We don't have much time."

We used the backs of two spoons to crush the pills the way we'd seen in the movies, and when it was all turned to powder, we swept it off the edge of the counter and into an old envelope.

"Are you sure this will be enough?" I asked.

"Should be."

"It should be? You don't know?"

"They said it would."

"Who's they?"

"Doesn't matter, just trust me. It'll work. It has to."

"Maybe we should wait. Maybe we should ask Mercy if this is a good idea. He's her daddy too."

Melody screwed up her face the way she did when she was five and tasted her first olive. "Mercy wants him gone as much as we do, Madelyn-May. What do you think he did to her all those years when we were still babies? He's a filthy child molester. A pedophile. We're his daughters. Have you forgotten this isn't normal?"

Had I? It had been happening for so long that when I tried to think back, there wasn't a time I could recall when I wasn't Daddy's 'special girl.' There were times I hated it. There were times it hurt and made me cry, especially when I was little. But it also felt nice to be loved and held and noticed by him. Sometimes it was hard to separate what he did from the emotion of it all.

"Madelyn-May... you don't actually like it, do you?" Her eyes were slits, and the word 'like' dripped from her lips like poison.

"Of course, I don't like it, Melody," I snapped, shame coiling around me. "What he does to us is gross. I hate..."

"...hate what?"

The sounds. The smell. The taste. "How he gets all sweaty. Like I said, it's gross."

"It's not gross, it's disgusting," she spat. "Unforgivable. And now I have one of his filthy little seeds growing inside me. How do you think that feels?"

I wondered as she stared hatefully at her own stomach - weren't we also his 'filthy little seeds'?

"I'm sorry, Melody," I whispered. "Does Mom know? About the baby, I mean?"

"God, no. Can you imagine?"

I shook my head. "No, I actually can't."

"Anyway, let's get this done. After that, I'll figure out what to do with the baby."

When Daddy came home, it was in a cloud of stale bourbon and with a look in his eye that I had seen too many times.

"Well, here's my two girls," he grinned. "You're both here together. How about that?"

"Hi, Daddy," I managed. "How was the tavern?"

"The tavern?" he slurred. "Now, why would you go mentioning the tavern right off the bat? Who are you, your mother?" He glanced around the trailer. "Where is that old bag of bones anyways? She ain't here."

"She's at the evening salon, remember?" Melody told him. "How about another drink before she gets home?"

A grin tugged at his lip, and he leaned down so he was face-to-face with my sister. "You're a smart girl, you know that? Smart and pretty. You might just be my favorite."

Melody cast her eye toward me and it was clear she had no intention of changing her mind.

"In that case, I'll make it for you," she beamed. "Bourbon, with lots of ice."

If it was true that our mother had acting in her blood, she definitely passed the gene on to my sister. I knew she was a churning turmoil of rage and hate and yet she was smiling at our daddy like a dutiful and loving daughter.

"And what about you?" He pointed at me with a half-drunk can of bourbon. "What are you going to do for me?"

From the fridge, Melody shot me another glance. Distract him.

"Well, Daddy, why don't you tell me about your day?" I began.

"My day?"

"Sure," I smiled. "What did you do?"

"Funny you should ask." He placed his can on the edge of the table and it immediately fell, splashing across the floor. "Shit! Now, look what you made me do."

"Sorry, Daddy, that was my fault." I hurried to the sink and picked up a towel to clean the mess.

"Look at both my girls taking care of their old man, treating me like a goddamned king." He sighed and sat back in his chair. "You know, your mother could learn a thing or two from you girls. I've taught you well. You know how to take care of a man. I did g ood."

In the kitchen, ice clinked against the side of the glass as Melody stirred his drink.

"In fact, since your mother's not home I think you both deserve a treat," he continued. "Something extra special this time."

Melody handed him the drink and he took a long mouthful. "You're both so good to your old dad. There's no need for me to play favorites anymore." He looked us both up and down. "Hows about you both come and have a lie down with me in the bedroom? Together, this time."

I swallowed hard and glanced at Melody. He had never asked us to do anything like that before, and I had no idea how to respond. All I could do was pray the drugs would kick in before I had to see something I would never be able to exorcise from my mind.

"No, Daddy," Melody chimed, in a pretty sing-song voice. "I don't want to share our special time." She rubbed his arm, and I was immediately filled with a mix of sadness, and I hated to admit it, jealousy.

"Now don't be selfish, sweetie," he told her. "Madelyn-May is your sister and I've got enough love for the both of you. Now come on, I'm not asking again."

Reluctantly, we followed him single file into the room he shared with our mother. We stood awkwardly side by side as he lay down and stacked the pillows behind his neck.

"You two shared a womb once," he smiled. "There's nothing more intimate than that, so this shouldn't feel strange to you girls. It's a beautiful expression of your love for each other and for me. You do love me, don't you?"

We looked at each other and I fought my bottom lip as it began to quiver.

"Tell me something," he tried again. "Have you ever practiced kissing, you know, with each other? It's one of the best ways to learn."

I fiddled with my heart-shaped necklace. There had to be some way to buy time until the pills kicked in. But it was Melody who broke the silence.

"I don't need any practice," she grinned. "I know how to kiss just fine."

We both knew where it would lead but at least it would delay anything that involved both of us.

I stood frozen to the spot as they began to kiss, slowly at first, and then harder. His hand reached under her skirt, and he scooped her up and onto the bed.

"Daddy..."

I had planned to say stop, but no more words came out. I wanted to shout at him that I couldn't watch. I wanted to scream that I hated him and loved him. I wanted to howl that I didn't understand why he was doing this to us. But there wasn't enough air in my lungs. My forehead burned and my knees trembled. When he peeled off her underwear and covered her body with his, something inside me cracked. I was overcome by the indecency, the violation, and the sickness of it all. But mostly I was outraged that he had left me standing there like an afterthought, like something he could so easily forget. I hated myself for thinking it, for feeling it, and the last thing I wanted was to trade places with her, but jealousy coursed through me like a fever. I wanted to peel off my skin and gouge out my eyes. I hated myself, and her, and him, and everything about my stupid, messed-up life. I wanted him to see me, to notice me, to love me, and to never, ever touch me like that again. He was my father. What was the right way to love him, or was it wrong to love him at all?

My head was spinning and all the questions started splitting apart. Sentences broke down and letters jumbled. I couldn't think. My vision blurred, soft and out of focus at first, then sharp shards of darkness cut through. I rubbed my eyes and willed myself not to stumble. I had to stay in control. Had to take control. Had. To. Make. It. Stop.

"No more," I mumbled. "Please, stop..." I covered my eyes, but all I could hear were the sounds coming from the bed. "Stop..." I tried again, my voice barely a whisper. "Both of you, please, I can't..."

But they didn't hear me. And they didn't stop. And then it happened.

Like a robot, I reached down and picked up the hammer Daddy had been using to repair the closet. I raised it up over my shoulder and stepped toward the tangled mess they had formed on the bed.

Sometimes on Sunday mornings, if Mom was in a happy mood, she would make eggs. When I was little, I used to climb up onto a box and watch her crack them on the side of the frying pan. I loved to see the yolk and egg white spilling and oozing out all over the place. A big, delicious mess served sunny-side-up.

As I brought the hammer down and smashed it into the back of his head, I thought about those mornings and how the sun had streamed in through the window. When his skull cracked, I heard the sweet sound of our Sunday eggs breaking against the pan. Somewhere in the distance, Melody screamed and I laughed, remembering the morning a fly had fallen into her juice and she drank it. I lifted the hammer back over my head and brought it down as hard as I could, again, and again, until his skull was nothing more than a scrambled mess of brain and blood. Tiny pieces of bone clung to my sister's skin like broken eggshell. Then, as our Sunday mornings slowly melted away, I realized Melody was still screaming.

"What the hell!?" Her bare legs were covered in blood as she frantically inched her way back toward the headboard, her legs tucked into her chest. "What did you do, Madelyn-May? What the hell did you just do?"

The hammer dropped from my hand and landed heavily on the floor.

"Answer me!" Suddenly Melody was off the bed and up in my face. She was naked from the waist down, his blood splashed across her thighs like the lashings of an angry artist. "Why

would you do that? He would have passed out any second. Fuck!" She stepped back and started to pace. "Look at this fucking mess! We can't cover this up. Why the hell would you do that?"

"I'm..."

"You're what?!" She gripped fistfuls of her own hair and stared at me. "What, Madelyn-May?"

My ears were ringing like a field of crickets in summer. "I'm sorry... I don't know what happened."

Her eyes narrowed. "You don't know what happened?"

"No, I just blacked out."

"Oh, you just blacked out?" She flung her arm toward his body. "Look at what the fuck you did! Why would you do that, Madelyn-May?"

Before I could answer, the squeak of the trailer door caught us both off-guard.

"What's all that yelling about?" our mother called from the kitchenette. "What's going on up there and what are you girls doing in my room?"

We stared at each other with wild eyes and my sister grabbed my hand. "Jesus," was the only word that escaped her lips before my mother appeared in the doorway and started to scream.

Chapter Twenty

SOPHIE

2004

*O*n the morning I went to see Gerard, my stomach was buzzing like I'd swallowed a jar of bees. I had no idea what he would say, or how he might react to the question I was about to ask.

When he saw me in the waiting room, his face broke into a wide smile. "Sophie, what a nice surprise. Come on through."

He ushered me into his consult room and memories immediately came rushing back. Samara holding my hand as he walked me through the egg-freezing process. Signing forms and learning how to inject myself with hormones to stimulate ovulation.

"Thanks for seeing me on such short notice, Gerard," I said. "I know you must be busy."

"Never too busy for my wife's best friend," he beamed. "Have a seat. Tell me what you need."

I placed the tote bag gently on the floor and searched my mind for where to start. There were so many consequences for what I was about to ask, but I only had one shot at getting him to say yes. My mother was all that mattered. I searched his face and tried to place my words. "My mother has taken a turn for the worse. It's her kidneys – they're shutting down."

"Oh, Soph..." He reached out and took my hand in his. It felt warm and reassuring. "I'm so sorry."

"She needs dialysis and then around-the-clock end-of-life palliative care. The doctor says it could run to $50,000."

He nodded and squeezed my hand. "If it's a second opinion you're looking for, I could recommend a colleague, but that sounds about right."

"No, it's nothing like that."

He released my hand and sat back in his seat. "Oh, Sophie – we don't have that kind of money. You know Samara and I would do anything we could to help, but we just don't have it. As you know, she's been dropping hints about getting engaged and I can't even afford a ring right now, not while we're trying to buy a house."

I hated that he thought I wanted to borrow money. It was the last thing I would ever ask. "I know, and I would never put you guys in that position," I told him. "Not when I know I could never pay it back."

"Then what is it, Sophie? How can I help?"

My hands felt clammy. "I have a way to pay for her care, but there's something I need to do. Something that can't happen without your help."

"Well, you've certainly got my attention." He smiled but looked nervous. "What is it?"

"What if there was something you could do that would help me give my mother the care and treatment she needs?"

He stood up and walked over to the window. "I'm not sure I like where this is going, Sophie."

"Just hear me out, Gerard, please. I met someone - a woman. Her name is Jane and she desperately wants to have a family with her husband. She agreed to buy my eggs. That money would be enough to pay for my mother's care."

"Sophie, the standard fee for egg donation is around $8,000. That won't come any-where close to the bill for your mother's treatment."

"I know, that's why there's a catch. He can't know."

Gerard's body stiffened. "Who can't know?"

"Her husband."

He turned and held his hand out palm up - a signal to stop. "Are you saying that you want me to transfer your frozen eggs in an IVF procedure that the father doesn't know about? Sophie, have you lost your mind?"

"He'd know about the IVF procedure, just not the egg donation."

The muscles in his jaw tensed and he shook his head. "Absolutely not. Sophie, how can you even ask me something like that? I'd lose my license."

"Please, Gerard, she's as desperate as I am. Trust me, she won't say a word. She's more scared of losing him than anything I've ever seen. Please, no one would ever know."

"No, Sophie. I will not do that. And honestly, I'm surprised you'd even ask."

"Here, look..." I pulled a pile of cash out of the tote. "$10,000 for you. You could buy Samara's ring."

"For Christ's sakes, put that away," he hissed. "Have you lost your mind?"

"Please, Gerard, I'm begging you."

"No, Sophie! I won't. Now, I'm sorry but you need to go. I can't believe I'm about to say this, but I wish you hadn't come here. You've put me in a very difficult situation."

I slipped the money back into the tote, but when I tried to stand my legs wouldn't hold me. It had been a year of pain and worry and guilt and fear and it was all about to come crashing down.

"Sophie, did you hear me? You need to leave."

I tried to tell him I was leaving, but no words came out. My knees buckled and I fell to the floor, my body wracking with uncontrollable sobs.

"Sophie..."

Whatever he said after that was a blur. My fingers clawed at the linoleum floor and Gerard's leather shoes shuffled across my field of vision. Then came a sharp jab to my upper arm.

When I next opened my eyes, I was lying on a gurney in one of the consult rooms. On the ground was my tote, the money still inside. I'd just managed to pull myself up onto one elbow when Gerard peeked his head around the corner.

"You're awake."

"I am."

"I gave you a mild sedative. You've been out for a couple of hours." He came in and closed the door behind him. "You had me worried there for a minute."

I sank back down onto the gurney, embarrassed he'd seen me in such a state.

"Sophie, what you asked me to do..."

"I know, and I'm sorry," I offered. "I shouldn't have come here. Please don't tell Samara."

"Where did you meet this woman?"

"Jane?" I paused and thought back to the day we met. "In Love Park of all places. I know how crazy it sounds, and when she first mentioned the idea, I said no. But then Mom's kidneys failed and it all just spiraled out of control. I didn't know what else to do."

He sighed and rubbed the back of his neck. "You really have no other way to pay for your mother's care? A second mortgage perhaps?"

"We've exhausted every option. We've hounded and harassed the VA, Dad already took a second mortgage back when she started chemo, and we've used up all our savings."

He paused, an agonizing frown clouding his face. "And you're certain we can trust this woman?"

"Wait, you're actually considering this? But you said—"

"How can I sleep at night knowing I'm the only reason your mother isn't getting the care she needs? I couldn't live with myself, Sophie, and I doubt Samara would forgive me either if she ever found out."

"I didn't know if I should tell her. If you'd want her to know?"

He rubbed his chin, and I could see his mind ticking over. "I've never kept a secret from her. To do so would be very difficult for me. But at the same time, it wouldn't be fair to burden her with this. The ethics alone are... no, this has to stay between us, and – what did you say the woman's name was?"

"Jane. Her name is Jane." He was going to do it. He was going to help me. "Gerard, this is incredible. I can't believe you're really going to help me."

"Well, I don't see what choice I have," he sighed. "But Sophie, this goes to the grave. Both our graves. Do you understand? If anyone ever found out then everything I've worked for, the life Samara and I have together, it's all gone."

"Yes, of course," I promised. "Gerard, I don't know what to say."

"You say nothing. Not ever. And you better figure out a way to explain where that money came from to your father and brother."

"I will. And here..." I sat up quickly and took the two stacks of cash from the tote. "This is for you."

"I don't want that. Put it away."

"Please take it, Gerard. I allowed for this. I want you to buy Samara the ring she wants so badly. It's the least I can do. For you, and for her. She's my best friend. I know what it would mean to her. Please take it."

His cheeks reddened, and he refused to meet my eye, but he took the money and retreated behind his desk. My mother was going to get the care she needed. And Jane... Jane was going to have a baby.

The plan was for Jane and her husband Ian to attend an initial appointment with Gerard to find out why they were not falling pregnant. After that, things would start getting a little tricky. When the initial bloods and other tests came back, Gerard would immediately rule out oligospermia, meaning Ian's sperm count was not the culprit. He would suggest a further ultrasound for Jane, conduct a pelvic exam, run more tests, and inevitably diagnose her with Polycystic Ovarian Syndrome, also known as PCOS, a condition that caused ovarian cysts. It was a leading cause of infertility in women and one that had no specific cause. In other words, it was an act of God, and no one could get angry at their wife for that.

Gerard would create a twenty-two-day preparation plan that directed Jane to self-adminis-ter a daily injection of Lupron. She would then move into FSH injections to stimulate ovulation and HCG injections to mature her eggs. According to the plan, on the tenth day Gerard would carry out the egg retrieval procedure. The clinic would fertilize the eggs with Ian's sperm and wait twenty-four hours to see how many became embryos. Viable specimens would be housed in special incubators until the magical morning of the transfer. But of course, Jane and Ian's journey would really begin on day seven, when Gerard began the careful process of thawing some of my frozen eggs and fertilizing them with Ian's semen, each in a separate culture dish.

The next day, as I ran over the plan with Jane she listened intently and scratched quick notes on a pad. She never looked up, and simply nodded every now and then to let me know she was listening.

"You'll have to become one hell of an actress if you're going to pull this off," I told her. "Are you sure you can do it? Faking injections and pretending to have egg retrieval appointments?"

She slipped the notepad back into her handbag and smiled. "Ian is at work most of the time, and I'll tell him I want to do the injections myself in case I need one and for some reason, he's not there. I read they have to be done at the same time every day, so that will make sense."

I pushed out a breath and looked at her closely. "You don't seem very nervous. Aren't you worried he'll find out?"

"I am," she nodded. "But at this point, I've already gone too far to worry about lying. We'll just have to be extra careful. Make sure it's all done right."

"It doesn't bother you that he won't know the truth about his own child?"

She sighed and twisted her wedding band around in circles. "The truth is a funny thing, Sophie. Sometimes telling it can be very selfish."

"Selfish?" I raised my brow. "You might have a hard time selling that to the person being lied to."

"What I mean is, the truth can be very powerful. It can set you free or put you in a cage," she said. "Have you ever noticed that people telling the truth are usually the ones who find freedom on the other side of it? Freedom from guilt, from burden. The guilty tell the truth, but the innocent receive it. Sometimes it's possible to measure our love by the secrets we keep."

Loving someone by lying to them. At face value, it sounded selfish and convenient. I was about to protest, but then considered my own situation. Would I tell my mother how I got the money or spare her the burden of knowing the truth? "I guess I never thought about it that way."

"It's the same for both of us, Sophie," she continued. "What are you going to tell yourself about what we did here today? Will you let yourself off the hook and move on with your life, thinking of this as a mutually beneficial business arrangement, or will you dwell on it, pouring over the truth and morality of what we've done? Will you walk away or will you become the architect of your own cage?"

I wondered if I would ever be able to see this as a simple business transaction. "Is that what you're going to do? Just move on with your life like this never happened?"

"I'm going to do what I have to. That's how I see it. Sometimes the things we must do are not the things we want to do. But they're often the things that matter most."

"You must really love him."

"I never knew how love could feel until I met my husband, but I guess that's the same for everyone." She thought for a moment and then smiled. "What about you? I never asked. Do you have someone special?"

"Me? No. What you're doing is something I could never imagine. I've never met anyone I would go to these lengths for."

She picked up another tote and placed it on the bench beside me. "The rest of the money is inside. The appointment for Ian and me is next Thursday?"

"That's right. Ten o'clock in the morning."

She stood up and turned to leave. "Thank you, Sophie. I mean it. I know you must think badly of Ian, the way he's so adamant about the whole baby situation, but please don't. You can't imagine how he's changed my life."

"You've saved me as much as I've saved you," I told her. "Whatever Ian thinks is none of my business. We all do what we have to sometimes."

She began to walk away but stopped and looked back at me. "You're wrong, you know. You do have someone in your life who is special enough to go to these lengths for."

"I do?"

"'Course you do," she smiled. "Give your mom a kiss and a hug for me."

And then she was gone.

Chapter Twenty-One

SOPHIE

As a mother, what lengths would you go to if it meant finding the missing piece of your heart? That is the question posed by Bastian's new author, Geraldine Jackson. When he gave me her manuscript, it was because he thought the story would resonate with me. A mother longing for her lost son, desperate to see him again at any cost. What he didn't know was how dangerous it could be in my hands. If he knew the truth, he would never have brought it anywhere near me.

I run my hand over the paper and stare down at the words on the page. Just like the woman in the story, my son is gone. But what if...

Jackson's story is as brilliant as it is haunting. In the book, the main character is a dying mother searching desperately for the son she gave up for adoption when she was sixteen. The primal need to tell him that she's sorry, to explain her absence, relentlessly drives her toward both insanity and the hope of redemption. Bastian was right to think it would strike a chord with me. Reading it, I once again experienced the pain of losing my mother and the tragedy of Josh's death, but he had no idea how deep the story would cut. Since I first read the manuscript, a thought has been hovering in my periphery, flickering in and out like the wayward reception of a broken television set. There have been glimpses, bursts of color, and pieces of broken words. What if...

I tuck a stray strand of hair back behind my ear and glance at Miss Molly lying at my feet. "What do you think?" I ask her nervously. "I can't, right? It's too risky." But she just stares at me, her eyes reflecting my own confusion.

When she suddenly barks, it crosses my mind that even she knows I'm being stupid. But when she leaps to her feet and dashes from the room, I know Bastian is at the door before I even hear the knock.

"What are you doing here at this hour?" I ask when I find him standing on the stoop. "It's after eight."

"Can I come in?"

I step aside, and he brushes right by me without so much as a kiss on the cheek. "Sure…" I murmur under my breath, "…come on in."

He flops onto the couch, one hand draped over the edge to scratch Miss Molly's ear.

"Problem?"

"Madelyn-May," is all he says.

Careful not to crowd him, I sit down in an armchair on the other side of the room. He's never shared much about his personal life – not the challenges of it anyway. Probably because he's always so busy dealing with mine. "You want to talk about it?"

"Got any wine?" he asks. "Nothing fancy. Just anything will do."

I pour him a glass of red and retreat to my chair.

"She's just so… argh." He lifts the glass to his nose and winces at the biting scent of my cheap Merlot. "I know you probably don't want to hear this, Soph, but I need… something. I don't know."

"You've listened to enough of my whining and woes. I owe you. So, let's hear it."

He takes a sip of wine, despite the fact we both know he'll hate it. "I don't get her. I've given her everything a woman could possibly want, and yet she's not there."

"Not there? She didn't come home?"

"Not present, I mean. She's in our house, at least *sometimes*, but it's like only her body is there. She's not. I feel like I've been married to a ghost for the past seventeen years."

"And you've tried talking to her about it?"

"Talking to her?" He looks at me as though I've gone mad. "You can't talk to Madelyn-May, Soph. I've tried so many times, but there's no point. She won't budge. She won't open." He sets the glass down to speak with both hands. "Do you know, she won't even talk about her childhood with me? Both her parents were killed when she was young, and I get that she's traumatized, or scarred, or something, but Christ… I'm her husband for God's sake."

I underestimated how much it will hurt to hear him talk about his marriage. For the past few years, I've heard so little about her that there is a part of me, and it's a large part, that almost believes Bastian and my relationship is the only one he has.

"I'm sorry, Soph," he sighs, seeing my face. "Shit, it was selfish of me to come here like this. I'll go."

He stands to leave but instead, I reach for his arm. "I won't lie, Bastian. This is a hard situation, but I care about you. And putting the other stuff to the side, I am your friend. So let me be that for you, at least tonight. It kinda looks like you need one right now."

His jaw is tense, but his eyes are tired, hollow. "I don't understand it. She loves her work. She must because it's not like she needs to do it. I mean shit, sure she makes a ton of money from what she does, but my business was always good and she's never wanted for anything, not even those stupid designer label shoes she likes so much. You have no idea how much I spent on that shit before she started making her own money. In the end, I even gave her an account of her own, so she didn't have to ask anymore."

I nod and wonder what it must be like to have someone cater to your every whim.

"Then we had the kids," he continues. "Two perfect kids. A boy and a girl. I don't know what happened to her after that. She just..."

"...she just what?"

"Changed," he says. "At first, I thought it was post-natal. We went to doctors and specialists. She took a bunch of medications and herbs. She even started yoga. Nothing worked. She just slipped further and further away. Then that blog she wrote about the challenges of the twins went viral or whatever, and that was it. She started her online site and we all got left behind."

"Online site?'

"She has a website about parenting of all things. Can you believe it? She's barely a wife, let alone a mother, and yet thousands of women worship every word she writes."

"She's a writer?" The idea of his wife as a writer is like a knife in my heart. Our shared love of literature and writing is our special connection. To find out she is part of that feels like a twist of the blade.

"Writer? No, she's not a writer," he says. "She has a blog about things she doesn't even do. It's just... I don't want to go into it, Soph, it'll just make me angrier than I already am."

"Did you eat?"

"What?"

He looks up, and I'm relieved to see my question has interrupted his train of thought. "Are you hungry?" When the first hint of a smile catches the side of his lip, I breathe out. "Tell you what, if you run to Joe's I'll make you dinner. Deal?"

"You'll what?"

His surprise is warranted. Cooking was something I always took such pride in doing for James. To do it for Bastian has always felt wrong. But he's hurting and after all the time he's devoted trying to *fix* me, the least I can do is make him a meal.

When he comes back with the groceries, I kiss him gently on the cheek. "Now, go pour yourself another glass of wine and find something to watch on the tele. Miss Molly will keep you company until dinner is ready."

He eyes me cautiously. "Who are you? Where's Sophie?"

I shove him away and laugh it off, but the truth is, this version of me was the real Sophie. The version he knows, the messed-up, incapable, unbalanced person is the impostor.

I boil a pot of water for the flat noodles and chop Spanish onions, coriander, and garlic. In a bowl, I combine sugar, lime juice, and fish sauce, with a dash of sugar, then set it to the side. The prawns Bastian bought from Joe's freezer are toss-fried in a pan, then I add the rest of the ingredients along with noodles and a couple of eggs. It isn't long before a very basic but delicious Pad Thai is almost ready to serve. My family loved this dish, and as I garnish each plate with a hint of chili, a tiny voice calls out to me.

"Not too much chili Mommy, it burns."

"What?" I clutch at my chest and spin around, one hand gripping the sink for balance.

"I didn't say anything," Bastian answers from the couch.

"Did you hear that?' I ask, stepping forward until I'm almost in the living room.

"Hear what?"

I battle to steady my breathing. *His voice.* "Nothing. Never mind."

"Are you okay? You look like you saw a ghost."

"No, I... it's okay," I tell him. "It was probably just the television."

But it was his voice. I know it by heart. I know it so well that my ears can hear what my heart is shouting. *My baby. How I miss you.*

I steady myself and take a long, deep breath. Not tonight. Tonight, I need to keep it together for Bastian.

"Alright, it's ready," I announce, desperate to put my memories to the side. "Try it if you dare."

Bastian smiles as I place the dish in front of him on the coffee table. "And I get to eat it by the TV?"

"What do you mean, *get to*?"

"At home, that's not an option," he sighs. "We have twins. They don't practice what you might call refined eating. Half of it ends up all over the floor and if we didn't eat in the kitchen our living room carpet would resemble a Jackson Pollock."

I nod and smile. "I remember when Josh first went onto solids, James and I..." I catch myself mid-sentence, a rock in my throat stopping the words from coming out. "Well, never mind that. How's your dinner?"

Knowing when to leave things be, Bastian takes a mouthful and cannot hide his surprise. "Holy shit, Soph! You can actually cook."

"Gee, I don't know what to say. Thanks, I guess?"

"I didn't mean it like that, it's just—"

"I used to cook for them... before... that was my thing, so it can be hard..."

"...to do for anyone else," he finishes.

Even amid his own chaos, Bastian is thoughtful enough to use the words *anyone else*, instead of *someone else*. Anyone means just that, anyone. *Someone* means so much more.

"Right, but it actually felt nice to cook again," I tell him. "I might have to do it more often, even it if is only for Miss Molly and me."

"Hey, if everything you cook is this good, you can count me in." He grins before a somber shadow falls over his face. "The truth is, it's been a long time since someone cooked for me, so thank you, Soph. I mean it."

"You're welcome. Now, eat before it gets cold."

He piles noodles onto his fork, and I make peace with my decision. He deserves to feel cared for. Don't we all?

We eat our dinner and afterward, he helps me clean up. We sit on the couch and watch a few re-runs of *Seinfeld*, and soon I find myself yawning.

"You're tired," he says. "I should get going."

I can't deny that I feel sleepy, but it has been so nice playing house for the night. So nice in fact, that I almost forgot why he came over. "You think things will have settled down by now?" I ask as he stands to leave.

"Settled down? No, I think everything will be exactly the same. We never fight. Tonight was an exception because I actually got angry for once, but she'll be the same. Silent, secretive, there but not there. It is what it is, I guess."

"For what it's worth, I'm sorry," I tell him. "You deserve so much more than that."

"Like your cooking every night?" He pulls me close, and we kiss for the first time since he arrived.

"Every night might be a stretch," I grin. "How about once a week?"

"Deal. Call you tomorrow."

After he leaves, Miss Molly follows me upstairs where I shower, slip on my nightgown, and pad over to the bed. My skin feels toasty from the hot water and my heart even warmer from a night spent with Bastian. For once, I wasn't the one in need of help. For once, I had been the one to give support and it feels good. Tonight, I have proven to myself that I can keep control when I need to. Hearing Josh's voice like that, even if it was only in my mind, was a curve ball but I regrouped. I kept it together. Slowly, slowly, little by little, the light might finally be finding its way in.

On my bedside table, the manuscript catches my eye. What if...

It's not like I would ever make contact or announce myself. Nothing like that. I just want to see. Just to know.

I flick off the light and sink into my pillow. They say that in the dark when your sight is challenged other senses become more acute. Smell, touch, taste, sound. I wonder if darkness can also heighten other physical reactions. The connection between your memories and your heart. The heart's ability to sway your mind, and your mind's capacity to justify unrealistic desires. For the first time, I allow myself to go there - to wonder about the child I helped conceive all those years ago. I can't know for certain how old he or she might be. I never saw or heard from Jane again, and it would come down to how many rounds of IVF it had taken her and her husband to fall pregnant. It could've happened right away or perhaps it took years. All I know for sure is that there's a child in this world who was conceived using my egg. I can feel it. That undeniable connection born of faith, blood, and a mother's intuition. Somewhere out there is a child who is the only living, breathing proof I ever created life. All I want is a glimpse, just for a moment to see what that tiny part might look like. Unlike the woman in Jackson's manuscript, I don't need to explain or apologize. I don't want to interfere. What I want, is to know whether the child carries any traits of my son. If there might be a tiny piece of him that still lives on in the child I helped Jane conceive.

Despite the dark, I squeeze my eyes even tighter. I wasn't there when Josh died, and in the morgue, I only pretended to glance at his tiny, pale frame. A mother doesn't need to see her child's body to know he is dead. The last memory I have of my son is watching him pull on his shoes and take his father's hand. He smiled at me, waved, and I blew him a kiss.

It's a blessing and a curse. I spared myself the pain of seeing my child's broken body, but how do you let go of someone you can't bear to believe is gone? How do you stop listening out for their footsteps, for the unmistakable sound of their voice? How do you stop thinking of things they'll like, and what they might say? How do you stop waiting?

It's a question that drives me closer and closer to insanity. But here in the dark, I finally allow myself to wonder if seeing this child might instead bring me closer to redemption. Would seeing a tiny piece of Josh walk safely into Jane's arms finally allow me to let him go?

Chapter Twenty-Two

LACY

I t's Saturday morning, and people are marching through the Philadelphia Mills shopping mall like brightly colored ants. They follow each other in long lines, this way and that, occasionally stopping to step awkwardly left, then right, then left again, to avoid bumping into each other. They laugh to try and hide their annoyance, but I can see it simmering there under the surface. What they really want to shout out is, *"What the hell are you doing! Move you idiot, get out of my way. Can't you see I'm carrying bags and trying to get to Cinnabon?"* But instead, they artfully dodge this way and that, smiling, apologizing, and pretending it's their own fault. I find it ironic that people are willing to apologize to the person they wish would get lost just because they're a stranger. If it was a family member or close friend, they'd probably tell them exactly what they thought. People.

Up ahead, Madelyn-May and the girl are making their way through the mall, drifting over to storefronts where they pause, occasionally point at something in the window, then navigate their way back into the flow of ants.

This is the first time I've seen Madelyn-May take either of the children out of the house. Usually, it's the husband who takes them to the park and to do activities, but from the shopping bags fastened to her arm, it looks like the girl needed to update her closet, and who better than the always-stylish Madelyn-May to lead the charge. It wouldn't surprise me if this whole trip is more of a branding exercise than anything else. With millions of followers watching their every move, the girl can't be seen bumming around in track pants and worn-out kicks, now can she? Even now, she's dressed in a white T-shirt with a frog on the front, which seems normal for an eleven-year-old girl, if it wasn't accompanied by Chanel jeans and a small Louis Vuitton shoulder bag.

I follow them as they make their way into Coconut Grove, a ritzy fashion store for young girls. From a safe distance, I watch as the girl pulls at dresses and shakes out T-shirts, Madelyn-May too engrossed in her phone to even look up. At the swimwear section, the daughter stops, balances her stash of clothes in the crook of her elbow, and picks up a leopard-print bikini.

"OMG, this is so cool," I hear her say. "Mom, I like, totally need this."

But Madelyn-May shakes her head and tells the girl to put it back.

"No, but I want this," she argues. "I'm trying it on."

Intrigued to see how the exchange plays out, I find a safe place behind a pile of summer knits and watch it unfold.

"Put it back," Madelyn-May tells her. "If you want a swimsuit, you can choose a one-piece. You're not wearing *that.*"

A smile creeps across my face as I watch the girl challenge her mother: "I'll try it on, then you can decide."

Realizing the swimsuit situation is about to escalate, Madelyn-May finally slips the phone back into her bag. "You're not getting that swimsuit and that's all there is to it, Harlow. Now put it back and choose something else or you can put everything back and we'll go home."

It's a stand-off, the two of them glaring at each other as shoppers unknowingly make their way around a bomb about to explode.

"Why are you so frigid and boring?" Harlow hisses. "Last week Kempsey posted a pic wearing a bikini exactly like this one on her Insta. What's your problem? It's not like you care anyway."

"My problem, Harlow, is that you're eleven years old. Kempsey shouldn't even have an Instagram account at her age."

"Well, she does. All my friends do. I'm the only one with no socials. You have no idea how you're killing my life, seriously. Not everyone wants to be a leper you know."

Beside me, a woman in denim overalls, and hair so short she looks like an ugly version of the actor Edward Norton, is staring at me. "You need something?"

"I want to see those knits," she says. "If you're not looking at them, can you move aside?"

I look her up and down and wonder if I should play the amputee card to make her feel bad or come up with something better. I quickly decide on the latter. "Sure, of course," I reply. "My apologies, and I hope you get better soon."

"Get better?"

"After your chemo," I tell her. "I mean... you are in treatment?"

"What are you talking about? I'm not sick."

"Oh... I just thought, well, with your hair, and this whole thing," I say, my finger indicating her overall appearance, "that you must have some kind of... anyway, my mistake."

I feel her staring after me as I wander off in search of another place to watch Madelyn-May's drama unfold. Sometimes people just need to be reminded they're not special. I consider it more of a public service than anything else. Once you start thinking you matter, disappointment is sure to follow because the truth is, no one cares about anything more than they care about themselves. The sooner people figure that out, the better off they'll be.

Over by the swimwear, Madelyn-May snatches the bikini out of her daughter's hand and throws it back onto the pile. "You do not talk to me like that in public. Not ever. You got it?"

"Why?" the girl challenges. "You worried it will hurt your brand?"

For a moment, Madelyn-May stares at the girl and I can tell she's at a loss for what to do next. If she makes a scene there'll be a video of the argument posted on social media before they make it back to the car – but if she gives in, the girl wins and life will unravel from there. As far as I'm concerned, either will suffice. My only disappointment is that I don't have a bucket of popcorn to snack on while I watch.

"Go and try on your other clothes," Madelyn-May tells her. "We'll discuss the bikini later."

"Does that mean I can have it?"

"I said, we'll discuss it later. Now go."

The girl huffs and pushes out her bottom lip. "Whatever... You're such a punish."

While Madelyn-May waits in the store, I follow the girl into the changing room. When the attendant is busy folding discarded garments, I grab a pen and scribble on a discarded piece of paper. As I fold it neatly into my pocket, to my surprise, Madelyn-May appears in the doorway. In a panic not to be seen, I turn too quickly and my prosthetic foot gets caught on a discarded hanger.

"Oh, my goodness," Madelyn-May gasps, as she catches me under the arms. "Are you alright?"

"I'm fine, thank you," I tell her, pretending to smooth down my outfit so that I don't have to turn around.

"You nearly took a fall there. Are you sure you don't need help?"

My heart is beating so hard that it echoes in my ears. The last thing I want is her feeling sorry for me. The very idea of her pity is enough to—

"Mom, is that you?" The girl calls out and despite my anger, I want to kiss her.

"I'm coming, Harlow, hold on..."

She excuses herself and walks toward her daughter's cubicle, where within seconds their bickering over the bikini starts up again.

"For God's sake, Harlow," I hear her say. "You are not going to parade around in a leopard-print bikini at your age. If you try to act like an adult, there are sick people out there who will want to treat you like an adult and I don't think I need to explain to you what that means."

"Maybe you do," the girl replies, her voice dripping in sarcasm. "I am only eleven remember."

"That's it, get changed. I'm taking this stuff back to the counter and we're going home. When you're ready to speak to me with a bit of respect we'll come back. Or you can wear the clothes you already have until you're older and can get an after-school job to buy your own. It's your choice."

"I hate you," the girl says flatly. "I wish you weren't my mother."

The girl's got balls, I have to give her that. And she's doing my work for me.

When Madelyn-May storms out from the dressing room, I slowly open the curtain of my cubicle. Any minute now...

Right on cue, the girl rips her curtain open with such force I'm surprised it doesn't tear from the rail. She stomps toward the exit, muttering curse words under her breath and I silently count. One... two... three – then step out. "Your name is Harlow, right?"

She stops dead and looks me over. "Yeah, so? Who are you?"

I search her face, so full of anger and disdain, and wonder if she might be the prettiest child I have ever seen. She is even more beautiful than—

"My mother will be back any minute to give me more shit and I really don't need it," she tells me. "So, whatever you want make it quick."

"I couldn't help overhearing your argument. I think your mother is being unfair about that pretty swimsuit."

"Yeah, well, no surprise there," she says, already bored and looking past me.

"Let me guess, you don't have any sisters. Maybe just a brother and your dad?"

"How did you know that?"

I have her attention. "I see it all the time, believe me. I'm part of the Philadelphia Big Sisters program. We support girls your age who are misunderstood by their parents and who don't have a female sibling to talk to."

She looks me over, and her eyes come to rest on the small visible section of my prosthetic leg. "You have a wooden leg?"

"It's not wooden, but yes, it's a prosthetic."

"Cool. What happened?"

My mind pulls back to the night of the fire. "You know what? That's something we can talk about when we catch up for a big sister chat. What do you say?"

She looks me over one more time, still not convinced. "You look a bit old to be a big sister. You look more like someone's grandma."

Spiteful little...

"Maybe... But I'm still a lot cooler than your mom." I grin through gritted teeth.

She finally smiles, and I take the opening. "Do you have your own phone?"

"Yeah, I'm just not allowed any socials."

"Alright, well take this..." I hand her the piece of paper I scrawled my number on. "Have you ever heard of AA – Alcoholics Anonymous?"

"Yeah, why?"

"The Big Sisters program is a bit like that. To make sure young women feel comfortable telling their big sisters anything and everything, we keep it just between us. That way meddling moms don't get in the way and you get all the support you need. Sound good?"

"So good," she smiles. "I hate my mom. Pretty sure she hates me too, most of the time anyway."

"Well, that makes you a perfect candidate. You text me whenever you need someone to talk to, alright?"

"Yeah, thanks. I better get going or you know who will be back."

She turns and trots out into the brightly-lit store where, despite their bickering, Madelyn-May places a hand protectively across her shoulders.

"Try all you like Madelyn-May," I smile. "But it's too late. I already have her."

Chapter Twenty-Three

MADELYN-MAY

Down the hall, Bastian is putting the kids to bed. It's been a long day, and Harlow really tried my patience at the mall with that whole bikini nonsense. If only she knew what happened when young girls try to act like women. I close my eyes as my father's voice whispers in my ear: *"You just need to seem a little bit older. A bit more mature..."*

That's the trouble with trying to put the past behind you. When you least expect it, it comes creeping up to tap you on the shoulder. I slow my breathing and run my fingers over the keypad of my laptop. An article online said that when bad memories threaten to pull you back to a place you don't want to be, touching textured items can anchor you in the present. I can't change the past but I can stop Harlow from posting images of herself on Instagram in a leopard-print bikini. Now all I have to do is stop myself from wanting to strangle her.

After a few minutes, my breath steadies and I reach around to rub at my neck. My shoulders are tight, crunchy. How long has it been since I relaxed? Maybe joining Bastian to say goodnight to the twins will prove cathartic. That is, if Harlow has managed to forgive me.

In Harry's room, the light is out but his face is bathed in the blue glow of his device. "Has Dad been in to say goodnight?"

"Yeah, I think he's gone in to see Harlow."

"Okay well, it's bedtime, buddy. Time to put that away."

Reluctantly, he puts the device on charge and I wait until the light goes dim. "Night, buddy."

"Night, Mom."

I smile to myself and move toward Harlow's room. It's been a week since Bastian and I fought over the box of matches, and each day I've been trying. Despite the fact my shopping trip with Harlow didn't exactly go to plan, it was a first step and—

A low murmur coming from her bedroom stops me in the middle of the hall. There's whispering, and then a giggle. My heart skips a beat as I try to make out what she's saying, but all I catch is the word "daddy." It's not unusual for Bastian to put them to bed, but there's something intimate about the tone of her voice, something that makes my stomach twist.

When I gather the courage to look inside her room, a sound escapes my lips that I have never made before. My hand flies up to my mouth, hovers momentarily, and then I find my voice. "What the hell do you think you're doing?! Get away from her!" It's a roar inside the stillness of her bedroom.

Bastian's head jerks up and he stares at me, his face a mask of confusion. He's tucked up in bed with Harlow, her head cradled beneath his shoulder.

"Why are you in bed with her?" I demand, my voice shaking. "Where are your hands? Show me. Harlow, get out of that bed. I mean it, right now."

Harlow immediately begins to cry, and Harry appears by my side. "Back to your room Harry. Now!"

He turns and runs back down the hall where his door slams. I forget to breathe as Bastian throws his legs over the side of the bed. He's wearing pajama shorts and a T-shirt. He turns and helps a now-hysterical Harlow out of bed and to my relief, she's dressed in pink summer pajamas, top, and bottom.

"What the fuck, Madelyn-May?!" he says, not caring that Harlow is by his side.

It's the first time he has ever cursed at me, but I'm too angry for the enormity of it to register. "Why were you in her bed?"

"What?"

"Answer me, Bastian. Why were you in her bed? She's eleven years old."

Blood has drained from his face, leaving it patchy with anger and confusion. "Jesus Madelyn-May, I was giving her a cuddle."

It's not good enough to calm me. Right now, nothing is. "Why do you need to be in her bed for that?"

He helps Harlow back into bed and pulls up her covers. "She was sad for Christ's sake. Can we do this downstairs? The way you're acting is—"

"Sad about what?"

"Like I said, can we do this downstairs?"

"No, you tell me now. Sad about what?"

"You won't let me have Instagram and everyone thinks I'm an idiot." Harlow's choked-up voice finds its place between us. "And the other day, Sarah Kentwell told everyone in our class that her mom thinks you're full of shit and that everything you write is a lie. They think you're a shitty Mom. They know Dad does everything and they all make fun of me because of you. I hate it!"

"Harlow!" I gasp. "Don't you talk to me like that."

"Well, it's true!" she shouts. "They call you a bitch and a phony and I hate you. I wish you'd just leave so we could live with Dad."

"Harlow..."

"Get out of my room. Get out! Get out! Get out!" She collapses into her pillow, her sobs loud enough to deafen everything but my conscience.

Frozen to the spot, I stare at her bird-wing shoulders and think of nothing except how fragile she looks. Beside her, Bastian's eyes are boring into me, but I can't look at him.

"Madelyn-May..."

Instead of answering, I turn and take the stairs two at a time in my hurry to get away.

Down in our kitchen, I pour myself a glass of red from one of the bottles of Cabernet Sauvignon we bought on our last trip to Napa. My version of comfort food.

"You want to tell me what the hell that was?" Bastian demands when he finally comes downstairs.

"Forget it, alright?" I say, the trembling glass a giveaway. "I was wrong. By the way, this whole thing is because I wouldn't buy her a leopard-print bikini at the mall today. Did she mention that?"

"You were wrong? Is that what you just said?"

"Bastian, you don't understand—"

"Well, you're right about that," he shouts. "Do you have any idea what you just did up there? To our daughter? To me?"

"Did you hear what I said? This has nothing to do with what anyone said at school. You spoil her so much that the minute I say no, this is what happens," I fling my free hand into the air for dramatic effect. "A leopard-print bikini, can you believe it? And not just that – she wanted it for Instagram."

He stares at me as though I've gone crazy. "I heard you Madelyn-May, but did you hear what I said? What the hell *was* that?"

"I'm sorry, alright? That was out of line, I know." Images of my father slipping into bed beside me creep in, and I push myself out of the seat. I need to move.

"Not good enough, Madelyn-May. I want an explanation. You don't just walk into a room and do what you did. You just don't."

He is on one side of the island bench, and I am on the other. It might as well be a continent between us. "It was a mistake, Bastian. I know that."

"It was more than a mistake, Madelyn-May. You practically accused me of molesting our daughter."

"Oh, don't be so melodramatic."

"Melodramatic?!"

Before I realize what's happening, he's up against me, his hand closing tight around my arm. "Bastian, let go. You're hurting me."

"You know what? I don't give a shit." His face is so close to mine that I can see the vein in his temple throbbing. "You've been hurting us for years. How dare you come in and accuse me of something like that, and in front of her? How dare you, Madelyn-May."

"You know, I'm getting pretty sick and tired of people in this family speaking to me like I'm a piece of shit," I counter. "Look around Bastian – everything this family has is because of me. I think I deserve a little respect."

"Are you kidding me right now?"

Everything I say is making it worse and from the look on his face, he's about to explode.

"Okay, alright, I didn't mean that." I glance down at his fingers, white-knuckled around my arm. "I'm tired and she really pushed my buttons today. I'm sorry."

"That's no excuse for what you did."

"I know, and I said I'm sorry. What do you want from me?"

"Something. Anything. An explanation. Give me something, Madelyn-May, because I'm drowning here. You're hiding things from me and acting in a way that, to be honest, is just pushing me further away. In fact..."

"...in fact what?"

"I can't do this anymore." He lets go of my arm and instead grips the bench with both hands. His head drops forward, and to my surprise, he begins to cry.

"Bastian?"

"Just go, Madelyn-May. Leave me alone."

My first instinct is to reach out and touch him but as I lift my hand, I think better of it. There's nothing to say that will explain my behavior other than the truth, and I certainly can't tell him that.

I turn and take the stairs, then pause outside Harry's room. Inside, he's crying. I consider going in but instead hover in the doorway. When he doesn't turn, I gently close the door.

Although she claims to hate me, I continue down the hall and dare to sneak a peek into Harlow's room. Her back is turned and she's eerily still. How can I possibly apologize to her for what I've done tonight? Technically, I didn't say the words out loud but I might as well have. Knowing she won't hear me, I whisper to her back that I'm sorry, then head up the hall toward our bedroom.

In bed, I pull the covers over my head. My family hates me and who would blame them? All these years, I've been terrified if I let them love me, really love me, I will fail them spectacularly. Tonight, it seems those fears have become a self-fulfilling prophecy.

Chapter Twenty-Four

MADELYN-MAY

1995

"*What in Christ have you stupid girls gone and done?*" *Mom screamed from the doorway. "You've killed him! Oh my God and Jesus Christ! He's dead. You really killed him." She tore her eyes away from Daddy's body and stared at us. "Which one of you did this, and don't you dare lie to me."*

"It was Madelyn-May," Melody shouted, pointing an accusing finger in my direction. "It was her. She did it."

I couldn't stop staring at the blood spiraling out of the crevice in Daddy's temple. It was soaking into the floral bedspread, turning it black like a cancer.

"Tell her, Madelyn-May," Melody was shouting. "Tell her you did it. Tell her it was you who killed him."

I tore my eyes away from the quilt and glanced at my sister folded up in the corner. All I could think was that she looked so much smaller than when we were crushing up the pills. "I did it," I said flatly. "I did it, Mom. I killed Daddy."

Without warning, she stepped in and slapped me hard across the face. "Do you have any idea what you've done?"

The blow snapped my head back and at the same moment, it struck me she hadn't asked Melody why she was naked from the waist down. "You knew, didn't you?" I whispered. "All this time you knew what he was doing to us."

"Don't you dare talk about your daddy like that." Her bangles bashed against each other as she pushed her hair back. "If anyone was doing anything wrong around here it was you girls, wearing skirts too small and trying to get his attention all the damned time. What did you think would happen?"

"That's not true. I hated him coming into my room. We all did and—"

She brought her hand down to slap me again, but I caught her wrist. "You knew and you didn't help us. Why didn't you stop him?"

"You couldn't leave well enough alone, could you? You needed his attention so bad, and oh, you got it alright, didn't you? All three of you and none of you ever stopped to think about me."

I glanced over at Melody, but she refused to meet my eye.

"None of you ever cared about me in all of this," she continued. "So long as you had him all to yourselves. And all this time I've had to live knowing what was going on, and not once did any of you give a damn about me. You never once asked me to make him stop. Three little mice all blind to how I felt."

"You can't be serious," I managed. "Have you lost your mind?"

She reached into her pocket, pulled out a cigarette, and lit it with trembling hands. "I must be insane to have put up with all the shit that's been going on behind my back. And now look what you've gone and done. How am I supposed to pay for the trailer now? That ever cross your stupid mind?"

"Didn't Daddy have an insurance policy?" Melody asked quietly.

"Policy?" Her head whipped around, and I finally let out a breath. It was Melody's turn. "Is that what this was about? Trying to cash in by killing your own daddy? Is that what I raised in this stinking trailer? Two murdering little whores?"

She took a long drag on the cigarette, then threw what was left onto the floor. When she looked away, I stepped forward and stubbed the glowing butt out with my shoe.

"It's true what Madelyn-May says," Melody tried. "We hated it, but he just wouldn't stop."

"Liar," she spat back. "And don't go thinking you'll be getting any of that policy money or living here off what you've done. That money goes to me. While ever I'm breathing, you two won't see a goddamned cent. That goes for Mercy too. Nothing will be coming your way because of what you've done. You hear me? Not a damned cent."

Melody finally met my eye, and we exchanged glances.

"You two are going to pay for this, you hear me? You've been trying to take him away from me since you were kids, and you've finally gone and done it. Well, we'll see."

"What are you going to do?"

I could hear the fear in Melody's voice.

"What am I going to do? I'm calling the police, is what I'm going to do. You two aren't getting away with this. You've ruined everything, and now you're going to pay for it."

"You can't!" Melody shouted. "They'll make us go to jail."

"And finally you'll be out of my hair. You know, it was always him that wanted kids, not me." She walked toward the bedroom door but stopped and looked back. "If it was up to me, I

would have had an abortion. Now stay put 'til I call the police. They're going to have a field day with you two and this godforsaken mess."

Melody and I looked at each other. She was wringing her hands and shifting her weight from one foot to the other. If Mom called the police, we would both be locked away for murder. I broke her gaze and looked back to my daddy's lifeless body sprawled out across the bed.

"We can't let her call the police," Melody whispered, her voice frantic. "Do you know what will happen to us in juvie?"

I nodded and without meaning to, glanced down at the hammer on the floor. Fragments of bone were stuck to the head, the handle spattered in red.

Melody followed my gaze. "You have to, Madelyn-May. You have to or both our lives are over." She glanced over her shoulder, then looked back at me. "You heard what she said. All these years she let him do this to us. All she cares about is herself. Do it, Madelyn-May. You have no choice. You have to."

I reached for the hammer. The handle felt cold in my palm. It was different this time. My mind wasn't fractured. I wasn't overcome with rage. Instead, I felt strangely numb, almost oblivious to the gravity of what was happening around me.

"Hurry, Madelyn-May. There's no time."

I stared blankly at Melody as my fingers wrapped tight around the handle. Outside the door, I could hear our mother rummaging through her bag in search of her cell phone.

I was only fifteen, but there had been times in my life I was afraid. Times when I hadn't known what to do. In those moments, my internal voice always ran rampant shouting this and that in a whirlwind of confusion and fear. But as I stepped out into the tiny hall and brought the hammer down against the back of my mother's head, my mind was silent and still. There were no frantic whispers. No chills of terror. My body was quiet and cold. If she screamed, I didn't hear it. If blood sprayed out, I didn't see it. One minute she was hunched over her bag, and the next she lay crumpled at my feet. I dropped the hammer and turned to my sister. "I don't..."

"...I know, but there's no time for a meltdown. We have to take care of this, Madelyn-May. We have to get rid of all this... mess."

I stared vacantly around the trailer, my eyes purposely skimming over her body.

"Snap out of it, Madelyn-May, there's no time," Melody ordered. "We have to get this cleaned up before someone comes."

I could see Melody with her wild eyes. I could see our mother's body, and there was a part of me that knew my daddy was lying dead in the other room. But none of it was real. A divider

*had fallen between my eyes and my heart. I could see what was happening, I just couldn't feel i
t.*

"Jesus Christ, Madelyn-May. Hello? Are you in there?"

"What?"

"We can't leave things like this. Do. You. Understand. What. I'm. Saying?"

*I squeezed my eyes open and shut, open and shut, open and shut. It had to be a dream. But
when I opened them again, Melody was staring straight at me. "Come on, Madelyn-May, help m
e."*

"They're dead."

*"Yeah, no shit they're dead," she repeated. "And you killed them, so let's sort this shit out
before we both go down for what you did."*

"For what I did?"

*"They're your fingerprints on the hammer, Madelyn-May. So either you help me sort this
shit out or I'm turning you in. I'm not taking the blame for this. So, what's it going to be?"*

"Mom's cigarette…"

"What about it?"

*"She didn't put it out properly, back there in the bedroom." I started to glance back but
remembering Daddy's body, stopped myself.*

*"Now's not the time to be worrying about a stupid cigarette, Madelyn-May," she snapped.
"If it started a fire…" She stopped mid-sentence and nodded quickly. "You're right. We need to
set the trailer on fire."*

*I followed Melody's directions as she barked orders to gather up all of Daddy's liquor from
the cupboard, and any old bottles of nail polish remover. Together we tipped what we had over
the kitchen, and onto the bed in their room. When it wasn't enough, I ran out to the carport
and rummaged through empty plant pots, tools, and tins. Eventually, I came back with a
half-empty jerry can of two-stroke fuel Daddy kept for the emergency generator.*

*"Get whatever you want to take, Madelyn-May because once I light this up there won't be
anything left. You understand?"*

*I nodded, then quickly started shoving clothes into a backpack, glancing back every so often
toward my mom's broken shape lying on the kitchen floor.*

"Don't look at that," Melody hissed, as she frantically packed a bag of her own. "It's over."

*I thought about Mercy and how she would react to what we'd done. Knowing me too well,
Melody read my thoughts. "Mercy will be fine. She left for a reason, Madelyn-May. She can
take care of herself."*

When my backpack was so full I feared the zipper was going to burst, I threaded my arms through the loops and took one last look around the bedroom we had shared. This was where it all began. This was the place he hurt me, where he broke me. It was also the place he had loved m e.

"Don't you feel sorry for him, Madelyn-May," Melody warned. "Or her. They chose their own fate."

I followed my sister out to the kitchen, where she found a lighter in Mom's purse and lit the ends of three dishcloths soaked in two-stroke. She threw the first one onto the bed. I hurried to the front door as she threw another outside our bedroom door, and the third into the tiny kitchenette. The pungent smell of gasoline suffocated the air. It coated the back of my throat and doused the hope of ever turning back.

"Go, go!" she shouted as the dirty lace curtains caught alight. "We have to get out of here."

I ran out into the warm night air, the smell of smoke chasing me into the darkened corners of the trailer park.

When Melody caught up, she took me by the shoulders. "We have to split up now, Madelyn-May. You know that, right? We can't stay together."

I nodded, even though I had no idea where I would go.

"Here..." She reached into her pocket and handed me a wad of $20 notes. "He gave these to me, one for each time... well, you know. It's all I have, but you take half. There's also a few notes I took out of Mom's purse."

Behind us, flames were already licking at the windows of the trailer.

"We have to go. I love you, alright? We'll always be sisters," Melody promised. "You were really brave back there. I couldn't have done what you did."

I choked back a knot in my throat. "Won't the police find out?"

"Don't worry about that. We'll be long gone by then, and there's no proof of who did what or anything. It will all be burned up by the time anyone gets inside."

I nodded and hugged her quickly. "I love you, too."

"Be careful out there, Madelyn-May, and don't ever look back. You hear me? Not ever."

I took one last look at the trailer, a cauldron of all our sins. They say fire is supposed to be cleansing, but as I watched it burn I felt anything but clean. I had committed an atrocity. I murdered my parents. I would never be clean again.

I reluctantly let go of Melody's hand and started to walk away. And that's when I heard it. Inside the trailer, my mother was screaming.

Chapter Twenty-Five

SOPHIE

Under normal circumstances, had I donated or sold my eggs to Jane, the child could legally request my identity when he or she turned eighteen. If I'd checked the box that allowed them to, that is. In other countries, like the UK, donor anonymity has been abolished but here in the US, technically it would be my choice. Then again, DNA testing, online registries, and ancestry websites make it easier than ever for a child to track down their donor, and perhaps someday when he or she was older, Jane's child could've looked for me. But the veil of secrecy the three of us had agreed to meant the only medical records in existence are for Jane and her husband Ian. Records show only that a couple had undergone IVF treatment under the care of Doctor Gerard Thomas, one of Philadelphia's up-and-coming fertility specialists. I do not exist. The child will never be able to find me. That was the promise, and the price tag for my silence was $60,000.

I clip Miss Molly's lead to her collar and we head out the front gate. Walking her helps me think and thinking distracts me from the fact I'm venturing away from the safety of home base. It's a win-win, especially for Miss Molly.

As we stroll, I wonder again whether Jane gave birth to a boy or a girl. Would there be any resemblance to Josh if it was a boy? Would there be any resemblance to me?

Egg donors are not technically considered biological parents. While it's true I only donated genetic material, in the culture dish Ian's sperm and my egg had been transformed into a beautiful and miraculous tangle, splitting and duplicating over and over. Two had become one, and one had become three, for him and Jane.

We turn the corner and I wave to Joe through the shop front window. He was there for every stage of my pregnancy. He knows I was a mother. He witnessed the miracle that was Josh. Deep down, I know it would be best to find contentment in that, to leave this whole thing alone. But as we walk on counting off the regular markers so I don't stray too far, my thoughts pull back to Josh and the child I've never seen.

How similar would they be? Is there a child out in the world whose face could give me one last glimpse of my son? Would they have the same eyes, the same dimples? Would the splash of their laughter sound the same?

Tears burn and sensing the change in me, Miss Molly glances up mid-trot.

"I'm okay, sweet girl," I reassure her. "I'm just being silly, and a little bit selfish."

We finish our walk and head back inside the house. The idea of seeing the child is tearing me in two and I silently curse Bastian for giving me that stupid manuscript in the first place. It has planted a seed. A seed that is growing and sprouting. A seed that is taking on a life of its own.

I let Miss Molly off her leash and she runs ahead to her water bowl.

Gerard will have Jane's details in his files. Contact numbers, emails, and most importantly, an address. So long has passed since the last time I saw her. Perhaps the details have changed. Then again, perhaps they haven't.

I flop down on the couch and close my eyes. I can't possibly ask Gerard to give me her address. To even bring it up after all this time would be like kicking a hornet's nest. We've all moved on with our lives since then. Gerard and Samara turned their engagement into a wedding and a wedding into a life. They have a beautiful, sassy, and way-too-smart daughter. Their life is everything they wanted it to be. And I had moved on too, hadn't I? James and I met just a year after my first encounter with Jane. We fell into each other and I found out quickly what she meant about the power of love and how it can transform you. From the moment we kissed, James became my world and I would have moved heaven and earth if it meant making him happy. I came to understand Jane a lot better after meeting James, and despite the moral questions that forever linger over what we did, I learned it was possible to love someone more than you love yourself. And that devotion can make someone do unimaginable things without ever questioning why.

For the past five years, I have lived in a cage too afraid to drive my car or go beyond a four-block radius, and while it might seem like a small feat, cooking dinner for Bastian marked a major milestone. It proved that in small doses I can administer my own form of therapy.

So, instead of tying myself up in knots again, I get busy cooking dinner for Miss Molly and me. Grilled chicken, rice, and vegetables. Nothing flashy, but it's something we can both enjoy and it makes me feel better to cook for a reason other than just myself. She's my dog but it provides a sense of purpose to cook for her. That night with Bastian, I realized that with the right incentives I could make great strides forward. That by doing something for someone else, it automatically made me the one in control and I liked the way it felt.

The dinner table was always for family time, and I need to do this step by step. When dinner is ready, I fill Miss Molly's bowl and then take my own plate into the living room. One reach too far and I will sink all the way back into the dark depths.

As I eat, I scribble notes in my diary about how I might start making my way forward. I write things like adding an extra street to our walk each day, not taking my phone on our walks, cooking three times per week, researching natural remedies that might eventually take the place of my medication, and generally taking better care of myself. When I'm done, I consider what I've written and realize it's been on purpose that I let myself fall this far. I have intentionally failed to practice self-love. Even thinking about the enjoyment of things like facials, yoga, meditation, and eating well creates a pang of guilt inside my heart. How can I spoil myself knowing I'm here and they're dead? How can I possibly make peace with anything resembling happiness or hope, let alone yoga?

Visions of a car crash I didn't see flash through my mind. Mangled, angry slices of metal. Bashed-in panels and crumpled-up doors. I hear the screeching of brakes and the smashing of glass. Screaming and the heavy silence that comes before the sirens. I should have been there. I should have been able to do something, anything. Why am I still here and they're gone? Every thought and plan they ever had ceased to exist the moment that drunk driver lost control and slammed into James' car. Every future embrace, kiss, touch, and flutter of their hearts, gone in an instant.

I carry my half-eaten plate of food out to the kitchen. James would not want this for me. He would want me to be healthy, safe, and happy even if I must do it without him. But how do I justify creating a future when they are forever trapped in the past? How do I ever find a way to let go?

Without thinking, I reach down and let my fingers trace the cesarean scar across my belly. My body has created two children, neither able to reach for me. One was taken and the other lives unaware that I even exist. An author once described grief as being, *"love with no place to go,"* and in my heart I know that's true. My love remains unrequited, my children carried away on the wind.

Chapter Twenty-Six

LACY

T heir weekly routine is like clockwork.

Every morning at eight thirty am, the husband leaves, drops the kids at school by nine, then heads into the city. Meanwhile, the Queen of Sheba herself is always at the office by eight am. Afternoons are the same. He's outside their school by five minutes to three, they come out, and he brings them right home. She usually gets back to the house around seven pm, sometimes later. Every day is the same, with one exception - Thursdays.

On Thursdays, the boy stays late at school for soccer practice and the girl plays tennis. He finishes a half-hour before her, then walks around to the courts where he opens his backpack, pulls out a piece of fruit, and waits. When she's done, together they stroll to the bus stop. It's the only afternoon they don't get picked up. Instead, they catch a bus that drops them two blocks from home right before six pm.

It's been two weeks now, and the routine has stayed the same.

From the safety of my car, I watch students filing into school like a herd of mindless sheep. None of them have any idea what's waiting out here, out in the real world. In school, they are placated and treated like they matter but in a few years they'll graduate, and that's when life will hit them like a smack in the face. Because guess what kids – the world doesn't give a shit about you and all your plans. It takes what it wants and there's no bell that rings at three pm when it's time to go home and put your feet up.

I take a bite of my breakfast burrito, a treat I gave myself this morning since we're getting so close to the end. Soon everything we've been planning will rain down on Madelyn-May's head like a shit storm.

When the twins finally come into view, I screw up the burrito wrapper and throw it onto the dash. The girl is a few steps behind and has her arm linked with a friend, a tall wiry thing with hair like a field of electric strawberries. The boy is alone walking off to her left, his hands shoved inside his pockets and his head so far down it's like the entire world is pushing against the back of his neck.

"Give it a rest, kid," I say with a sigh. "You haven't got anything to be miserable about... yet."

When the girls drop arms and Harlow steps away, I grab my phone and click a few pictures. A pretty portrait of what's to come.

When they disappear into the school, I flick through the images and choose one I like best. "That's nice," I whisper. "Perfect."

When it's attached to the message app, I type a quick note and check it over one last time. Satisfied, I hit send:

Lacy: *Your photo as promised*

I start the car. Everything is on track.

Chapter Twenty-Seven

SOPHIE

The phone rings: once, twice, three times. I know from Samara that Gerard keeps Mondays clear for consultations, so he should be in. When the receptionist finally answers, I tell her my name is Sophie and that it's a personal call. A few seconds later Gerard's voice comes onto the line.

"Sophie, how are you?" he chimes.

"Hey Gerard, sorry to call you at the office. I was hoping to make an appointment, but the thing is, I just wanted to talk to you about it first."

"Appointment? Is everything okay?"

"I'm okay. I actually wanted to chat with you about possibly having another baby. I'm just not ready for a relationship, so I thought maybe with a donor…"

The line falls silent, and I hope he won't hang up. When he eventually speaks, his voice is low and serious. "Sophie, have you really thought about this?"

Wanting another baby is the only excuse I could come up with for needing to make an appointment. "Maybe it's that I'm turning thirty-five in a couple of years, I don't know," I tell him. "But I'm thinking this might be the only way I'll ever have another child, Gerard."

On the other end of the line, he sighs out loud. "If you're sure, then we can discuss it. Have you spoken about this with Samara?"

"Not yet. I wanted to talk to you first to see if you would be willing to help me. Obviously, I'd have to come in for an appointment to discuss it properly."

When he agrees, I thank him for his help and make an appointment for later in the week. With any luck, it won't be too hard to find Jane's file on his computer and copy down her details. All I'll have to do is get him out of the room.

I put down my phone and sink into the couch, guilt already creeping over me. It took so long to make the decision. Back and forth, to and fro, always worrying about how to broach the subject with Gerard. On the afternoon it happened, I had no idea a simple walk to Joe's for milk would become the ultimate decider for everything that was about to unfold.

He had been two houses from the corner of Brown and North 25th when I saw him. A twenty-something kid dressed in cargo pants, a black T-shirt, and the item that caught my attention - a camouflage-print Philadelphia Eagles cap. I had sent the same one over to my brother when he was still in active service. Before the communications bunker in Afghanistan was raided. Before they sent him home to wake up each night, drenched in sweat and re-living the honorable horrors of serving his country. The hat was meant as a bridge, something to connect his love of the Eagles with his dedication to the service. But when I saw the kid on the street with his camouflage print Eagles cap, it struck me what a ruse it all had been. Not the NFL's Salute to Service military recognition campaign – God knows veteran's support groups need all the help they can get - but the pride I once felt at being a military daughter. Conflict is ugly and no amount of camouflage can ever cover that up, but it did get me thinking. If I concealed my plan and camouflaged my intentions, created a ruse of my own, perhaps I could avoid conflict altogether. If Gerard didn't know I wanted Jane's details and believed our consultation was about something else, then maybe I could achieve my mission without ever upsetting anyone. And that's how it happened. That's how a simple ruse would start a war.

On the morning of my appointment with Gerard, I text Samara from the waiting room. Knowing them inside out will work in my favor, and as much as I know this is wrong, I can't leave anything to chance. It's the only shot I'll get at seeing the files and I can't afford to blow it. In my text, I tell her I'm thinking of using a sperm donor to have another baby. I tell her I'm not exactly sure how I feel about it and am going to discuss the logistics with Gerard. Since Josh ended up being conceived naturally I don't expect any issues, I say, but it's important to go over everything just to be sure. I also suggest dinner at my place tonight where together we can pour over every detail. As I hit send, right on cue Gerard appears at the door and calls my name.

I follow him into the room and sit down.

"Now, Sophie, before we start..."

And just like clockwork, his cell phone rings. I knew without a doubt that Samara would call him the moment she read the text. I also knew he wouldn't ignore the call or take it in front of me. He glances down as their wedding photo lights up his phone screen. "Do you mind if I take this? I'll only be a moment."

I sit quietly as he makes his way out into the hall but the second he closes the door I leap into action. I minimize the window on his computer and search frantically on his desktop for something labeled as medical files. My legs feel giddy and my heart is racing as I move the search arrow across the screen looking for anything that resembles Jane's file. "Shit, shit," I whisper. "Where are you?"

Trying another tact, I click on the search bar and type in my own name. The procedure will only relate to Jane and her husband, but they used my eggs so there might be a connection. Instantly my name pops up and I click the link. It takes me to the medical history files I was looking for, but they are password encrypted. I quickly glance over my shoulder and wonder how much time I have before he comes back. "Password, password," I wonder aloud. "What would he choose?"

I type in SAMARA and hold my breath. No luck. I try his birthday but it's another fail. I might only have one more shot before the program locks me out, so I type in their daughter's name JADA. And I'm in.

Knowing I'm on borrowed time, I click the link and it takes me to a file with records of my egg harvesting procedure and cryopreservation but there's nothing about Jane. I try typing her husband Ian's name into the search bar, but once again it comes up empty.

"Shit, maybe her full name is Janelle or maybe Janet," I think out loud. "Why didn't I ask her surname? *Stupid.*"

I scroll all the way to the bottom of the screen and notice a code with a hyperlink. It's a numerical sequence with no letters or words, but I click the link anyway and hold my breath. I can hear Gerard saying goodbye to Samara down the hall.

A new screen loads and the first words are IVF procedure and 2004. This has to be it.

"I love you, too," Gerard says. He's right outside the door.

I scroll down and find the words I've been looking for - Patient Details. I click the link and open the camera on my phone, ready to snap a picture of her address.

But when the new page loads and I see what's in the file, my hand flies up to my mouth and my phone clatters to the floor. "Oh my God," I whisper. "What have I done?"

Chapter Twenty-Eight

MADELYN-MAY

1995

*P*eople were gathering around the trailer to watch it burn, shadows hollowing their faces and making them look like gargoyles. A man I recognized as Jim Clancy from six trailers over tried kicking at the front door a couple of times, but embers quickly lit up the sole of his boot and he kicked it off, cursing out loud, something I couldn't make out.

"Mom's still alive," I whispered frantically to Melody. The sharp edges of my keys pressed through the pocket of my jeans and into my hip. "We have to go back."

But Melody grabbed my arm and spun me around to face her. "We can't Madelyn-May, not now. It's too late."

"But we can't just leave her in there."

"We have to. If we go back, they'll ask too many questions. The only chance we have is if we disappear. It's done. Let it be."

I glanced back at the burning trailer. A long plume of black smoke billowed up from the roof, twisting and coiling like a dark genie. Had I wished this upon us? All those nights I cried myself to sleep, wishing it would stop – had the night sky heard me?

"I can't just stand here," I told Melody. "I know what I did, but she's still alive in there. I have to go back." I pulled my arm free from her grasp and started running toward the trailer. "Go," I shouted over my shoulder. "Don't wait for me."

It was an inferno. Heat radiated through the dark, and as I drew closer the air felt like it was on fire. Tiny sparks and pieces of burning debris lit up the sky like fireflies, the wind carrying them off into the distance. A window exploded and flames licked their way along the outside walls.

"What are you doing? Get back!" someone screamed.

But I wasn't listening. With a sweater wrapped around my hand for protection, I ran to the door and shoved my key into the lock. Ash fell into my eyes and sweat beaded across my forehead. Coughing and choking from the smoke, I shielded my eyes and turned the key.

"Do not open that door!" someone shouted. "The flames will—"

I pushed the door and fell back as fire punched its way through, scorching my hand and wrist.

"Someone help her," a woman shouted. "She's hurt. Someone help..."

I screamed and frantically rolled my arm back and forth across the grass, trying to put out the flames. The burning material tangled around my wrist. The pain was excruciating, and again I screamed out. Two men rushed over and worked quickly to unravel the smoldering sweater. When it fell away, fibers and melted fabric were stuck to my skin but I didn't dare pull at them. Instead, I hoisted myself up to my knees and nursed my burning arm across my chest.

"Are you alright?!"

"Let me see."

"What were you thinking?!"

People rushed forward, trying to see my injuries. They asked questions and tried to get a better look at my face despite the dark. "I'm fine," I snapped. "Just leave it. I can take care of it."

Behind us, three fire trucks rolled in, the firemen already out and uncoiling their hoses before the wheels came to a stop. "Out of the way!" a burly man dressed head-to-toe in yellow PPE shouted. "Was there anyone inside? Are there people trapped in there?"

"A woman was screaming," someone told him. "Five people live there. A man, a woman, and three girls. We don't know who was inside."

The firemen turned on their hoses as the main drive of the trailer park flooded with even more red and blue lights. The police. I glanced back to see if Melody was still hiding over by the trees, but to my relief she was gone. I had to make a choice. Own up to what I did or try and get away before it was too late. Melody was already gone. Mercy would have the alibi of being with her boyfriend. That only left me.

"Are you alright? How bad are you burned?" It was Avril Beanie, a nice enough but strange woman who lived in a trailer over by the playground.

"I'm alright, Avril, thanks for asking."

"Which one are you, dear? I never can tell you and your sister apart. You look so much alike."

"We don't look that much alike," I told her. "My sister is much prettier than me, everyone knows that. But I'm okay. Thanks for asking, but I need to go and find my sisters."

Avril nodded, and I ran off toward the trailer Mercy's boyfriend lived in, hoping it would throw her off my trail. When I was satisfied that everyone was busy watching the burning spectacle that had once been our home, I turned and snuck along the outside of the park, careful to stay in the shadows. I tracked back to the leafy spot where I had stood with Melody and picked my backpack up off the ground. I winced at the weight of it on my burned arm and glanced down to see pieces of dead skin already flaking away. Gritty ash spread further across my cheeks as I flinched from the pain and tried to wipe away my tears.

The rocky track behind the park led past the sewer pipes and through the riverbed that always dried up in summer. The ground was littered with loose rock and broken twigs. It was difficult keeping my balance. The air felt damp and humid. Thin moonlight fell across the surrounding bush. I stopped and clutched at my chest in fright when an owl hooted from somewhere off in the distance. At any moment, I expected the weight of a hand to fall across my shoulder or a spotlight to shine in my eyes. But when nothing happened, and I was safe inside the big pipes that ran under the main road into town, I crouched down and rested my burning skin on the cold cement. Melody had given me what I guessed was about $300. I also had a few hundred dollars of my own saved up from helping at the hair salon on Saturdays, but it wouldn't be enough to hide nearby for any length of time. People had seen me at the fire. They knew I was there. My only option was to get as far away as possible, and like Melody said, never come back.

I got to my feet and clawed my way up the embankment and onto the main road that led out of Sonoma. My plan was to take the local bus to Santa Rosa and from there take the first Greyhound to somewhere on the East Coast. I didn't care where - I just wanted to get as far away from California as I could.

I had been walking for about ten minutes when the sound of car tires crunching in the gravel sent a pulse of fear running through me. Terrified it might be the police, I dropped my head and kept walking. But when a woman's voice called out, I stopped and turned around. Her headlights were blinding, and I couldn't see her face. "Hello? Who's there?"

"Sweetheart, do you need a ride?"

I still couldn't see her, but there was something soft about the tone. Something nurturing. "Umm..." I glanced down at my filthy clothes. How would I ever explain the blood? "Thanks, but I'm alright."

She took a few steps toward me, not so close that I would run but enough for her to see my face. "Sweetheart, it's past ten pm and you're alone on the side of the road. That's no place to be for someone who's alright."

The truth was, I had never been further from alright and I did need help. But after one look at me, anyone in their right mind would surely call the police.

"I can help," she offered. "I can see you've been in an accident and I mean you no harm. I just want to help."

My shoulders fell slack. I was so tired. I turned, and against my better judgment, took a few small steps back toward her car. When I got closer, she caught her breath.

"Oh my, you are definitely not alright are you?"

I flinched as she placed her arm around my shoulders.

"Whatever happened to you?"

"Umm... I was in an accident like you said."

"And your parents?" Her voice held a downy timbre of kindness that I'd never heard before. She smelled like lavender and had a simple gold band on her ring finger.

"My parents, they're..." And that's when I started to cry. A flood of emotion finally pouring out for everything that had happened. For my childhood, for my sisters, for my parents, and what I had done to them.

"Never mind that for now," she told me. "First things first, we need to get home so you can clean up."

"No! You can't make me go anywhere." I pulled away, panic coursing through me. "I just need to get to the bus stop."

"It's alright," she said quietly. "You'll get cleaned up, and then I'll take you wherever it is you need to go. No questions asked. I assume you have clean clothes in that backpack?"

I eyed her cautiously and noticed a small gold cross hanging around her neck. "You're from the church?"

She took the pendant between her fingers. "You mean this? No, I'm not from the church. But I do work with teens who get themselves in all sorts of strife. They don't always hang around, but they leave in better shape than I found them."

"So, you're some sort of counselor then?"

She smiled gently and thought for a moment. "I like to think of myself as a rescuer, of sorts. I lost my husband a while back and it's good for me to have life in the house. I was a teenage girl once myself you know."

I figured she was probably used to drugs and teenage pregnancies but had she ever taken in a girl who'd killed her own parents?

"Will you let me help you? Just to get cleaned up?"

I weighed my options and quickly realized I had none. If I went to the bus stop covered in filth and blood they would call the police and child services in a heartbeat. So, I quietly followed her back to the car, and once we were inside, stole a better look at her. She had a heart-shaped *face and wavy gray hair pulled into a loose knot at the nape of her neck. I could tell she paid no mind to things like styling or make-up, but that didn't matter because all I could think was that she felt like coming home. She had an elegant nose that seemed in contrast to the deep lines etched around her eyes, and there was something about her, a certain fragility, that made me think of burnt orange leaves falling in autumn.*

"Why were you driving so late?" I asked as we pulled out onto the road.

"I was actually on my way home from a friend's place. Book club night."

The words sounded foreign to me, and I tried to imagine the kind of life that included a book club.

"I usually get home a little earlier than this," she continued, "but there was a fire back at the trailer park grounds. They blocked off the road so I had to take a detour."

"Oh yeah," I mumbled. "I heard the sirens. Some coincidence, I guess."

She glanced over at the burn on my arm. "There are no coincidences, sweetheart. Sometimes things just happen for a reason."

"Thank you, ma'am – for stopping I mean. I'm Madelyn-May."

"Well, you're very welcome, Madelyn-May," she smiled. "And please, call me Mary."

Chapter Twenty-Nine

MADELYN-MAY

Any trust I gained with Bastian after our argument about the matches had gone up in flames when I lost it over Harlow. The morning after my outburst in her room, I considered packing a bag and writing a note telling him it was best for everyone if I left for a while. But despite my failings, I am still Harry and Harlow's mom and Bastian's wife. I may not know how to emotionally connect with them, and maybe all my good intentions inevitably make things worse, but they are my blood and this is one family I could never run away from.

When my phone lights up with a call from school my heart flip-flops in my chest. "This is Madelyn-May. Is everything alright? Is one of the twins hurt?"

The school principal reassures me they're fine but asks if I can come and pick up Harlow. Apparently, Bastian isn't answering and my daughter has been suspended for fighting on school grounds.

"Could you repeat that?" I ask. "Did you say *fighting*?"

According to the teacher on playground duty, one moment Harlow was sitting on the seats by the school's community garden, and the next she had her classmate Lola Rifkin down on the ground and was, *"wailing on her with both fists, in a sight that was quite disturbing, to say the least."*

I try Bastian's cell phone. When he doesn't pick up, I call his office. "I'm looking for my husband," I tell Val, his receptionist. "Is he there?"

"I'm sorry Mrs Marozzi, he stepped out for a lunch meeting with one of the editors. Is there anything I can help you with?"

I glance at my watch. Twelve-thirty pm. Harlow's fight must have happened on her lunch break. "No, it's fine. Have him call me when he gets back."

Untangling the jumble of questions and trying to figure out what I'm going to say to my daughter, is no easy feat. What do you say to an eleven-year-old girl who carries a Prada school bag and beats on her friends?

"Mrs Marozzi, thank you for coming in," Principal Laura Waters says when I sit down. "I appreciate your time. I know you must be very busy."

Before I can respond, the door opens and a teacher I am not familiar with escorts Harlow into the seat beside me. There are grass stains on her sleeve and one of her braids has come undone. I immediately want to scold her but can see in her eyes she is struggling to keep it together.

"As you know Mrs Marozzi, Harlow was involved in an incident at lunchtime that included physical contact with another student," the principal says. "I don't need to tell you that we have a strict policy around physical contact that results in immediate suspension. So, while we understand your family is a friend of the school, and we greatly appreciate your ongoing support, our policy requires Harlow be suspended as a consequence of what she did today."

Instead of scolding my daughter, I instantly scold myself for wondering how Bastian and I are supposed to go to work with a suspended eleven-year-old at home.

Next to me, Harlow mumbles something I can't quite understand, and I snap back into the room. "What's that, sweetheart?"

"I said, she started it and don't call me that. You hate me and you think Dad is—"

"Harlow," I cut in, "don't be silly. I don't hate you." But it's too late. The principal and the teacher have already exchanged glances, and now they're both staring at me.

"Harlow, why would you think your mom hates you?" Principal Laura asks. "I'm sure she loves you very much."

"Because she won't let me have Instagram. No Facebook or TikTok either. And the shit she writes makes other kids hassle me."

"You see," I say to the principal. "It's nothing more than typical antics. And we'll address the language when we get home."

"And last night she burst into my bedroom and accused my dad of touching my—"

"Harlow!" I gasp.

"Well, you did."

Principal Laura and the teacher exchange another glance, and I want to disappear beneath the desk. "That's... that was a misunderstanding."

"Mrs Marozzi, I didn't introduce our school counselor earlier. This is Heather Jenkins."

"Mrs Marozzi," the counselor says, "I've been noticing for some time that your daughter seems... troubled."

She has mousy brown hair cut into a bob that falls over her eyes in a way that is annoying, to say the least. "You think my daughter is *troubled*?"

"She's been exhibiting what we call 'signature warning signs'. At times she is withdrawn and not a moment later she verbally lashes out at other students. Her grades are suffering and her friendships are strained – as we witnessed today." She takes a moment, and then adds, "If there's an issue in the relationship with her father, then perhaps—"

"I beg your pardon?"

She ignores me and redirects her attention to Harlow. "If there's something you need to share about your dad, this is a safe space. We're here to listen and your mom will believe you. Isn't that right, Mrs Marozzi?"

In one sweeping motion, I pick up my bag and get to my feet. "Come on, Harlow, we're leaving."

"Mrs Marozzi, I think it's best if we let Harlow tell us what's on her mind," Principal Laura says in a well-rehearsed, calming tone. "I understand you have a great deal of parenting experience which women the world over read on your blog, but I would appreciate it if you could take a seat and give your daughter that opportunity."

"Fine. Harlow, tell the principal and your counselor what's troubling you."

But in true Harlow fashion, she just shrugs and tips back in her chair. "Like you care."

The metallic tang of blood drips onto my tongue as I bite my lip in an effort not to shout at her. "Harlow sweetheart, your principal and therapist are concerned you might be troubled so if there's something bothering you here at school or at home, now is the time to tell us about it."

They exchange another glance and I force myself to envision a beach somewhere, water lapping gently against the sand.

"Harlow is there anything you want to tell us about your dad that makes you uncomfortable?" the counselor pushes. "This is a safe space."

I look at my daughter willing her to tell them what a good man Bastian is, that he would never do something like that.

"No," Harlow says eventually, "my dad is fine. It's *her*."

"And what is it about your mom that's making you upset?" the curtain of hair asks.

I want to roar that it's all about my refusal to buy her a leopard-print bikini to wear on Instagram but instead, I keep quiet and bite even harder on my lip.

"I told you already," Harlow says. "She makes me look stupid and my friends make fun of me. All their moms think her blog is a load of shit. Everyone knows my dad is the one who takes care of us."

"And your dad, has he ever touched you—"

"Eww, no, gross."

I sigh and get to my feet. "Like I said, this is all just normal rebellious behavior. I'll talk to her about what she did today but for now, I'm taking her home."

"Well, it's not quite that simple," Principal Laura tells me. "There's still the matter of her physical contact breach."

"Look, you got me, alright? Things aren't perfect at home. My husband and I have been arguing more than we should and that's on us, but don't punish her for that. Harlow is a good girl, and sometimes even good kids act out. I believe my daughter when she says the other girl's moms say derogatory things about me and my business, I mean... have you met some of these women?"

"Mrs Marozzi, that's all well and good but we believe in our policies here at school and Harlow will have to be suspended."

I lean in and look at them, one to the other, and right in the eye. "Well, since this is such a safe space, let me open up to you both about what's troubling *me*. I believe what took place in this room, the way you tried to push my daughter into saying her father touches her inappropriately, is a disgrace. The only reason I didn't interject is because I wanted you to hear her say, in no uncertain terms, that it's not true. My daughter might be spoiled, and I'll take that on the chin, but she's a good girl who gets good grades and loves her father. She was upset today because last night I had a verbal argument with my husband that got out of hand, and there's every chance it upset her. Now, I apologize for that and I will talk to my daughter. We both will. But you will not punish her with something as severe as suspension for acting out because of my mistakes. Am I making myself clear?"

"Mrs Marozzi, I'm sorry but rules are rules."

"Then my rule is that I no longer contribute to this school's annual fundraising," I tell her. "Perhaps I'll pledge my support to an animal charity or donate it to the public school system. The options are endless. So, if that's all, I'll have my lawyers draw up the paperwork to cease my ongoing financial commitment. Harlow, get your bag – we're leaving."

Principal Laura stands up from her seat, her fingers splayed out across the desk. "Okay, let's call this a warning and I trust both you and Mr Marozzi will speak to your daughter to ensure this never happens again."

"Wise decision, Principal. And if either of you ever speaks about my husband that way again, my lawyers will be drawing up more than financial documents. I trust we understand each other?"

When we walk out to the car, Harlow surprises me by climbing into the front. Any other time she barricades herself in the back, her headphones silencing any chance of a conversation.

"OMG, that was incredible!" she gushes the minute we close the door. "You owned them back there."

"I did, huh?"

"They're such bitches."

"Hey, no cursing," I tell her. "And by the way, you're not off the hook yet. We still need to talk about this with Dad tonight. What you did today is not okay. You get that, right?"

"Yeah, I know. Sorry, Mom," she whispers. "For all of it. Yesterday too. But you know Dad would never do that, you know... what you thought last night in my room."

"Oh Harlow, I know," I gush. "Of course he wouldn't, and I'm sorry for what I said. When I was your age something bad like that happened to a friend of mine and I got carried away. It's not an excuse for what I did, but I want to make sure you're always safe – and you are safe with Dad. You always are. I was being stupid."

"I know, Mom."

We share a smile and my heart swells. "How about we go home and watch a movie, maybe make some popcorn?"

"Can we make brownies?"

"Sure, but you might have to take the lead on that one."

She smiles and for the first time, I dare to hope we might finally begin to bridge the divide.

A message alert sounds on her phone, and she reaches into her blazer pocket.

"Is that Dad?" I ask. "They tried calling him earlier to come get you."

As I wait for her to respond, my phone rings and seeing that it's Bastian, I let my question go and answer his call.

"What the hell is going on?" he demands, the moment I pick up.

"Nothing, it's fine. Harlow got into a fight at school but it's over now. They tried calling you. I did too. Who were you meeting with?"

"What?"

"Val on the desk said you were in a meeting with one of the editors."

"Oh... just a freelancer. You're sure everything's okay with Harlow?"

"We're heading back to the house to have a girl's afternoon. We'll talk when you get home."

"Is she suspended?"

"No, I took care of it. Didn't she just text you back?"

"Harlow? No."

I glance over at my daughter as she slips the phone back into her pocket and stares innocently out the window.

Chapter Thirty

MADELYN-MAY

1995

*M*ary was the first person I ever felt like I could trust. The relationship was short, lasting only a few hours, and yet she changed my life forever.

After I cleaned myself up in her bathroom, she asked me to stay but I refused. She was lovely, the kind of woman I wished my mother could have been, but it wasn't safe to stay so close to the trailer park. Instead, I thanked her and asked for a ride to the Greyhound Terminal at Santa Rosa. When she asked where I would go, I told her truthfully that I had no idea. The east coast, far from California, was where I wanted to be but exactly where I didn't know. Thankfully, Mary had been kind enough to call a friend in Philadelphia, a woman she had known since college, who would give me a place to stay until I got on my feet.

Seven hours and thirteen minutes after the fire tore through our trailer, the bus to Philly pulled out of the station at Santa Rosa carrying me and my sins across the country. True to her word, when I arrived three days later, tired and more than a little disheveled, Mary's friend was at the station to meet me.

Anna was a sturdy woman with a generous smile. She wore a bright blue dress, and when she stepped forward to greet me it was with open arms and the warmth of an old friend. Just like Mary, Anna had an affinity for finding things that were lost and when she took me to her home, I realized I was not the first wayward teen to take shelter beneath her roof.

To anyone else, the tumbling brownstone in Fairhill might not have felt like home sweet home, but to me it was everything. My bedroom was pink and flowery, and the bright yellow kitchen felt like sunshine. The fridge was full, the rooms smelled like vanilla, and warm morning light shone in through the windows. Outside, festive murals brightened the walls of buildings that had seen better days, and I loved the way people congregated on their front stoops, sharing food and laughing out loud. I had never lived in a suburb with storefronts and homes and streets so long they melted into the horizon. I'd only ever lived in the trailer, so Anna's narrow brownstone was the first place that ever felt like solid ground.

Over the years, other girls came and went. They fought with Anna, and sometimes tried to steal from her. They lit glass pipes that smelled strange and scratched at things that weren't there. I didn't like any of them and for the most part, I kept to myself. The only issue Anna and I ever had happened six weeks after I arrived.

When I missed my period and took a pregnancy test from the pharmacy, I discovered that just like Melody, I too had fallen pregnant. Terrified Anna would kick me out, I searched online for the nearest clinic willing to perform a termination on a minor without parental consent. When I'd crossed off almost every option on my list, I finally found a nurse who agreed to perform the procedure at her home for $150.

She lived two blocks away, and after moving a stack of books and lying out a sheet of plastic, the woman ordered me to climb up onto her kitchen table. Three minutes later, I passed out from the pain. The only thing I remember is waking up to see Anna's face looking down at me and the feeling of being lifted. I found out that the nurse discovered Anna's emergency contact in my purse and called her to come and get me. Anna carried me the two blocks home in her arms. She also called a doctor who examined me and immediately called an ambulance. It was the only time Anna ever spoke crossly to me. She used words like trust and faith and other things I didn't understand. She told me I could count on her, and that I was safe. I stayed with Anna until I was twenty. Then, just one day after my birthday a massive stroke stole her away.

When Anna died, I took the money I saved working at the local supermarket and rented a room in a share house in North Philly. I kept to myself and attended classes at the local night school. I learned to use computers, and how to keep records, and soon enough I got a job working as a secretary at an accounting firm in the city. Mario Marozzi was a smart accountant, known for his fairness and for giving the downtrodden a hand up through small, no-interest loans. As fortune would have it, Bastion took after his father when it came to taking chances on people, and on his third unnecessary visit to the office he asked me out to dinner. Three months later, we were married.

Chapter Thirty-One

LACY

Beyond the dirty curtains of the hotel room stretches a vast sea of gray concrete, a few scattered dumpster bins, and the shape of a Wawa convenience store to break the horizon. But it won't be long now. Soon we will have ourselves a mighty fine view, one that's a damn sight better than this.

I move away from the window and balance myself on the edge of the bed. The map I brought is so worn that the folds are starting to fray, but it doesn't matter. I know the route we need to take by heart. Maryland, Virginia, Alabama, Louisiana, Texas, over the border, and south into Mexico.

When I was a girl, I dreamed of being a movie star, of seeing my name up on the big screen. In those days I imagined traveling in style. Private jets, limousines, and an entourage catering to my every whim. I was going places. Going to be somebody. Somebody who mattered.

All those years stuck in that God-forsaken trailer, I always figured somehow, someway, I would eventually make it out. I never gave up. I fooled myself there was still time to make my dreams come true. But that all went up in flames the night of the fire when those girls left me there to die alongside that piece of shit husband. If only they knew that I'd been dragged out of purgatory and into a whole new kind of hell.

The fire left me with fourth-degree burns to the lower half of my body which was traumatic enough, but worse was the infection. Despite the hospital's best attempts to treat my legs with antibiotics, sepsis took hold in the left, and eventually they had no choice but to amputate. You could say I was lucky – I escaped any severe injury to my upper body and face, but I can't say luck comes to mind when I look at that stump.

It had taken me a while to come to after my daughter tried to bash my skull in, and by then fire had spread from the bedrooms and out across the floor of the trailer. It was the smell of my own flesh burning that pulled me back to consciousness and when I looked down my legs were already on fire. I screamed and screamed. Flames engulfed the doorway, and my only option was to try and pull myself up off the floor. The curtains over the sink were already ablaze, so I had to use the kitchen table. Despite the pain, I climbed to the center of the table and was forced to watch as flames quickly licked their way up the wooden legs toward me. It was Salem, and those girls had sentenced me to burn at the stake.

It had been a mistake to underestimate them. Turns out they had the type of guts I never gave them credit for, or one of them at least - Madelyn-May. She surprised me. For a stupid girl, she'd played it smart. Smarter than me. But that won't last. They say being a mother is about teaching your kids a thing or two. Up until now, she has been the one dishing out lessons, but that's all about to change. There's still one lesson yet to come, and Madelyn-May is about to learn it the hard way.

Chapter Thirty-Two

MADELYN-MAY

2004

*E*xplain to me why you can't just let it happen when it happens?" I shouted. "What's the rush?"

"I shouldn't need to give you a math lesson, Madelyn-May," Bastian said. "You're twenty-five this year. We've been trying for three years and you're still not pregnant. There has to be a reason this isn't working."

It was our third wedding anniversary, and we had planned a romantic picnic in the park. A quiet moment between the two of us. But before we even left the office, he'd gone and brought up the one topic guaranteed to start a fight.

"In fact," he continued, "I think it's time we got you checked out."

"Me?" I shouted back, defensiveness quickly becoming a state of mind. "What about you?"

"Okay, alright," he conceded. "We both should get checked out."

I thought back to the kitchen table covered in plastic and knew exactly what the tests would show. "And if we can't get pregnant?"

"Can't?" He repeated the word like it was a vile taste on his tongue. "That's not an option, Madelyn-May. I want a family. You've known that from the beginning. Whatever it is, the doctors will find it and we'll get it fixed."

"There are some things, Bastian, that you can't just fix."

He shoved his hands into his pockets and looked away. "Well, that's something I'll have to deal with, if and when the time comes."

Something he would deal with – not we, but he. Clearly, there would no longer be a 'we', if baby didn't make three.

When there was nothing left to say, I took the elevator down to the street and walked out onto JFK Boulevard. I didn't bother stalling or looking back. He wouldn't come after me, not after the fight we just had. Bastian didn't like to argue, and it was clear we both needed time to cool off.

As I made my way toward the park, I silently cursed myself for not telling him the truth back at the start. But there was so much to tell, and I knew without a doubt he wouldn't be okay with any of it. We had fallen in love so quickly. One moment it was just me, and then before I knew it, for the first time in my life, the word 'us' found its way in. I had never felt the warmth of being an us before, the way it could wrap its arms around you even when you were alone. When he asked me to marry him, I knew I should've told him the truth but who would love a girl like me? Instead, I promised myself to be the best wife he could ever want. I would dedicate my life to making him so happy, that eventually, children wouldn't come into the equation. I hoped if I loved him with all my heart, then maybe I would be enough.

I sat down on one of the park benches and watched a man and woman strolling toward the iconic red Love sculpture. A little boy was swinging happily between them, each of their hands taking his weight. They were perfectly balanced. Man, woman, and child, just as Bastian wanted us to be. But as I watched the family, I felt the weight of eyes on me and glanced over to see a young woman looking in my direction. She was one bench over, and when our eyes met, she immediately looked away. I had so much on my plate, and the last thing I needed was some girl staring. I got to my feet, determined to go over and tell her as much but as I drew closer, her puffy eyes told me she'd been crying.

"You were looking at me," I said, in a voice softer than I'd intended.

"I was, and I'm so sorry," the girl mumbled. "I was... looking for a distraction I guess."

I pointed to the space beside her and when she made the obligatory motion, even though there was more than enough room, I sat down. I didn't know what I was going to say, and it was clear from her red-rimmed eyes and blotchy skin that things were not going well for her either.

"Do you think they're happy?" I eventually asked, looking over at the family.

She followed my gaze and thought for a moment. "I think everyone is happy sometimes."

"Are you?"

"I was... before."

I nodded and folded my hands into my lap. "Can I ask what happened?"

"My mother is dying," she said, her voice little more than a whisper. "I have no money left for her care. I feel like..."

"...a failure."

"Yeah, pretty much. And you?"

"My husband wants children."

"And you don't?"

I fiddled nervously with my wedding band, sliding it up toward my knuckle and then down again. "It doesn't matter whether I want to or not. I can't."

"There's other options," she suggested.

"Not to him."

We sat quietly, both lost in our own thoughts, and I searched for something comforting to say. I knew what it was like to watch someone die but had no idea about how to save a life.

"And your husband, he can't accept the idea of you guys not having kids?" she asked.

"He doesn't know, and I can't find the words to tell him. Having a baby is all he cares about."

"I'm sure that's not true."

"You don't know him." I paused for a moment. "And your mother? There's no hope?"

She shook her head and gazed out over the park. "Not for recovery, no. I want to take care of her until it's time. She's always taken care of me. I just... don't know how to give that back to her."

We both stared out across the park and a part of me wished I could help her somehow. "Can I ask what condition she has?"

"Cancer. It started in her cervix, then spread. We tried every treatment possible, but all we can do now is keep her comfortable and provide end-of-life care – if we could afford it, that is."

"That's tough."

"Tell me about it." The girl threw up her hands in frustration. She told me how she had used all her money having thirteen eggs cryogenically frozen in case the hereditary condition inevitably came calling for her as well. As I listened, my heart began to beat faster. "How much do you need for her care?"

But she just shrugged and pushed back her hair. "Too much."

"Ballpark?"

"$20,000, give or take."

And just like that, I knew what I had to do. "I have money."

At first, she didn't react and I wondered if I had said the words out loud or just rehearsed them in my mind. "I have money, and what I'm about to say might sound crazy, but I believe that things happen for a reason."

"What are you talking about?"

"I have money, enough for what you need. Maybe we could help each other?" I continued.

"Help each other how?"

I took a deep breath and surprised myself by reaching for her hand. "I could buy some of your eggs. If we kept it a secret, my husband would never have to know."

"What?" She pulled her hand away as though she'd been burned. "You've got to be joking?"

"Think about it," I began, adrenaline pulsing through me. "I buy your eggs for $20,000. I tell my husband I want to try IVF, but we use your eggs instead. He would never have to know."

"No!" she exclaimed. "That's crazy, and it's lying. Just tell him the truth and use an egg donor. It's still his baby. I couldn't..."

Bastian and his family were practicing Lutherans, who believed the introduction of donor eggs or sperm would violate the one-flesh rule of marriage. The best I could hope for was his agreement to IVF because it was still my egg and his sperm just as God intended.

"No, he would never allow that," I told her.

"But I don't understand?"

"You don't have to understand. All you need to know is that you can pay for your mother's care and the child my husband and I have will be loved. He or she will never want for a thing. You have my word."

She searched my face clearly trying to figure out if I had gone mad. "That's... no, I couldn't."

"Tell me something," I said. "Why did you come to this park?"

"Huh?"

"This park. Why did you choose here to come and think?"

"I don't know, I guess I like the sculpture."

"Because it makes you think of what love can do. The way it can turn everything on its side?"

She looked at me closely. "I suppose you could say that."

"Don't you see? There are no coincidences. Sometimes things just happen for a reason."

I had no idea what she might say next, but it came to mind that I hadn't even introduced myself.

If by some chance she might agree to this, I couldn't risk her knowing my identity. If Bastian ever found out, it would be over between us – worse than that, it would hurt him in a way that could never be healed. Instead, I searched my mind for a name to give her. If I could be anyone, who would I want to be? I thought back to the night of the fire, and the woman who saved me. She had introduced herself as Mary but later told me her friends called her by her middle name - Jane.

"I'm sorry," I apologized. "All this and I haven't even introduced myself. I'm Jane."

Chapter Thirty-Three

SOPHIE

After spending the entire afternoon agonizing over what I found in Gerard's medical files instead of cooking for my friend, the kitchen feels lifeless. There is no spicy paella aroma floating up from the dinner that I promised to make, or warm smell of homemade flatbread. Of course, right on time, she knocks at the front door.

"Talk to me," she says before she even gets inside. "What's all this sperm donor talk about?" On her way in she glances through to the kitchen and if its stillness surprises her, she doesn't show it.

"Samara, I have no idea where to start."

"Well, you can start by telling me why you've been lying to me all day."

"Lying?"

She dumps her bag on the couch and stares at me. "Girl, we've been best friends since college. Did you really think I'd believe you're planning to have another baby, and with a sperm donor? Please, give me some credit."

I want to smile – and I want to cry. I should have known Samara would see right through my story. She's my best friend, and that's what friends do sometimes – they call you on your shit.

"Tell me, has this got anything to do with that egg donor caper you and Gerard pulled like a million years ago?"

Without meaning to, I push her shoulder in surprise. "You knew?"

"Of course, I knew Sophie... jeez." She shakes her head and looks disappointed. "You really think my husband has the balls to propose to me with a ring bought with ill-gotten gains without telling me first?"

"I can't believe it," I tell her. "I don't know what to say."

"Gerard and I don't have secrets, Soph, you know that. It took him a few days to work up the courage of course, but eventually, he told me."

"So why didn't you say anything? It's been twelve years and you've never mentioned it once."

"Because I know why you did it. Gerard did too, that's why he agreed to go through with it. I know you, Soph, and if it was something you wanted to share with me, you would have. I also know you didn't tell me because you wanted to protect Gerard. I figured one day when it felt right, you'd confess."

"I don't know what to say..."

"Well, you can start by telling me what's going on now. Gerard was busy with Jada from the moment he got home, and he couldn't say much when I called him earlier. So, what the hell is happening because I know you're not planning a pregnancy?"

I drew a deep breath. Samara knowing what we did is a monumental relief, but there's still so much I need to tell her. "We may need a drink for this," I warn her. "At least, I will."

Knowing my house inside out, Samara grabs a bottle of wine from the rack in the kitchen and pours two glasses. "Alright, I'm listening."

"Okay, so you already know the back story which makes this a lot easier," I begin. "But what you don't know is how this all started, and who used my eggs."

"A woman you met at Love Park, right? At least that's how Gerard told it back then."

"Right, Jane. And she told me her husband's name was Ian. But there's been a development."

I explain about the manuscript, the effect it's had on me, and why I wanted to find Jane. When I reach the part about my fake appointment with Gerard, she immediately frowns and clicks her tongue. "You lied to my husband? Shame on you, Sophie. Now, why would you go and do that after what he risked helping you?"

"I'm sorry, Samara. I didn't want to involve him in this all over again. I thought I was doing you both a favor by keeping my plans to track Jane down a secret. I never intended to contact her. I just wanted to see the child, even from a distance. I know you understand why."

"I do understand but I don't like it, especially the lying. But keep going... You said there's been a development?"

"Right, so when I looked at the files on Gerard's computer, I found out Jane wasn't really Jane at all."

"She used a fake name?"

"To me, yes, but obviously she had to use her real name for the appointment because her husband was there. Did Gerard ever mention their names or anything like that to you back when all this was happening?"

"He told me enough so that it wasn't a lie but I didn't ask a lot of questions, Soph. Seemed like the two of you had it under control so I left well enough alone. Figured the less I knew, the better."

"Well, brace yourself because it turns out Jane, the woman in the park, is actually Madelyn-May."

Confusion pulls at her brow. "And Madelyn-May is?"

"Madelyn-May Marozzi. As in... wife of Bastian Marozzi."

Her hand freezes, mid-sip. "You mean..."

"I mean Bastian's twins were conceived using my eggs." We stare at each other in silence until I can't take it anymore. "Samara say something, please."

"So, what you're telling me is that his kids are really your kids, like *together*?"

"Well, that might be a stretch, but yes, you could say that."

She takes another moment and lets the information sink in. "Have you told him?"

"Are you serious? Of course not."

"Are you going to?"

"Well, that's why you're here – to tell me what the hell I'm supposed to do now."

She drains what's in her glass, and immediately refills it to the top. "Wait, I'm confused – you said before her husband's name was Ian?"

"Bast*Ian*," I explain. "It's just a clever way of covering up his real name by shortening it. They do say all lies have a portion of truth to them."

"Wow, Sophie," Samara says, with a shake of her head. "Curiosity really has killed the cat this time. And right now, the cat is you."

I rub at a headache starting to form behind my brow. "The thing is, all I can think about is how much I want to see them. Is that awful? I mean I know they're not *my* kids, but this is huge. When I decided to look for Jane it was because I wanted to see if there was any part of Josh in the child I helped conceive, but now..."

"...there's Bastian to consider," she finishes.

I search my mind, trying to make sense of the multitude of questions vying for my attention. "I think the main thing I need to remember is that they're not *our* children, right? Thinking about it as though they are Bastian's and mine makes things so much more confusing."

"Honestly? I have no idea."

"Okay, that's not helping."

Samara puts down her drink. "But I don't know how to help, Soph, not with this. It's not as though we have a precedent to draw on here. I mean, come on, this is unbelievable, right? The chances of this happening are..."

"... a million to one?"

"I don't know. Do clichés go any higher than that?"

We finally laugh, and the release feels good. "I guess it's not *that* strange," I begin. "His office has always been right near Love Park. If they had a fight, it's not a stretch to imagine she might go to the park to think. On that day, I had been at Penn and needed to clear my head. I guess it's not so absurd to think we crossed paths."

"Soph, I have to say, as much as I hate that you lied to Gerard and broke into his medical files, which is completely and utterly unacceptable by the way, I'm actually proud of you."

"Proud of me? Why?"

"Have you stopped to think about what you did? You went to Gerard's surgery, came up with a way to get him out of the office, then hacked into a medical database – all without having an anxiety-fueled meltdown. Can you imagine yourself doing that a year ago – shit, forget that - a month ago?"

Samara is right. I hadn't stopped to think about what I did. I just knew I had to do it.

"It is pretty out of character, I guess."

But Samara gives me a smirk. "Not for the Sophie I knew before the accident. She was a fighter, and one hell of a great mom. The Sophie I knew would've fought a lion for someone she loved. What you did, I'd say, was in perfect character."

What I did was extreme and off-the-charts crazy – but it was a lot more proactive than anything I've done in the past five years. I wonder quickly if acting crazy might be the only way to find your sanity.

"So, now what?" she asks.

"I have no idea. I can't tell him, so..."

"You can't?"

"It would ruin his life. I can't do that, not to him."

Samara looks thoughtful, and I know that whatever she says next is likely to have me lying awake all night.

"Sophie, I know you're going to say this is stupid – but what if it was all meant to be?"

"If all what, was meant to be?"

"Everything. You meeting Madelyn-May. Having frozen eggs stored. Madelyn-May offering to buy your eggs. You being in a situation where you had no choice but to say yes. Knowing Gerard and him agreeing to help you. And of course, Bastian being the father. I mean, come on Sophie. You must admit a lot of things had to fall into place for this to happen. It can't be all a coincidence."

"Then what else could it be? God's plan?" I ask with a roll of my eyes.

"How about fate?"

I scoff and look away. Fate would mean Bastian and I are inevitably and irreversibly linked - that we are meant to be. But James was my soulmate. There could never be another, and as much as Bastian and I have used each other's shoulders, I find it hard to believe there is anything divine about our situation. "No, I think it's just an unimaginable chance of timing. That said..."

"Okay, well it was just a thought, and I know I'm not being much help. I think the only thing we need to figure out here is how you feel about all this. I know you said you can't tell him, but the real question you need to ask yourself is - do you want to tell him?"

I think back to the park, to her terror at the idea of her husband finding out. "I can't tell him. If I do, then I'm responsible for breaking up his marriage, and worse than that, their family. And then what? He and I and the kids live happily ever after? That's just not going to happen."

"Because you don't want it to?"

"Because it's not right, Samara. It's turning the world on its axis. That's not the life he signed up for. I'm not their mother."

"Well from what you've told me, neither is she. And things change, Soph. What you want matters too."

"But it shouldn't. I took the money. I gave my word and there's two sides to every story Samara. I only know what Bastian tells me – and besides, what about the kids and what they want? Imagine what finding out something like this would do to their lives, to their sense of identity. I can't be responsible for something like that, it's too much."

"You were a great mom, Soph. You could be again, and maybe that's what those kids need. Have you thought about that?"

"No, I haven't," I tell her, a defensive tone creeping into my voice. "And it's not about that. I know what kind of mother I was. I don't need you to tell me I was a good mother. I'm just saying that I don't think it's right to interfere and risk messing up their entire life."

Samara raises her eyebrows. "Well, I don't want to be the one to tell you this Soph, but I think sleeping with him is kinda already doing that."

The pain that started as a dull ache has spread into my temples and down behind my eyes. The last thing I want is to end up in a fight with Samara. "Look, all I know is that I just want to see the twins from a distance, without dismantling anyone's life. After that... I don't know."

"And you're sure?"

I put down my glass, and nod. "About seeing them? Yes, that much I am sure of. Otherwise, what was all this for?"

Chapter Thirty-Four

LACY

I found the fake Gucci scarf in a small fashion store in Center City. As I try it on with jeans and a white shirt, the kind of simple classic outfit the mother of a millionaire might wear, I can't help but marvel at the irony of the situation. It will take an imitation scarf to convince anyone I am genuinely Madelyn-May's mother. If I was to present myself at the school in my usual jeans, sweater, and frayed canvas tennis shoes, biology alone would not be enough to convince anyone she was related to a person like me. But I have no doubt this $18.00 forgery and a pair of new loafers will be more than enough to do the trick.

I check my phone for any new messages from Harlow. It had taken no time at all for her to contact me after I gave her my number at the mall. To be honest, I thought it would take longer, at least a week or two but once again, Madelyn-May is doing my work for me. The text she sent was simple.

Harlow: *Hi it's Harlow we met at the mall on Sat. Got into a fight at school cause of moms work. Sick of no1 ever getting what it's like 2 b me. MayB we could meet soon?*

I hadn't messaged right back. Instead, I gave it an hour to make sure I didn't appear too enthusiastic. She must be the one to come to me. If I go in too hard, there's every chance I'll spook her and she'll alert Madelyn-May before we reach our endgame.

Big sis: *Sorry 2 hear that and hope ur ok. Lets make a time soon.*

Said the spider to the fly.

She responded with a smiley face emoji, and I left it at that. A couple of days have passed since then, and now it's time for my next move. Wrapped in soft tissue and tucked away in the zip pocket of my suitcase, is a gift I plan to leave for Harlow at her school. My plan is to seal it up in an envelope, along with a note, and explain to whoever is on the desk that my granddaughter left her watch at home.

If they ask any questions about why I've never visited the school on family or sports days, I'll simply tell them the truth. I live in California and am here to re-connect with my family.

I take out a pen, and on a piece of paper write what might turn out to be the most important letter of my life:

> Hi Harlow, I wanted to drop off this little gift to say I hope you're feeling better after the fight at school. I noticed the frog T-shirt you were wearing at the mall the day we met and thought you might like it. I have some free time tomorrow afternoon. I could pick you up from school and we could go to a café. I will be outside the school gate tmrw when you finish. If there's any problems text me. Your Big Sister

I carefully fold the note in half and slip it inside the envelope. Then unable to resist, I unwrap the tissue and take one more look at the gift. The fact it survived the fire is remarkable. Madelyn-May's watch, with the leather band and green frog on the face. I had taught her to tell time with it when she was seven years old. Now it will tick down the minutes until the world explodes around her.

Chapter Thirty-Five

SOPHIE

"Are you sure about this?" Samara asks as I click my seat belt into place. "You said she has a parenting blog. We could have looked them up online."

I've considered the same thing. I even looked up her site, but quickly pulled the laptop closed before I found the courage to click any of the links.

"I know, but it's not the same," I tell Samara. "I want to see them in real life – their mannerisms, the real them. A picture won't tell me if they have the same walk as Josh, or if their laugh sounds the same. I want the first time I see them to also be the last, so it has to count."

She looks me over one last time, clearly trying to assess whether I'm still in my right mind. When she turns the key and the engine comes to life, I figure she's convinced. "Alright then. Let's go."

As Fairmount fades into the rear vision mirror, we snake our way through city traffic and eventually pull into a marked loading zone half a block from the parking garage by Bastian's office.

"And you're sure this is what he does every afternoon?" Samara asks, for the third time.

"He picks up the kids from school. That's who he is. Trust me, Samara, I know him."

She drinks from her water bottle while I stare straight ahead, petrified we'll miss his car.

"Let me ask you something, Sophie. What do you think he'd say if he knew we were out here right now?"

It's the same question I've been asking myself since we left the house.

"Honestly? I think he'd be disappointed. I think he'd expect me to be rational, to sit down and explain what happened."

"So, tell me again why instead of that we're out here like Sherlock Holmes?"

I stifle a grin. In the worst situations, somehow, Samara can still cheer me up. "Because I can't tell him what happened. If there was any upside I would. Believe me. But what good can come from that? It would cause irreparable damage to everyone involved."

"If you say so."

"I mean it, Samara – if there was any reason that would benefit him, I'd spill the beans. I've given this a lot of thought, but he's..."

Samara lowers her water bottle, and peers over at me. "...he's what?"

"He's Bastian," I say with a shrug. "He matters."

"Enough to make sure he doesn't know the truth?"

"Exactly."

"Well, that's about as clear as mud."

I screw up my face. "You're so—"

"Wait, Soph," she says, and points at the windshield, "did you say a black Lincoln? Is that him pulling out?"

I recognize Bastian's car and we quickly pull into the traffic keeping a safe distance, three cars behind.

"This would be a lot easier if you knew what school they went to."

"I know, but like I told you, he never talks about the kids. Her either for that matter. I know there's a boy and a girl, Harry and Harlow, and they're both eleven. That's about it."

Saying their names out loud has an undeniable effect. Harry and Harlow. A little boy and girl, created with my egg and his sperm. Two little lives I helped bring into the world.

I allow myself to wonder for the millionth time what they will look like. I wonder how I might feel when I see them. Will I be drawn to them? Will we be the north and south poles of a magnet instantly and undeniably pulling each other in? Or will seeing them have the opposite effect? Maybe I'll be overcome with guilt at the idea of searching for Josh in the eyes of another child. Perhaps I will feel that in some morbid, misconstrued way I might be trying to replace him.

"You okay over there?" Samara asks.

"Just thinking."

"You want me to keep going?"

I nod and force a smile. "It's a big day is all."

"It doesn't get much bigger than this, Soph," she agrees. "You're about to see yours and Bastian's children – who you never knew you had."

"Samara, they're not *our* children," I remind her.

"Fair enough, but they wouldn't exist without you. Their very DNA was created from you and him."

"Yes, well, DNA doesn't make you a parent."

"No, being a parent also takes love, compassion, sacrifice, and a damned lot of patience – believe me, I know. But has she given them that, Sophie? If she hasn't, then I'm sorry but in this case, nature wins out over nurture. You are hard-wired into them, you and Bastian. That has to count for something."

"You're not helping me. You know that, right?"

"I just want to make sure you look at this from every angle," she says. "You're my best friend, and you're a good person. I know you want to do what's right and for you, that means leaving well enough alone – but Sophie, we're out here following his car. This clearly matters to you, so try to think about what might be best for them, and you, long-term."

"What's best for them is to be with their mother, Samara, and that's not me. Like I said, biology doesn't make you a mom. I don't exist to them."

We follow Bastian across the Schuylkill River, and he turns northwest on Seventy-Six. We drive past the golf club and through Northwest Philly. A few minutes later, I see a sign for Newmarch College. "I think we're getting close," I whisper, as much to myself as Samara.

"Damn, that's one expensive school." Samara lets out a long whistle, then clicks her tongue as we draw closer. "Damned expensive."

When he pulls over, we slip into a space a few cars back, and Samara turns off the engine. Neither of us speaks as we stare out the window, collectively holding our breath. The minutes tick by and my chest begins to burn. I remind myself to breathe, slowly in and slowly out.

Eventually, two children make their way toward his car and Samara glances over at me. They are almost the same height, except the boy is a hair taller. Harry. I lean forward until my nose is almost touching the windshield. Samara reaches for my hand and squeezes it. "That's him," I whisper. "I know it."

I watch as he lumbers forward, his messy chestnut hair just long enough to tickle his eyes. His hands are shoved deep into the pockets of tan slacks, and a navy blazer hangs unbuttoned around his shoulders. He's so much older than Josh, and it's difficult to tell from a distance if there's any real resemblance, but the tug on my heart is undeniable. Trailing behind him like the pretty tail of a kite is Harlow. She shares his mess of chestnut hair - the only exception are some highlights around her face. I quickly think back to Madelyn-May's hair the day we met in the park. It was so dark, almost black, just like Bastian's. I marvel at the realization my lighter genes have forced their way in and colored the children's hair to match Josh's. I don't dare to move my eyes as Harlow half skips along behind her brother, keeping the beat of a song only she can hear.

"You see it, right?" Samara asks. "Their hair? It's the same."

"I know," I whisper. "It's just like his."

"It's just like yours."

They climb into the car and when the car's turn signal comes to life, I finally let out my breath.

"You want me to follow him?" Samara asks.

"Follow him?" I've been so preoccupied with seeing the children, the idea of following him home never crossed my mind. "I don't think we should. I mean, isn't that a bit much?"

"We're here now. You must be curious to see where they live."

The idea of infiltrating his private world, the one he shares with her, has always been so far off-limits that the thought never occurred to me, until now. "I don't know, Samara. If I see the house, I can never unsee it. If we go there, his whole other life will be undeniable and so will all my guilt."

"And you'd prefer to keep living in denial?"

"I don't know."

She pulls out and keeps a low profile four cars back.

"What are you doing?"

"If you don't make a choice soon, he'll be gone. I'll drive, you think about it. I can pull away anytime."

Once the car is in motion, the decision makes itself. "For the record, I think this is a mistake."

"You've been living in this state of denial for years, Sophie," Samara says. "You don't move forward – you hang suspended in mid-air. The way I see it, you either tell him the truth and see what happens or take a good hard look at his life and let him go."

Living in a house haunted by memories and pretending Bastian's wife doesn't exist, is not a healthy way to live. I can feel a change coming, the same way a spring breeze drifts in and warms the cold. Every season has its end and perhaps one way or another, my winter might be beginning to thaw.

Up ahead, Bastian turns right into Chestnut Hill Avenue, and I shift nervously in my seat. The narrow street is lined with tall trees standing sentry over homes set on endless, green lawns. As the homes drift by, they pull my imagination back to the days of Jane Austen.

Their grandness, mixed with English pastoral elegance, sings of old money and delicate fixtures.

Next to me Samara sighs and cranes her neck for a better view. "I thought Gerard and I were doing alright but Jesus, Soph. I had no idea Bastian's business was at this level."

"It's not," I sigh, already defeated. "This has to be her."

Samara slows the car and drops back, the narrow street making it difficult to follow without catching his attention. "What website did you say is hers?"

"It's called *Love, Mommy*."

Samara's eyes widen, and she pounds the wheel. "Holy shit, Soph, it's the most popular online site for moms in North America. Probably globally. Jesus, she started that?"

I shrug and shrink lower in my seat. Bastian's life is so much bigger than I imagined. He has a successful wife, two perfect children, and a home that by the look of this neighborhood must be worth millions of dollars. By comparison, I live in a brownstone that I barely leave and celebrate the ability to cook a meal without experiencing a full-blown meltdown. To say I have been living in denial might be the understatement of the decade.

When he pulls into a long drive, Samara passes by the house, then pulls over. While most of the homes resemble English manors with extensive stonework, peeking attics, and curated cottage gardens, his looks more like a sprawling Hampton's estate, surrounded by perfect lawns and trees so tall they must be hundreds of years old.

"Well, I guess the lesson for the day is that money doesn't buy happiness," Samara says.

His car snakes up the drive, then disappears around the back of the property. Coming here was a huge mistake. I feel silly at best, and inferior at worst. Madelyn-May is clearly in a whole other league. I slump even further in my seat. "Can we just go, please?"

Samara re-starts the car and shifts into gear. "I'm sorry, Soph. I shouldn't have followed him. You were right. It was a mistake to come here."

My stomach feels nauseous. All I want to do is go home, snuggle up to Miss Molly and disappear beneath the covers. But as the car moves forward, something catches my eye and I tell Samara to stop. About a meter behind the car a strange light is moving near one of the trees. "Can you move the car back just a bit, but super-slow?"

Samara backs up, and I train my eye on the strange light. As we draw closer, I realize what I'm seeing - a lit cigarette. It's difficult to see her at first, but she's there. Dressed in dark clothes and standing in thick underbrush on the other side of the road, is a woman smoking a cigarette.

"Do you see her? There, behind the tree." I watch as the woman smokes the last of the cigarette and stamps it out on the ground.

"I do," Samara nods. "She seems out of place. Creepy."

The woman's eyes are focused on Bastian's house. She is so fixated that I wonder how close we can get without her noticing us. "Go a little closer," I whisper. "But really slow. Actually... wait." I unclip my seat belt and climb over into the back.

"Sophie, what the hell?"

"I can see better from here. Now, go slow."

Samara reverses back, turns off the engine, and climbs over the seat to join me. She holds up her phone and zooms the camera in on the woman. "What do you think she's doing?"

"I don't know," I whisper. "But whatever it is, it can't be good."

Chapter Thirty-Six

MADELYN-MAY

This morning marks the first weekday since I built my company that I haven't gone into work. It would be lovely if I was taking the day off to relax – maybe I'd pour myself a glass of wine and watch a movie. But unfortunately, that's not the case. Since Harlow's fight in the playground, an uneasy feeling has settled in my stomach and I haven't been able to shake the sense she's hiding something from me.

Standing my ground with the principal and counselor allowed Harlow to realize for the first time that, despite my shortcomings as a mom, I'm on her side. So, it is with trepidation I begin the task of rummaging through her life. When I was eleven, in all of two seconds my mother could have upended my two drawers and lifted my mattress in search of a diary, and the job would have been done. But these days it's a much more arduous task. I need to log onto Harlow's laptop and go through her files. I must search her iPad, and the external hard drives she has, then move on to the cloud storage allocated to her phone – and then finally comb through her actual bedroom.

She must have taken her iPad with her to school, but any information it holds is stored, along with content from her phone, on our Cloud. But first things first. When the screen of her laptop lights up, I whisper a silent plea for forgiveness, and also to not find anything I don't want to see. I scroll through the main drive of her laptop, looking through photos and Word documents. There are homework sheets and other allocated schoolwork, but nothing that draws my attention. I click on her browser history and smile when I see that the last eight searches were about how to convince your parents to buy you a dog. I scroll down further and find that she has also searched for something called the Philadelphia Big Sister Program. When I click the link it takes me to a site about mentors for young girls, and the first hint of a niggle tugs at my insides. I can't imagine why she has visited this site. But when I'm satisfied there are no more clues on her laptop, I close it and stand quietly in the middle of her bedroom.

Compared to the space I shared with my sisters, Harlow's room is every girl's dream. Instead of the bunks I had to share with Melody, my daughter has a king-size bed complete with white comforter, white pillows, and a white throw. Bright-blue scatter cushions complete the look, and above her head is a white tulle canopy, sprinkled with fairy lights. Her closet is brimming with clothes, mostly designer labels, and she has already started her handbag collection. Two Chanel, one Louis Vuitton, and one Gucci. When it comes to providing for my children I spare no expense, but what have I really given her other than a room so beautiful it's been featured in *Vogue Kids*, and a collection of overpriced status symbols? When I was a child, I never could have dreamed I'd be able to provide for my family this way, but despite the pride it gives me to buy them the world, in my heart I know kids don't care how luxurious their bedroom is. I mean, don't get me wrong, Harlow is the first to invite other girls over to show off, but at the heart of it, if a mother's love is absent, how bright can a room ever really shine?

Since I'm already inside her inner sanctum, I begin the slow task of going through every drawer, careful to put everything back exactly where I found it. If I'm being paranoid and there are no secrets, the last thing I want to do is break the trust that has finally started to build between us.

I check beneath clothes and rifle through her sock drawer. I pull old books and toys she has grown out of from cane storage baskets and tear up when I see her first bunny, Mr Jenkie, crumpled under a pile of magazines. I pull out board games and books and come across one of my own favorites, *The Velveteen Rabbit*. I sit cross-legged on the carpet and pore through the pages until I find my favorite paragraph:

> *You become. It takes a long time. That's why it doesn't happen often to people who break easily, or have sharp edges, or who must be carefully kept. Generally, by the time you are Real, most of your hair has been loved off, and your eyes drop out and you get loose in the joints and very shabby. But these things don't matter at all, because once you are Real you can't be ugly, except to people who don't understand.*

I am not Real. Here in this beautiful room, in this sprawling house, I am not Real. And that's the whole problem. My eyes have not been loved off. My joints are not loose, but strict and tight. And I have made myself untouchable. Maybe if I was Real, I think to myself, my family would understand and I wouldn't need to be in here trying to figure out what my daughter is keeping from me.

I pack the baskets away and move to the last search area - her bedside drawers. If there's anything hidden in her room, it's likely to be stashed inside one of these drawers. As I open the first one my stomach twists. I move discarded bottles of nail polish, hair clips, and about a thousand scattered beads that are supposed to be housed inside a jewelry-making kit. There are tubes of glitter and torn-out pictures of Harry Styles and Niall Horan. All typical items for an eleven-year-old. And then I find the envelope. On the front, her name has been handwritten in an unfamiliar scrawl, and inside is a small, discarded sheet of tissue wrapping, and a note. With trembling hands, I unfold the paper and begin to read. The first thing I notice is the writing, all loops, and long strokes. Distinctly female. I try to take consolation in the fact that it wasn't written by a man, but I have no idea who this woman signing off as Harlow's *'big sister'* could be. Was there an email about this Big Sister Program sent from school? Did Harlow mention it, and as usual I wasn't paying attention? Why does this woman want to drop off a gift, or collect my daughter from school?

Bastian and I are already walking on eggshells. The last thing I want to do is overreact—but with everything that's been going on, I need to be sure this program is legitimate. I text Bastian, then think back to the way Harlow was messaging in the car the day I picked her up from school. My gut feel says that she was texting this woman from the program, and if that's the case, the storage cloud should tell me more. Our children's data is saved to our Cloud account – a provision of them having their own phones and tablets. So, while I wait for Bastian's reply, I go into our home office and click on Harlow's phone backup. Like a detective, I quickly scroll through all her messages looking for anything out of the ordinary. Most of the texts are from Bastian, telling her he's out the front of the school. There's a few from her friends and one or two from me, but when I get to the date of her fight at school an unfamiliar number pops up:

Harlow: *Its Harlow we met at the mall on Sat. Got into a fight at school cause of mom's work. Sick of no1 ever getting wot it's like 2b me. Maybe we could meet?*

Big sis: *So sorry to hear that and hope ur ok. Let's make a time soon.*

The mall? I cast my mind back to the weekend and try to think who she could have met. Aside from when she went into the change room, I was with her the entire time. I scroll down to the next time the number appears:

Harlow: *Thank you so much for the gift. Yes lets do that. I'll make an excuse and tell Haz 2 get the bus like we always do. Meet u out front*

Big sis: *Gr8 cu then*

The spit disappears from my mouth, and I forget to breathe. My daughter has agreed to go off with some random woman she met at the mall last weekend. I tell myself there's still the possibility that this woman, whoever she is, could be from a legitimate program. It could've happened by chance. Maybe she saw Harlow and me arguing over the bikini and wanted to help. I remind myself not to overreact, but the ache in my stomach and the pounding of my heart quickly overrules my mind. I read over the text chain again, and my eyes freeze on the bus reference.

"*I'll make an excuse and tell Haz 2 get the bus like we always do.*"

The only day they catch the bus is Thursday. Today is Thursday.

In my hurry to call the school, I drop my cell and it bounces beneath my desk. To make matters worse, as I lean over to pick it up, the letter falls out of my pocket, and I curse out loud. When I finally manage to grab the phone, I pull open my desk drawer with the intention of stashing the note inside, but the first thing I see is the box of matches. At this moment, in my heart, I know the woman contacting my daughter is not from any Big Sister program.

I dial the school and pace the length of my office three times in the seconds it takes for someone to answer.

"This is Madelyn-May Marozzi," I say, my voice bordering on panic. "You cannot let my children leave school grounds today with anyone other than me. Is that clear?"

"Of course, Mrs Marozzi – we would never allow children to be collected by anyone other than a family member. It's our policy," the woman on the other end tells me.

"I know that, but what I'm telling you is not to allow *anyone at all* to collect them other than myself."

"Not even Mr Marozzi?"

"I'm coming to get them now."

"Mrs Marozzi, is everything alright?"

"Was a package dropped off at the school for my daughter earlier this week? It would have been an envelope with her name handwritten on the outside?"

"Yes, actually there was," she replies. "Harlow forgot her watch and your mother dropped it off at the office. It was lovely to meet her. We certainly hope we'll be seeing more of her at school."

I grab onto the edge of my desk to stop myself from falling. "Did you say... my mother?"

"Yes, Harlow's grandmother. Oh... I'm sorry, is she Mr Marozzi's mother? When she referred to you as her daughter I just assumed—"

"I'm on my way. The children are not to leave school grounds, is that clear? Not under any circumstances."

"Of course."

As I run to the car, I dial Harlow's cell but it rings out. I try Harry's next, but it's the same. The school doesn't permit students to answer calls during class, so I text her that she is not to speak to anyone other than teachers until I get there.

In the twenty minutes it takes to drive to her school, I pick up the phone to call Bastian, then decide against it at least five times. Instead, I dial 911, then hang up before it rings. My mother is alive. She survived the fire. She's the one who's been threatening us. I glance down at the phone to see if Harlow has read my message. It says the message has been delivered, but not read. I look back to the road and slam on my brakes, missing the car stopped in front of me by inches. My heart is racing. I can't think straight. My mother is the one coming after me. How is any of this possible?

When I reach the school, I park illegally in front of the main building and run inside, caring little for airs and graces. "Where's my daughter?!" I demand, the top half of my body leaning over the front counter. "I want to see her right now."

"Mrs Marozzi," the clerk says, clearly startled. "Let me check for you."

She types something into her computer, then tells me Harlow is doing her physical education lesson on the field by the gardens. "But you can't go out there," she calls as I dash out the door.

Up ahead, I see the girls gathered in a group on the field. It strikes me that the activity looks more like a gossip session than exercise, but right now it doesn't matter. All that matters is ensuring my daughter is safe.

"Harlow!" I call, as I get closer. "Harlow!"

She turns and physically shrinks when she realizes it's me storming across the field.

"Mom? What the—"

"What the hell were you thinking?" I demand when I reach her. "Do you have any idea what could happen if you let a stranger pick you up from school?"

It feels odd to refer to my mother as a stranger, but it's been more than twenty years since the night of the fire. Until moments ago, I didn't even know she was still alive.

"Mom, chill," Harlow tells me, hand on her hip and flicking her hair. "It's no big deal."

The other girls are closing in around us, jackals waiting for their piece of prey. Lithe and hungry, their eyes are trained to look for weakness, and right now, I can see they think they've found it. The girl standing closest to me takes out her phone and unabashedly points it right at us.

"Don't you even think about filming this," I warn her. "This is between my daughter and me."

She ignores me and continues filming.

"Mrs Marozzi, is there a problem?" Harlow's fitness teacher strides over, all dark skin and white shorts, a whistle around his neck and clipboard in hand.

"I'm taking my daughter, and I don't want any of these girls filming me while I do it," I tell him. "Is that clear?"

"So not on-brand," one girl whispers, and they all laugh.

Harlow looks from me to her friends and back. "I hate you so much," she hisses. "Why are you doing this to me?"

As she points her finger, the light catches something shining on her wrist, and I grab her arm. The little frog watch my mother gave me on my birthday. "Take that watch off right now."

"No, I like it. It's kinda retro or something. Besides, it was a present."

Happy Birthday, Madelyn-May...

"I don't care. Take it off now right now, Harlow. I mean it."

Every time the big hand moves one little tick, a minute has gone by. You must pay attention. Time ticks by so fast. If you blink for a second, you'll miss it...

"No, it's mine."

Thanks, Mommy. I love my present...

Without thinking I launch at her and forcibly try to remove the watch from her wrist.

"Let me go!" she shouts, twisting her entire body away from me. "I hate you! You're not having it!"

"Mrs Marozzi, this isn't the time or the place," the teacher interjects. "I suggest you let go of your daughter and we all take a breather for a minute."

"Fine, I'm sorry." I let go of her arm and step away. "Harlow, just come with me alright? We have to go."

But my daughter is having none of it. She crosses her arms firmly against her chest. Her face is flushed, her back rigid. "No, I'm not going anywhere with you. You're acting insane."

"I'm not telling you again," I say, stronger this time. "It's not safe here."

"Mrs Marozzi, I think it would be best if we discussed this inside. Also, I can assure you the school is a safe space for your daughter."

"Oh, just shut up with your safe space bullshit," I snap. "I'm sick of hearing it. I'm taking my daughter, and it's not up for discussion. Harlow, we're going. Now."

She turns to follow me, but not without twisting the knife. "I wish you were dead," she whispers as she trails along behind me.

I wish you were dead. And my heart breaks in two.

Chapter Thirty-Seven

LACY

I haven't slept a wink in the past forty-eight hours. After all our planning and preparation, the day is finally here. We're so close now. Only minutes remain until Harlow walks out of school and climbs into the car. A smile pulls at the corner of my lip, but I shake it off. Not yet. Once she's inside, that's when I'll allow myself to declare victory – not a moment sooner.

I park just outside the school gate and crane my neck to see if she's coming out. After ten minutes pass and she doesn't appear, I pull out my phone and call her mobile. It rings twice, then connects.

"Harlow, I'm out front like we planned. Are you coming out?"

But the voice that answers is not Harlow.

"No, she's not coming out, Mom," Madelyn-May hisses into my ear. "But I am."

The phone disconnects and a shadow falls over my car window. It's her.

"Get out of the car, right now!"

Up close, she seems a lot taller than I imagined and even more beautiful than in her pictures online. And she's angry.

"I said, get out!"

She bashes her fist on the glass, and I hate that it makes me flinch. She'll think I'm weak, pathetic. I can't afford to let her gain the upper hand. Not when we're so close. I've already checked out of the motel, and all my belongings are in the trunk of the car. All except the essential items I keep in my handbag.

"What were you going to do, huh?" she yells. "Take my daughter for coffee and try to turn her against me?"

I lower the window a crack, just far enough to meet her gaze. "No, Madelyn-May, you've already done that yourself."

She smashes her fist against the glass, but this time I don't budge.

"What do you want, huh?" she shouts. "What do you want from me?"

I simply smile. "We'll meet again soon Madelyn-May, that's a promise."

"You stay away from us. I don't want you anywhere near my family."

I reach over and open my handbag, allowing her to see the gun inside. "You had your chance back at the trailer and you took it. Now it's my turn."

My plan wasn't to take Harlow to a café. My plan was to take her far away from here. Once she was in the car, I would have locked her in and driven. When we reached the rendezvous point, my part would be done. Someone else would take it from there and I would just be along for the ride. But as usual, Madelyn-May has messed everything up - again.

"If this is about money, then tell me what it will take for you to leave us alone," she pleads. "Just tell me what you want and it's yours. But don't hurt my children, please."

"It's funny," I say, "how a gun can change someone's attitude so quickly."

She shrinks a little, her posture betraying her, and I know I'm back in control.

"Why are you here after all this time?" she asks. "Why now?"

I think about the real reason I'm here and do my best to suppress a smile. If only she knew. "A long time ago, you took something from me. In fact, you took everything from me. The way I see it, it's only fair you give something back."

"You want to take my daughter?" She steps back, her fingers splayed out across her heart. "I'm calling the police."

She pulls her phone from her jeans pocket, but I know she's bluffing. "Go ahead. Call. Maybe I'll call them as well, tell them I know the whereabouts of a murderer. I'm sure your husband and kids will come to visit you in prison."

As suspected, she lets out a breath and lowers the phone. "You can't take my daughter. You just can't. I know everything that's happened, but you're not a monster. This is not who you are. So just tell me what I can give you to make this right."

"There's no satisfaction in you giving me what I want," I snap. "I'm going to take it from you. Only then will this be made right."

I start the car and look her over one last time. "You were such a pretty child, Madelyn-May. I thought you'd grow into a beautiful woman. Looks like I was wrong."

Chapter Thirty-Eight

MADELYN-MAY

I have indisputable proof my children are in danger but if I go to the police there will be questions and background checks. I've been lucky until now, especially given my public profile. All those years ago, I was a teenager with long ebony hair, pale skin, and limbs I hadn't grown into. By the time I did my first media interview for *Love, Mommy*, I was twenty-seven years old, with a woman's body, and hair the color of champagne. Thanks to Bastian, I have been able to create a new life. One I never could have dreamed possible back in the trailer. A life with children and family. A life I can feel proud of. Calling the police would be the first tug, the first strand of that life unraveling.

Seeing my mother this afternoon felt like someone took a knife and hollowed out my chest. She looked so hard compared to my memories. So bitter. When we were young, she was soft and lovely with gypsy skirts and bracelets that jangled like wind chimes. She reminded me of a field of dandelions, delicate and fragile, likely to blow away on the slightest breeze. But not anymore.

I'm the one to blame. That much is true. I'm responsible for my father's death, for the fire, and for whatever happened after that. Everything she lost is because of me and now she wants to take my daughter. She knows I can't call the police, and she's already managed to infiltrate Harlow's life. She knows where we live, what school they go to, and probably everything about us. She has a gun, and from the way she looked at me, so full of hate and anger, I know today will not be the end of it.

With so much to hide, I've never formed any real relationships other than with Bastian so there is no one I can turn to for help. I look at him sitting across the kitchen and try to prepare myself for what I am about to say.

"Harry, Harlow, can you go up to your rooms so I can talk to Dad, please?"

He peers over the top of his reading glasses and watches them go. When they are safely out of sight, he shakes invisible creases from his newspaper and turns to me. "Madelyn-May, I'm not in the mood to talk, so whatever it is, can we do it some other time?"

For the first time in a long time, I look closely at my husband. The gentle slope of his cheekbones, and the brightness of his eyes. I admire the generosity of his bottom lip, full and plush, and think back to the way I used to catch it gently between my teeth just to tease him.

"Madelyn-May, did you hear me? I said I don't feel like—"

"The kids are in danger and I don't know what to do."

He leans in, his eyes searching mine. "What did you just say?"

I open my mouth, but nothing comes out. Instead, I hunch over, my body heaving as heavy sobs gasp and splutter their way across the room. Unabashedly I cry, loud and ugly, as my body tries to purge its secrets out into the light.

He puts down the paper and strokes my hair. "Hey, come on now. Talk to me, Madelyn-May. Tell me what's going on?"

I wait for the lump in my throat to fall away. Despite what I've put him through, his eyes are soft and kind. He covers my hand with his and it feels warm.

"It's my mother... she's alive."

His chest rises and falls, slow and steady, a sign he's trying to calm himself. "Alright. Well, I need you to tell me everything. No more secrets."

I start from the very beginning - the trailer back in Sonoma. As I explain my childhood, and what my father did to us, I watch his face closely looking for any hint of disgust or shame. Seeing none, I move on to the afternoon of the fire but when I reach the part that involves picking up the hammer, he holds his palm up signaling for me to stop.

"I'm doing my best here, Madelyn-May, and I'm not saying he didn't deserve whatever comes next, but I'm going to need some time. This is an awful lot for anyone to take in. I understand now why you never wanted to talk about your parents, but like I said... it's a lot. For now, just tell me about the kids. How do they come into all of this?"

"I've been receiving anonymous threats for the past few weeks. I didn't finish explaining the whole story about what happened back at the trailer park, but there was a fire. My sister and I lit it to cover up what we did. The threats began with an email asking how long I could hide the truth, then someone sent the box of matches you saw in my office. That's when I realized that whoever it was knew about the fire. At first, I didn't know it was my mother, but when Harlow and I went to the mall last weekend she must have been following us. She approached Harlow in the changing room and pretended to be from some big sister project. She got Harlow's phone number, and Bastian, she tried to pick her up from school today."

His jaw clenches, and I can tell he is doing all he can not to explode. "She what?"

"I saw the texts on Harlow's Cloud, so I went back to the school this afternoon at the time they were supposed to meet. She was there. She told me she wants to take Harlow to make up for what I did."

He pushes out from his seat and paces back and forth across the kitchen. "And you're just telling me this now?"

"I didn't know how... Bastian, please try to understand."

"So, she didn't die when you were young?"

"She was inside the trailer when it caught alight. At first, we thought she was dead but then I heard her screaming. I tried to go back, honestly, I tried – that's how I got this scar on my wrist," I hold out my arm as though it might prove I'm not a monster. "But the fire was too big. I couldn't get in. The emergency crews arrived a few minutes later. They must have pulled her out."

Bastian's parents live on a leafy street in a two-story cottage where the fridge is always full, and the gardens are always manicured. They laugh, hug, cook, and love each other with the kind of loyalty and ferocity for which Italians are famous. I can only imagine what he must be thinking about my family – about me.

"I don't know what to do, Bastian. She's so far ahead of us. She knows everything, even their schedule."

"Well, the first thing we need to do is call the police."

He reaches for his cell, but I stop him. "We can't. When they investigate, I'll be charged with murder. I killed my father."

He throws up his arms and walks in circles around the island bench. "Then what, Madelyn-May? We just wait around until she really does take Harlow?"

"I'm sorry..." I collapse onto one of the bench stools, my head in my hands. "I never meant for any of this to happen. It was another life. I honestly feel like it wasn't even me who did it."

"Well, clearly she doesn't share that view."

"Are you going to call them?"

He leans against the bench and rubs his forehead. "And send the mother of my children to prison for something she did when she was fifteen?"

"Then, what?"

"I have no idea."

I approach him cautiously, with the stealth and quiet of someone about to throw a towel over an injured bird. "I know this is a lot for you to take in, but I think we should get away from here. Let's just take the kids and go, even for a few months. They'd be safe, and you and I – we can figure this out and try to start over. You know the truth now, and if there's any way you can try to understand what it was like for me, why I did it, then maybe we can try again. You and me, no secrets this time. What do you think?"

Chapter Thirty-Nine

SOPHIE

When Bastian finally comes over, I can tell right away he's not himself. He kisses me absently on the cheek, then wanders into the kitchen where he plants himself by the sink and stares out the window.

"Want to tell me what's on your mind?"

He doesn't answer, and completely ignores Miss Molly's attempts to get his attention.

"Bastian, talk to me," I try again. "I can't help if you don't tell me what's wrong."

He shakes his head and refuses to look at me. "You can't help."

"Well, you don't know that until you tell me what's going on." I wait for him to respond, and my mind drifts back to Harry and Harlow. Their hair was just like mine.

"I can't tell you this, Sophie," he says eventually. "I'm sorry."

The words stab at my heart. He's never kept a secret from me, so why would he start now? Then again, I remind myself, who am I to judge? I have a pretty big secret of my own.

"That's not like you. It must be bad."

"It involves the kids."

Instantly, my skin prickles. If they're in trouble I want to know, but how can I get him to tell me without revealing too much? "Bastian, you know you can trust me. You always have. Let me help, even if it's just by listening."

Eventually, he turns, his arms folded tightly across his chest. "Someone's been threatening Madelyn-May and the kids."

My hand flies up to my mouth. I have so many questions, but no sound comes out.

"It's to do with Madelyn-May's past," he continues. "Her mother, if you can believe it."

I immediately think back to the woman standing under the tree. "What do you mean, *threatening* them?"

"She knows a secret about Madelyn-May's past and has been threatening to involve Harlow somehow. She tried to pick her up from school a few days ago. Madelyn-May thinks she was trying to take her. Maybe she's just trying to scare us, I don't know…"

My mind is reeling. Madelyn-May's mother knows about the egg donation. "And you know what the secret is? I mean… she… Madelyn-May told you?"

"I can't tell you any more than that, Soph. I'm having trouble coming to terms with all this myself, and to be honest, given the enormity of what she did and what she's kept from me, I really don't know if I can. I agreed to go away as a family until this all blows over. I don't want to," he sighs, "but regardless of what she did, she's still my wife, so I need to at least try and get past it. That's what I came over to tell you."

I can't make this about my feelings for Bastian. Like him, I need to focus on the kids and keeping them safe. But the thought of them going away together as a family makes my chest feel empty. "Well, that might be just what you need," I manage. "Some time away."

"Come off it, Soph," he sighs. "First of all, save the act. Second, the last thing I feel like doing is going away with her. I told her it was fine, and that I could deal with what she told me, but this whole thing just feels like a punch in the face. I don't know who she is anymore. To do something like that and never tell me is…"

"I understand. It must be very difficult."

"You couldn't possibly understand this."

Then without meaning to, I think out loud. "But how could her mother know?"

"What?"

"Huh?"

"You just said, *how could her mother know*? Why would you say that?"

"No reason," I say too quickly. "Just that if her mother is crazy, then I can't imagine why Madelyn-May would confide in her about anything, not to mention a secret. That's all."

"Just… look, Sophie, this doesn't concern you, okay? So just leave it." He pushes himself away from the sink and fiddles with his keys. "Anyway, I better go. We're leaving tomorrow. Fiji, then Tahiti. I know it's not what you want to hear, but I don't have a great deal of choice right now."

"Yeah… of course. Fiji and Tahiti. Sounds awful."

"Look, I said I'm sorry, okay? What do you want me to do?"

I ask myself the same question. What do I want him to do? Do I want him to leave her and be with me? Do I want the twins to call me Mom, instead of her? Or do I want him to walk out the door so I can dedicate the rest of my life to pretending this whole thing never happened?

"Soph, did you hear me?"

"I heard you," I tell him. "Was that question rhetorical or are you actually asking?"

"Honestly, I don't know. You know I can't leave the kids, so..."

"I know." *But what if you knew they were our kids?*

"I am sorry, Soph. I didn't mean for this to happen."

"I know that too." *And so am I.*

"The main thing is keeping the kids safe," he says. "Who knows what this woman is thinking, and to be honest...."

"...to be honest what?"

"It's nothing, never mind."

"You might as well tell me now."

He rubs at the back of his neck, a sign all of this is weighing heavily on him. "The way Harlow let this woman in so easily. It's a clear indication that she was longing for a woman in her life, someone she could talk to. Obviously, she's not getting that from Madelyn-May."

Samara's words echo in my mind: *Being a parent also takes love, compassion, sacrifice, and a damned lot of patience, believe me, I know. But has she given them that, Sophie?*

"And you've called the police?"

"I wanted to, but Madelyn-May wouldn't hear of it. The secret is something that must stay a secret, I'm afraid. If the police were involved it would get complicated, so she thinks it's better if we go away for a while instead. Let things calm down."

I think back to the woman standing outside Bastian's house and the look in her eyes. "So, what happens when you get back from the trip? What if she's still hanging around outside your house?"

"Well, it's my hope she loses interest by then, and... Wait, hanging around outside my house? Who said she was outside the house?"

"What?" *Shit.*

"Outside my house, that's what you just said. Sophie, who said anything about her being outside the house?"

My heart races. Stupid. Idiot. Just. Keep. Your. Big. Mouth. Shut. "Oh... no... it was just a figure of speech."

"Sophie…" He steps forward, the light gone from his eyes. "Don't you mess with me right now. I know you inside out. You may not want to admit it, but it's true. I know you, maybe not like your husband did, but enough to know when you're lying."

"I'm not lying."

"Stop!" His anger bellows across the room and Miss Molly immediately cowers at my feet. "These are my kids for Christ's sake, so if you know something tell me. I've been lied to for the past seventeen years by my wife, and I deserve someone to tell me the goddamned truth, just for once. So, what's it going to be, Sophie? Are you going to be that person for me, or are you no better than her?"

Anxiety finds its way in, and the room begins to spin. Deep breaths… in through the nose, out through the mouth.

"Sophie!"

"Okay, alright," I concede. "The secret. I know what it is."

"What did you just say?"

Slow and deep. Just breathe. "The woman, Madelyn-May's mother," I say. "She was outside your house last week. I know, because I saw her there."

His chest rises and falls, and he bites down hard on his lip.

"I know you must have a lot of questions, but I only found out myself a couple of days ago, and I know I should've said something, and it was stupid to follow you, but I just wanted to see them. I was never going to let them find out, I promise, and—"

"Stop rambling, Sophie, Jesus Christ! What are you talking about?"

"What I just said… That I didn't know, and obviously I should've handled things differently."

He paces back and forth, stopping only to fire off questions. "You were outside my house?"

"Yes."

"Why were you outside my house?"

"Bastian—"

"And how could you possibly know Madelyn-May's secret?"

"If you'll let me explain—"

"Do you two know each other?"

"Not exactly."

"What does that mean?"

I stare at the ground, terrified of what's unfolding around us.

"Sophie!"

"I met her once. In the park. It was a long time ago, obviously."

"That doesn't explain how you could possibly know the secret she told me or why you were outside my house."

My heart races and my stomach folds over. Tingles of anxiety creep along my wrists. "She didn't do it to hurt you."

"Do what? Sophie, you're not making any sense and I'm losing my patience."

"She wanted to give you a family. How could I possibly know that one day I'd work for you and that this, whatever this is between us, would happen."

He stops pacing and stares across at me. "Just tell me what you mean."

"The secret she kept from you about the egg donor. Bastian, it was me. That's how I know."

He doesn't blink and he doesn't move. "Say that again."

"Which part?"

"All of it."

"When I met her in the park all those years ago, it was only by coincidence," I begin, my voice trembling. "But we got to talking about how I couldn't afford my mother's end-of-life care, and how stupid it was that I'd spent all my savings on freezing eggs. She said she'd do anything to give her husband a family, but couldn't fall pregnant, so we came to an arrangement. She'd buy my eggs and I'd use the money to help my mother die in as little pain and with as much dignity as possible. It wasn't supposed to get so... complicated."

When he doesn't respond, I try again. "That's the secret. That she used an egg donor and didn't tell you."

"No, Sophie," he says quietly. "The secret is that when she and her sister were teenagers, they killed their father because he was molesting them."

My head spins. The walls close in. "No, but..."

"You sold your frozen eggs to my wife so she could get pregnant?"

"Bastian—"

"Yes or no?"

"I..."

"My children were conceived using your eggs and not hers?" He swallows hard and looks everywhere but at me. "How could you keep this from me?"

"I only just found out. Back then she said her name was Jane. I didn't know."

"And what? You thought the best way to respond was by stalking my children?"

My bottom lip quivers and I will myself not to cry. "I didn't want to tell you and upset everything in your life. I just needed to see if there was any of Josh in them. Please tell me you understand."

"Josh?" he spits. "That's sick, Sophie. You're sick and you need help."

Was it sick to hope some part of Josh might live on in Harry and Harlow? With everything that's happened, I can't tell anymore. "I'm sorry. The last thing I ever wanted to do was hurt you."

"This is unbelievable," he curses. "How the hell is this even possible?"

I stay silent, too afraid to respond. Beside me, Miss Molly is curled into a quivering ball.

"What the hell, Sophie? Do you have any idea what you've done?"

"I'm sorry," I whisper. "I didn't do it to you on purpose. I didn't know."

He doesn't answer. He just takes one last look at me then turns and walks out the door.

Chapter Forty

MADELYN-MAY

The door slams as Bastian storms into the living room, his face contorted and red with rage. "Upstairs," he bellows at the kids. "Close the doors and put your devices on. Headphones too. Now!"

Harry and Harlow run from the room, the sound of their feet taking the stairs two at a time echoing back at me. "What the hell is going on?" I demand. "Why are you shouting at them?"

Instead of answering, he pulls me up off the couch by my arm and drags me through the kitchen and out toward the patio.

When we're outside, he turns on me with a ferocity I've never seen before. "Tell me what I need to know Madelyn-May."

"What you need to know about what?"

His nostrils flare and his hands are trembling. "About my goddamned kids. Tell me what I need to know about *my* kids."

"*Your* kids? What's that supposed to mean?"

"Well they're not yours, are they?" He's screaming now. "Are they! Tell me what you did that day in the park!"

Terrified of doing or saying anything that will make this worse, I retreat into myself searching desperately for the eye of the storm.

"Is it true, Madelyn-May? Did you use some other woman's eggs to get pregnant and not tell me?"

My eyes dart this way and that, searching wildly for any way out.

"Answer me, goddamn it!"

"I..." With no other way out, I summon all my strength and attempt to turn this around. "Who told you that?" I shout with as much rage as I can muster. "Where were you just now?"

"Don't you try and turn this around. Answer my question."

But I can't back down. Not now. "How about you answer *my* question? Don't come barging in here with accusations like that unless you can back them up. Where were you?"

"It doesn't matter where I was, Madelyn-May. All that matters right now is that you stop playing games and tell me what I want to know."

"Well, it matters to me. Listen to what you're saying. You told me you had to stay late at work to tie up loose ends so that we could go away. Clearly, you were lying. So, where were you?" My construed anger quickly escalates into a legitimate demand. He couldn't have been at the office, so the question remains. Where has my husband been?

He throws up his hands and turns in a disorientated circle. "Tell me, Madelyn-May. For once in your life, just be straight with me. I'm losing my mind here, alright? After everything yesterday, and now this, just tell me. Did you do it?"

"First, you tell me where you were because obviously you've been lying. Where were you, huh? Who were you with to come back here with an accusation like that?"

"Seriously? Is this how you're going to play it? After all the secrets you've kept? You've got some nerve trying to put this back on me. Our daughter is in danger because of you and your lies, and even now you still can't tell me the truth."

"Well, it's starting to look like I'm not the only one who's been keeping secrets."

"It's not the same."

He glances up toward the kid's bedrooms and my stomach twists. I've heard women describe a unique coil of the gut that comes only from having a cheating husband, but until now I've never suspected a thing. Maybe I should've been paying closer attention.

"Bastian…" I slowly exhale his name and my shoulders drop. "You're having an affair?"

"Don't turn this around," he tells me again. "You're in no position to get all high and mighty after what you did."

"You are. You're having an affair. I can't believe it."

Perfect Bastian, with his cute notes in the kid's lunchboxes and thoughtfully packed school bags. Perfect Bastian, with his rational arguments and never-ending patience. Perfect Bastian, with his undivided attention and flawless school pick-ups. All these years I've been too afraid to show myself to him, to let him see the cracks and flaws because I believed he was perfect. Now I see that I'm not the only one who has been keeping secrets.

"It's not that simple, Madelyn-May," he tells me. "I wasn't… I didn't set out to."

"Oh, so it's my fault you're sleeping with someone else?"

"Not your *fault*, but you were never present," he says. "After the twins came, it was like you disappeared. Then there was your website and it felt like you just forgot about us."

"I forgot about you? Is that what you think?"

He sits on the outdoor lounge, and it strikes me how vast the empty space around him feels.

"Well, that's how it felt."

"Well if I did, it's because after the twins came I felt like you didn't see me anymore. God Bastian, you were always so fixated on having kids. It was obvious that if I couldn't get pregnant you were going to leave me." I walk in a slow circle, hands on my hips, trying to figure out what to say next. "How do you think that made me feel, to know that without kids I wasn't enough for you?"

"Why would you think that?" He looks at me, his eyes a mix of sadness and confusion.

"You made it pretty clear. I remember you specifically saying that if I couldn't fall pregnant it was something *you'd* have to deal with. Not we, but you."

"Madelyn-May... I meant I'd have to deal with being disappointed. I'd have to deal with the idea of starting a family some other way. I never would have left you, not ever." He gets to his feet and moves toward me. "We could have adopted, I mean... Would I have been disappointed? Of course. But I wouldn't have left you."

He finally reaches out to me, and the enormity of the lies I've told pulls the breath from my lungs. "I thought if I didn't give you a family..."

But it's too late. Now that someone has told him what Sophie and I did, Bastian will leave me and it's all been for nothing. Worse is the sudden realization that like my own mother, I've spent the past eleven years being jealous of my own children. I believed I had to contend with them for his love, and thinking I could never win, I didn't even try.

"Madelyn-May," he begins, "please tell me you didn't do the things she said. Please..."

Hearing the word, *she,* buckles my heart. "Tell me who you've been seeing, Bastian. I need to know."

As I wait for him to answer, my mind works overtime sorting and unpacking every possible option for who could possibly have that kind of information. The receptionist at the clinic? The nurse in the theater?

"Sophie," he sighs. "Her name is Sophie, alright?"

They say there are three stages of shock. Stage One begins with a sudden loss of blood pressure that causes your body to overcompensate. Your heart beats faster, blood vessels shrink, and your kidneys work harder to keep blood flowing to the heart and other organs. Stage Two begins when that process fails, causing a lack of oxygen to your brain. You become confused and disoriented. By Stage Three, severe shock results in the complete shutdown of your kidneys, and then your organs begin to die. The result of Stage Three is usually death. Hearing Bastian say her name feels at least like Stage One.

"Did you say, *Sophie*?" I repeat.

"She works for me. She started in the office about six years ago but moved to working from home not long after. You've never met her, or so I thought."

I quickly run through the calculations in my head. Could she have known Bastian when I first met her? Had she strategized this entire thing to steal my husband? No, I remind myself. She was twenty and still in college when we met in the park. *There are no coincidences. Sometimes things just happen for a reason.* "And you've been sleeping with her for, what? A few weeks? A month? How long?"

He looks away, and I know it's been longer. Stage Two.

To stop from becoming disoriented, I focus on my breathing and silently scream at my organs not to shut down. "And she told you this story about the frozen eggs, when? While you were at her place?" I take his silence as a yes. "Wow, Bastian, I don't know what to say to you right now."

"Stop twisting this," he demands, anger returning to his voice. "I want to know if what she said is true. Did you meet her in a park? Did you lie to me about all those shots and medications? Did you somehow convince a doctor to create embryos with her eggs and my... and not tell me? Did you really do all those things?"

"You make it sound ridiculous."

His face turns scarlet. "Because it *is* ridiculous! Who does something like that?"

"I don't know, Bastian." I throw up my hands. "I guess someone who doesn't want to tell their husband they can't produce eggs naturally because an illegal abortion at sixteen ruined any chance of that. A person whose ovaries were so infected with bacteria they had to be removed by a surgeon."

His face drains from scarlet to gray. "A backyard abortion... Madelyn-May, why would you do something like that?"

"Because I didn't want to give birth to my father's baby, alright? Is that an acceptable enough reason for you?" Stage Three. The next is death.

He folds himself into one of the outdoor seaters and rests his head in his hands. Unable to watch, I stare out over the pool its depths calling for my surrender.

There was a time, back when we first met, when I could hide who I was behind a shiny veil. I could pretend I had my life together, that I was fresh and lovely, a clean slate for him to write his life upon. But that's all gone. Now he knows exactly how perverse and disgusting

my life has been. He has pushed his way through the dusty webs, and with dirty hands
pried open a box that can never be closed.

"I don't know what to say," he whispers. "You should have told me. About the
abortion and everything else."

"Oh, come on Bastian. How was I ever supposed to tell you something like that?"

"You should have given me the choice."

"Well, what about my choice?" I turn back to him. "My choice was stolen before I
even broke double digits. I was eight years old when he first came into my room."

Finally, he looks up and meets my gaze. "That's right. I was eight when he came
calling, and it never stopped. Even after I left, he was still there inside me. He was
dead, and yet there he was, still penetrating every part of me from the inside out. What
would you have me do, huh? Have my own father's baby?"

"Stop it, Madelyn-May."

"No, you wanted to hear this. All the gory details. So I'm telling you, and you're
going to listen. I was sixteen years old when I begged a nurse to get that thing out of me.
She had a dirty kitchen table, a set of surgical implements wrapped in a dishcloth, and
the pain... was excruciating. Then, a woman I barely knew had to carry me two blocks
home in her arms, the insides of my legs covered in blood. A fever set in, and I shook
so violently I thought I was going to snap my own spine. I had no health insurance
but she took me to a hospital anyway where a real doctor removed my ovaries. It's a
miracle I even had a womb left to carry your babies."

"Madelyn-May, what happened to you is—"

"But you were my choice," I tell him, emotion causing my voice to break. "All my
life, everything was decided for me – but not you. You were the one thing I chose for
myself and the idea of losing you, of you looking at me the way you are right now, was
the most heartbreaking thing I could imagine. So I lied to you, Bastian. I hid what I was
and where I came from so I could turn myself into your Madelyn-May. The woman
we both wanted me to be."

"I never asked you to be anyone but yourself."

"You say that, but I can see from the way you're looking at me that you never would
have married me if I'd told you the truth. You wanted a wife you could take home to
your family, a partner to have children with, and I wanted to be that for you. I wanted
the chance to be that for myself and by your side, I finally could."

He runs a hand through his hair and looks away. "I've heard everything you've said, Madelyn-May. But I need time. You've lied to me in a way that is insidious and despicable. The things you've done, they're all but unforgivable. I'm sorry for what happened to you, I honestly am. No one should ever have to go through even one of those things, but that doesn't give you the right to do what you did. You could have talked to me, you could have... I don't know, trusted me. But instead, you lied and snuck around behind my back. You put other people in terrible situations and caused them to make hard choices." His eyes take me in, and I know he is looking at a stranger. "Right now, I just need to be somewhere other than here."

I wipe roughly at my tears, frustrated at not knowing what else to say, but mostly because in my heart I know he's right. "Are you going to be with her?"

"She's the least of your problems, Madelyn-May. I think it's best if you take the kids and go overseas tomorrow like we planned. It's safer for them, and I need some space. I'll be in touch after I've had time to think."

"You're not coming?"

"I can't be around you right now. The flight is at six pm. I'll come back to the house after you're gone and start trying to get my head around all of this. I know that's not what you want to hear, but it's the way it has to be."

"But you'll come and meet us eventually? This isn't..."

"I don't know what this is anymore. I need to think about what's best for the kids."

"What do you mean, *what's best for the kids*?"

He steadies himself. "I mean, I have to put them first. I know you're their mother... to a point. But that doesn't mean you're what's best for them."

"Bastian... how can you say that?"

"Think about it, Madelyn-May. You've never been their mother, not really. Not emotionally, and now apparently not biologically either."

"That's so unfair."

"What's unfair is letting me think they were our kids for eleven years, when this whole thing, this whole marriage in fact, has been a lie."

"Well, you'd know all about lies, wouldn't you," I hiss. "You're the one sleeping with someone else."

He takes a deep breath and looks at me. "Take the kids and get on the plane tomorrow, Madelyn-May. I need space. I need... to be away from you. If you can't do that, then you'll leave me no choice other than to contact a lawyer."

Chapter Forty-One

LACY

I glance up at the house and then check my watch again. It's almost eleven am, and still no movement.

I call Madelyn-May's office to check if she went to work, and some girl tells me that as of today she's taking extended leave. In the meantime, she asks, would I like to leave a message? Not bothering to respond, I hang up and toss the phone aside.

With the blinds drawn, the house looks like a sleeping giant. Quiet and still, but about to explode. Despite the red-and-white *No Smoking* sticker plastered across the dash of my new rental van, I light up a cigarette and draw long and deep. I would normally make an effort to get out and smoke so I don't lose my deposit, but these damned mornings are still too cold to care about shit like that. And besides, I'm pissed. Yesterday, Madelyn-May ruined everything. She unraveled all our plans. But I can't let that stop me. I made a promise, and it's one I intend to keep.

Across the road, a delivery truck slows and pulls into the drive. I flick my cigarette out the window and watch with interest. "Well, what do we have here?"

The driver leans out to press the gate intercom, and I roll the window further down. On the third ring, Madelyn-May's voice crackles across the gate speaker. "Yes?"

"Delivery for Marozzi."

"Who is it from, please?"

"American Airlines."

"Come on up."

The eight-foot-high wrought iron gate slides open, the van makes its way up the drive, and for what feels like the millionth time I curse out loud at Madelyn-May. As usual, she is messing up all my plans.

"Shit, shit, shit! American Airlines. You can kiss my ass if you think Harlow is making it onto any flight."

She's already taken a leave of absence from work, so there's every chance they could be flying out as soon as today. With money like that, they can do whatever they want, for as long as they want. For all I know, they might not be back for months.

"I've messed up," I curse at myself out loud. "Now what?"

If I miss my chance, I may never get it again. All my planning and promises will have been for nothing, and that won't be acceptable. I have come too far and waited too long.

"Alright, Madelyn-May," I breathe. "Looks like you've left me no choice. Today it is. I guess we'll just have to improvise."

Chapter Forty-Two

MADELYN-MAY

S ince the moment the kids woke up, they haven't stopped asking questions. Why didn't they go to school? Why are we going away in the middle of a semester? And most of all - where's Daddy? If truth be told, I've been asking myself the same question.

I've called his cell over and over, but it goes straight to voicemail. At eleven am I called his office, but Val said he hasn't been in. I try to push the idea of him and Sophie out of my mind, but inevitably it comes creeping back in, whispering and taunting. *There are no coincidences. Sometimes things just happen for a reason.*

If that's true, and this was all meant to be, will the ending be Bastian and Sophie together with our twins? Would the courts allow that? Technically, Sophie is not considered their biological mother because I was the one who gave birth to them, but genetically they are irreversibly intertwined.

I look over at the kids, staring at the screens of their devices oblivious to what's going on around them. They know something is up, that Daddy has gone away, but they are blissfully unaware their entire lives are hanging in the balance. I picture Sophie reaching out for them and a shiver runs through me. I imagine her and Bastian walking through a park holding hands while the kids run ahead laughing, all of them lost in the joy of finally being together.

What kind of mother would she be? Loving, kind, compassionate? Would she bring them joy in a way I've never been able to? Would she bake cakes and watch movies?

What about Harlow? Would Sophie be the role model my daughter so badly needs?

And Harry. Could she pull him close, fiercely and without fear?

Thoughts run rampant through my mind, but it really comes down to one question. Would she be a better mother for them than me?

For eleven years I've remained cold and distant. Bastian must have been drawn to Sophie's warmth like a shadow longing for the sun.

The thought pulls me to my feet, and I begin to pace. Bastian and I have both lied. We've both kept secrets. But if he came back, we could try to start over, together this time. No more pretending, and no more lying. We could talk, really talk, and maybe through forgiving each other we could become stronger. We could finally be together like a real family.

I glance at my children, and my heart swells. I felt them growing beneath my heart, but is it too late to let them inside it? Until now, I have always taken solace in the fact their DNA is not mine, that they are not infected with the flaws I carry. But as I think of losing them, my body takes over and it's molecular. A warm tingle of hope rushes through me, pushing its way into every cell.

"Harry, Harlow, get changed," I tell them quickly. "And put some decent clothes on. Harry, jeans, shirt, and a belt, and Harlow, your blue dress, that one with the white flowers you like. We're going for a drive."

Five hours remain until we need to check in for our flight. I can make it.

From my laptop, I log into Bastian's office account. A few years ago, I created a profile for him in case he was ever sick and had to work from home. Inside are most of his basic records and access to current client files. I flick through his payroll program, and there she is. Sophie Miller and her address. If that's where he is, then that's where we're going. I want my husband back, and Sophie needs to see that Harry and Harlow are *our* kids, that we're a family. There's more to being a mother than DNA, and if she thinks she can step into my place, then she has another thing coming. I am their mother. Then, now, and always.

Chapter Forty-Three

SOPHIE

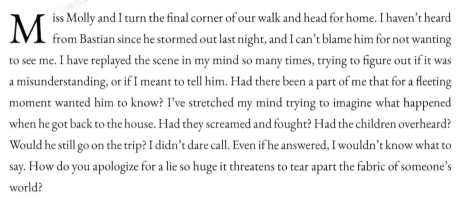

M iss Molly and I turn the final corner of our walk and head for home. I haven't heard from Bastian since he stormed out last night, and I can't blame him for not wanting to see me. I have replayed the scene in my mind so many times, trying to figure out if it was a misunderstanding, or if I meant to tell him. Had there been a part of me that for a fleeting moment wanted him to know? I've stretched my mind trying to imagine what happened when he got back to the house. Had they screamed and fought? Had the children overheard? Would he still go on the trip? I didn't dare call. Even if he answered, I wouldn't know what to say. How do you apologize for a lie so huge it threatens to tear apart the fabric of someone's world?

As we draw closer to home, I notice a car parked out front I've never seen before. To most people, it would sound crazy to say you know every car that frequents your street, but as a person who spends almost all their time at home, I know every detail of what happens outside from all the regular cars in our street, to which baby sparrow belongs to which bird. I know how long it will be before my neighbor's grass needs mowing again, and what time I need to be at the window to see the two brown sausage dogs trot by each afternoon in their pink harnesses. But I have never seen this white Audi SUV before.

We approach slowly, and I notice the shapes of three people inside the car. An adult in the front, and two children in the back. When the driver's door opens, Miss Molly barks and a woman in tailored gray trousers and a pastel knit sweater steps out. I unconsciously glance down at my dirty sweatpants and worn-out sneakers.

"Sophie." She says my name as though it were inevitable.

"Madelyn-May."

Her eyes take in my disheveled clothes then she looks past me to the house. "Is he in there?"

She looks so different from the last time I saw her. Long, inky hair has been replaced with cool, blonde waves, and the way she is standing, poised and proud, makes me feel small. Her eyes are hidden behind gold-rimmed sunglasses, and all I can think is that she is a perfect reflection of her Hamptons-style home. Fresh, clean, lovely.

"No," I manage. "He's not here. I haven't seen him since... Well, I guess you know what happened."

Through the car's side window, I can see the shapes of Harry and Harlow sitting in the backseat.

She follows my gaze and wastes no time putting me in my place. "You're not their mother. You do know that?"

She is looking at me the way a lion might stare at a lamb. "Yes, I know that."

"Are you trying to take my family from me?"

I reach down and scratch Miss Molly behind the ear, more for me than for her. "No, Madelyn-May. I would never do that."

"So, you would never do that, but you would sleep with my husband? I'm sure you can understand my confusion."

"I didn't know he was *your* husband," I tell her. "Not that it should matter. I know what I did was wrong." The familiar creep of anxiety begins in my stomach and inches its way toward my chest. I glance longingly at the house and want more than anything to go inside where it's quiet and safe.

"Why did you tell him what we did?" she hisses. "I paid you well, more than I had to. We had a deal, Sophie. Do you have any idea what you've done?"

"I do, and I'm sorry, honestly I am. I didn't mean to... I don't think I did, anyway. It all just happened. He told me your mother was threatening you over a secret, and I assumed it was ours. I said something stupid about seeing her outside your house, and it all unraveled from there."

"You saw her?"

"I know I shouldn't have been there... stalking.... wow," I gasp. "That sounds bad out loud. But it wasn't like that, not really."

I'm rambling. I'm dressed in old clothes and battered sneakers. I am outclassed, out of my depth, and out of excuses. "For what it's worth, I'm sorry, Madelyn-May. I don't know how it happened. It just came out."

"Yes, well, it seems secrets tend to do that."

I don't know what else to say, so I train my eyes on Miss Molly's coat.

"Sophie, I trusted you. You were the only person I ever trusted like that and look what you've done." She follows my gaze down to Miss Molly, then to the gold band on my finger. "Where did you get that ring?"

"My wedding ring?" I twist the gold band, a stark reminder that forever can slip by in an instant. "It's not from Bastian if that's what you think. I was married. We had a son. His name was Josh. They were both killed in a car accident when he was six. That's why I wanted to find you after all these years, Madelyn-May. It was never to disrupt your life. I just thought..."

"...you might see your child in my son."

I dare to meet her eye. "You understand?"

"You know, until today I probably wouldn't have, Sophie. But yes, I understand." She catches me off-guard by turning and opening the back door of the car. "Harry, Harlow, can you come out here please."

"What? What are you doing?"

Wide-eyed, I watch as Harry and Harlow climb out of the car and walk timidly toward me.

"Hi, I'm Sophie and this is Miss Molly," I manage. "You can pet her if you like. She doesn't bite." I crouch down, but Harlow ignores me and makes a beeline straight for Miss Molly. "How about you, Harry? You want to pet her?"

He reaches out to stroke her head, and I take every part of him in. His chestnut hair. His eyes with the same mix of green and brown I admired every time Josh looked at me.

Harlow finally tears her eyes away from Miss Molly and holds a fistful of her hair against mine. "Hey, we have the same hair. Sophie, do you see? It's the same."

"Yes, sweetheart, I see." I bite down hard on my bottom lip to stop from crying.

Madelyn-May looks at me, and I nod in gratitude. What she has done for me might be the kindest gesture I have ever experienced.

"Alright you two, you've patted the dog – now back in the car, please. Say goodbye to Sophie."

They chime their farewells and pile back into the car, none the wiser for the gift they have given me.

"I've made mistakes, that's a given," Madelyn-May tells me when they are out of earshot. "What Bastian did, a lot of that was my fault. But I love my family. I hope today has given you what you need. Now all I ask is for you to be kind enough to do the same for me."

"Madelyn-May—"

She cuts me off. "Goodbye, Sophie."

"Goodbye, Madelyn-May."

I lock the memory away safe and sound, never to be forgotten. "Well, there you go, Miss Molly," I say as we head inside the gate. "That was your brother and sister. What do you think of that?" She barks and I allow myself to laugh, the gentle sound blowing away on the breeze.

Behind me, the sound of a car ignition interrupts my moment, and I turn in time to see a blue van roar down the street, following Madelyn-May and the kids. At the wheel is a face I can never forget - the woman who was outside their house.

"Oh no," I whisper. "Miss Molly, come on, quickly."

It's been more than a year since I've driven, but as I bustle Miss Molly into the back seat all I can think about is warning Madelyn-May. It's unlikely Bastian would answer my call, so instead of finding my phone, I fumble with the keys and finally shove the right one into the ignition. Miss Molly looks at me as we fly backward in the driveway and all I can see are the whites of her eyes.

"I'm sorry, sweet girl, but I didn't catch either of the plates," I tell her. "I just need to catch up enough to call it in. The kids could be in danger."

I press my foot on the accelerator and hope to God I don't lose my mind. Catching up is going to take some speed, and fast-moving cars don't sit well with my anxiety. "Hold on, Miss Molly. I'm as scared as you are right now."

I blast my horn and swerve wildly between two cars. Up ahead, the van is stopped at the traffic lights connecting Fairmount and Pennsylvania avenues. So far, so good. I press the phone icon on my dash, and it comes up with a message: No Device. So much for my great idea of leaving the phone at home on our walks. Up ahead, the lights change to green and I shift gears. "Hold on, Miss Molly, here we go again."

I follow them onto Kelly Drive, past the rowing club and the trees of Fairmount Park.

Soon the cars around us start to fall away, and I finally have a clear view of Madelyn-May's SUV and the van following close behind. I only know what Bastian has told me – that Madelyn-May's mother is unbalanced and has threatened the children. I glance into the rear-view mirror at the empty road snaking out behind us. I have no phone, and there is no one around to help. I pound the wheel and consider intentionally cutting off the next car I see just to use their phone. Then, up ahead the lights turn red. We all pull to a stop, and I unclick my belt and take a deep breath. The only way to warn Madelyn-May is by dashing past the van and banging on her window. She'll have a phone to call the police. But before I can open the door, the woman in the van gets out of her vehicle and runs toward Madelyn-May's car. And there's a gun in her hand.

I look in every direction, my eyes searching wildly for another car. *Oh my God, what do I do?* In the backseat Miss Molly stares at me, my terror reflected by the exaggerated whites of her eyes. *I need to do something. Shit, what do I do?!*

Up ahead, the lights change to green but Madelyn-May's car doesn't move. The woman is in the passenger seat, and I can see the shape of a gun pointing back at the children. I open the door and step out onto the road. If ever there was a time to be brave, this is it.

Chapter Forty-Four

MADELYN-MAY

"**G**et in the back!"

We were so close. In a few hours, we would have been tucked into our seats on the plane, Harlow watching a movie and Harry playing on his iPad. I would've let my shoulders fall slack and asked the flight attendant to bring me a glass of full-bodied red.

"I said, get in the damn back, Madelyn-May," Lacy orders again. "Do not mess with me."

In the backseat, Harry is crying, those messy blubbering sobs that boys do when something really bad happens. I can't hear Harlow, and when I turn, she is staring straight at my mother, her eyes brimming with confusion and hate.

"Please put the gun down. You're scaring my children. There's no need for this."

She glances back at the kids, Harlow first then Harry, and I search her face for any softness, any hint of compassion. "They're your grandchildren," I whisper. "Please, stop."

"Just shut up and get in the back. Now."

The last thing I want is to turn my back on her, even for the few seconds it will take to climb from the driver's seat into the back. But she has a gun pointed at my children. "I'll do whatever you want, just don't point the gun at them. Point it at me – it's me you want to hurt, so point the gun at me."

"I'll point my gun wherever I damned please. Now, I'm not going to ask you again."

With no other option, I begin climbing over into the back but she stops me.

"Not that way. Get out and go around."

"I'm not getting out of the car while you have that gun pointed at my children," I tell her. "That's not going to happen."

"Get out or I swear to God, you'll leave me no choice but to use it. And unlike you, I'd rather not turn myself into a murderer. That wasn't the plan. But it can be."

Her face is strained like someone is squeezing her too hard around the waist.

"For God's sake, they're eleven years old," I try. "You must have some compassion left."

My mother's reaction is to cock the hammer of the revolver, the ominous click causing the hair on the back of my neck to stand on end. "Okay, alright, you want me to say it? It was my fault. Everything that happened was my fault. What happened to Daddy and to you, it was all me, and I'm sorry for what I did, but I can't take it back now. I was just a kid."

"You were not just a kid, Madelyn-May. You were fifteen. You knew what you were doing. Don't try to make excuses for what you did."

I glance back at Harlow. She looks defiant and brave. Next to her Harry's entire body is heaving.

"You have no idea what it was like back then," I whisper. "I wanted so badly for you to love me but you just wouldn't, Mom. We were never your daughters. We were a crutch for you to lean on. You hated your life, so you blamed us and we swallowed every word. What I did has been hanging over me every day of my life. If I could take it back I would, you have to believe that." I choke back tears, and finally, it hits me. All this time, it wasn't Bastian's forgiveness I craved. It was hers. "I didn't want to kill him. You have to know that. But he wouldn't stop. He was doing it to all of us. Melody too. You must be able to understand that. Melody, she—"

"Melody's dead."

"What?"

"She's dead. Mercy's in prison. Drugs on both counts."

"Melody came back?"

"Yes, Madelyn-May, she came back. Unlike you."

"What happened?"

"Everything unraveled after what you did. All your Daddy's insurance went to paying for medical bills after what the fire did to my leg. We couldn't even eat. The girls figured that selling drugs for that idiot Mercy was screwing was our only way out."

Over the years, every time I pictured Melody she was happy. Maybe in a little house somewhere with a garden and a dog. I saw her with a daughter of her own, and a husband who loved her. But none of that is true. My twin sister is dead.

"You can't hold me accountable for every decision they made." My voice is trembling. I long to cry for my sister, and I will after my children are safe. "You could've helped us. If you did, maybe things would've turned out differently."

"Don't try and blame what you did on me," she spits. "You killed him. End of story."

She will never forgive me. That much is clear. All I can do now is try to get my children away from her before she does something stupid. "I loved Melody," I say. "Probably more than you did. I'm sorry she's gone, but taking my children isn't going to bring her back."

"The sooner you get in the back, the sooner this will all be over."

"Okay fine, have it your way." I reach over and touch Harry gently on the knee. "I'm going to come around and hop in with you guys, alright? Everything will be okay. Don't move and keep your eyes on me. I won't let her hurt you, I promise."

But Harlow's hand reaches out and wraps around my wrist. "Don't get out, Mom, please. She'll take us."

The fear in her voice tugs at my heart, and I hate myself for all the lost moments I could've spent with her. "It'll be okay, sweetheart. When this is over, Dad and the three of us will all go on our trip, the one we talked about. How does that sound?"

My mother gestures with the gun for me to get out, and as my feet touch the road, I know in my heart this is a bad idea. No one knows where I am, and Bastian isn't going to call anytime soon. I look back, and Harlow meets my gaze. She doesn't speak but I can read her thoughts. *Don't get out Mom. She'll take us.*

"Undo your belt, sweetheart, and slide over toward your brother," I tell her. "I'm going to come sit by you."

She does as she's told, and slides toward Harry. When their legs touch, she laces her fingers through his and whispers something into his ear.

I set my second foot down on the road, and slowly lift my rear off the seat. At the same time, my mother lifts herself over the console and takes my place, her hands gripping the wheel before I even stand up.

"Don't you do it..." I warn her. "Let me get into the back with my children."

But before I can reach for the door handle, I hear the doomed click of my car's central locking and spin around. "No! Don't!" I pound on the glass as hard as I can, but my pleas go unanswered.

Harlow's fingers spread out across the glass, and for a moment our eyes meet. Then the car roars away with my children trapped inside.

Chapter Forty-Five

SOPHIE

It happened in the blink of an eye. One minute, the woman was pointing a gun at the twins, and the next Madelyn-May was standing in the middle of the road watching helplessly as the car accelerated away.

I jump back into the driver's seat and glance into the back. "Hold on, Miss Molly, we have to chase that car."

My body is vibrating. My thoughts smash and collide, each idea shattering before it has the chance to form. Blood is rushing. My heart is pounding. But I must keep it together. If panic rules, chaos will ensue.

Don't be weak, don't be weak, don't be weak. The new mantra finds its way onto my lips. "Don't be weak, don't be weak, don't be weak."

For the past five years, I've let anxiety win. I've allowed it to take me over. I don't know whether it's the crippling fear of being alone, relentlessly wondering why I'm still alive and they died, or just a longing to follow them deep into the abyss. But whatever the reason, my discomfort with life vibrates on a cellular level. Stronger than sadness, deeper than depression. When it hits, it's like my body is screaming. My heart pounds against my rib cage, angry and trapped. A desperate need for change vibrates through me like an errant live wire, a hot trail of sparks left in its wake. The power of it is overwhelming. I live in fear of the day I inevitably implode, a supernova of light spewing out and disintegrating anything I've allowed to stray too close. But keeping my distance is no longer an option. I've already let them in. Miss Molly. Bastian. Samara. Gerard. Harry and Harlow. And it would seem, even Madelyn-May. If I implode, I will take them all with me, but I need to try. I must be stronger than my fear.

I pull up next to a distraught-looking Madelyn-May and push open the passenger door. "Get in! Hurry!"

"Sophie? What... Where did you come from?"

"Get in!" I shout. "There's no time."

She climbs in and I slam my foot on the gas.

"She has them, Sophie." In the time since Madelyn-May left my house, her face has aged. Worry lines I didn't see have creased their way across her forehead, and her eyes have clouded. "She took Harry and Harlow. Do you have a phone? I need to call 911."

I don't dare take my eyes off the road, but I can tell from the tremble in her voice that she's crying. "I don't want to have to tell you this Madelyn-May, but no, I don't have a phone. I left it back at the house."

Up ahead, her SUV weaves and swerves between cars, and I hold my breath. All we need to do is keep the car in sight until we figure out a way to contact the police.

"Shit," Madelyn-May curses. "My phone is still in the car. What are we going to do?"

I follow the SUV as it exits right onto City Avenue. "This goes to Interstate Seventy-Six," I say. "Looks like she's heading west. Any idea where she might be taking them?"

"I have no idea what she's thinking about any of this. None of it makes any sense."

"Bastian said she tried to pick up Harlow from school yesterday. Did you ever think she would actually kidnap them?"

"He told you about that?"

I realize right away I shouldn't have mentioned it. Once again, I have put my foot well and truly in my mouth. "He did, but—"

"Did he tell you everything?" She pauses. "Did he tell you about what happened to me?"

"Ummm..."

"He did, didn't he?"

She falls silent, and the impact of our betrayal is undeniable. She doesn't say anything more because there are no words to describe it. The intimate bonds that he and I have shattered go further than the physical. We have broken promises, vows, and trust. We have broken her heart.

"I'm sorry, Madelyn-May... about everything."

"The kids are all that matter now, Sophie," she says bluntly. "The rest is—"

Up ahead, the SUV swerves onto an exit lane, and I push down hard on the gas. "Where is she going?"

"I wish I knew."

I steal a quick glance in her direction and can see her mind working overtime.

"She has to know she can't get away with it. Not like this. You don't think she'll hurt them, do you?"

"No, she could have done that back there."

"Then, what?"

"Well, first of all, she didn't expect me to be behind you guys."

She nods and I can see she's trying to steady herself. "You're right, at least we have that in our favor. Don't lose her, Sophie. Everything depends on us not losing her. If we do…"

I keep my eyes trained on the road ahead. I don't need to hear the rest of the sentence to know that if I lose the car, we lose the children. "I won't. That's a promise."

"I want you to know that I had no choice," Madelyn-May says quietly. "You have to know that. I'm not a murderer. What happened with my family back in Sonoma was… unimaginable."

Determined not to say anything that might make her feel worse, for once I choose my words carefully. "Bastian didn't say much, just that you did what you had to. No one would judge you for that, and for what it's worth, if I was in your situation I can't say I wouldn't have done the same thing. I know I broke our promise, but what we did in the park that day meant something to me. If it hadn't been for you, my mom wouldn't have found peace at the end of her life. You and I have a bond that can't be broken, Madelyn-May, regardless of Bastian. I would never tell anyone what happened to you or how you chose to save yourself. You have my word on that."

She opens her mouth, but before she can speak, up ahead the SUV swerves violently left, and we both stare wide-eyed unable to believe what we are seeing.

Chapter Forty-Six

LACY

The wheel pulls away and the car swerves into the middle lane. Harlow is pressed against the back of my seat, her hands wrapped around my face like suffocating tentacles.

"Let go of me you little shit," I curse, struggling to pull her hands away from my face and eyes. "I can't see..."

"Stop the car," she screams. "You lied to me, and you're not going to take us away from Mom. I don't want to go with you."

"I. Said. Let. Go!" I sink my fingernails into her skin expecting her to cry out, but instead, she digs deeper into my eyes.

"Stop the car!"

The car swerves right as I try using one hand to correct the vehicle and the other to grab at her hands. "Get your hands off my goddamn eyes!"

"Take us back!"

"Sit down. You're going to get us killed." I ease my foot off the gas and manage to yank her hands away from my eyes. With all my strength, I reach around and shove her back into her seat where she slumps down against her brother. "Jesus, kid, you're eleven years old. What are you trying to do?"

I wait to hear the click of her seat belt and when it doesn't come, I glance at her in the rear-vision mirror. "What are you doing back there? Put your belt on."

She returns my gaze and for a moment I swear it's Madelyn-May's scheming eyes looking back at me. "What the..."

Suddenly, she launches forward and wraps her brother's belt around my throat. The buckle clicks as she pulls the leather through the clasp, tighter and tighter until it cuts into my throat.

"Stop the car and let us go!" The change in her voice is unmistakable. Gone is the shrill tone of a little girl's fear and panic. Instead, her tone is solid, determined.

"Get off..." I cough, already feeling light-headed. "Let go..."

But instead of letting go, she pulls tighter. Unable to breathe, I have no choice but to release the wheel as my fingers claw at the leather. Tiny lights buzz in front of my eyes like mayflies in the spring. "You want to try and kill me?" I whisper. "Fine, but this time you're coming with me." I plant my foot hard on the gas and close my eyes. "Finally, you're going to get what you deserve Madelyn-May. Now it's your turn to watch something you love go up in flames."

Chapter Forty-Seven

SOPHIE

I can't tell whether it's coming from Madelyn-May, the car in front, or my own lungs but amid the sound of breaking glass and twisting metal, it's the screaming that finds its way in. Primal and raw, it is the screaming that will forever echo through the chambers of my heart.

Madelyn-May's SUV smashes into the middle barrier, the impact flipping it up into the air where it hangs suspended long enough for us to see Harlow's tiny body tumble forward and smash through the windshield.

I slam on the brakes, my own tires squealing and suffocating the car in a cloud of stinking smoke. In one motion I leap out and run toward the carnage ahead of us.

"Harlow!" Behind me, Madelyn-May's scream cuts through the silence, and I stop where I am. Two lanes over, the little girl's body is lying broken on the motorway.

I think back to what was happening in the car right before the crash. Harlow was standing up against the back of the seat.

"She wasn't wearing a seat belt." The whisper hangs on my lips as I scan the road in every direction searching for Harry. *He had his belt on, he must be trapped in the car.*

I turn and almost run head-on into a balding man standing on the roadway. Cars have stopped all around us and people are spilling out onto the road. His hands are on his hips and he's shaking his head. "Do you know them? Is there anyone else in the car?"

"Yes, a boy," I say, as my mind crashes and the present collides with the past. "My son."

"Your son is in the car?"

With no time to explain, I run toward the overturned SUV. Inside, Madelyn-May's mother lies unconscious in the front seat, her head buried in the deployed airbag. In the back, still strapped into his seat, is Harry. Upside down, his head is hanging forward and his eyes are closed. He isn't moving.

"Harry, are you alright?" I shout. When he doesn't move or answer, I do my best to get in closer.

"Don't move him," someone says.

"The paramedics are on their way," says someone else.

Their voices wrap around me, but I can't make sense of anything they're saying. All I can see is the dark rainbow of gas leaking out from beneath the car. "I have to get him out," I point toward the pattern forming on the road. "Right now!"

"She's right!" a man shouts. "I'll get the woman. Someone help me."

Without waiting, I throw myself down onto the road and crawl in through the broken back window. Shattered glass cuts into my knees and palms, but I don't feel a thing. "Harry..." I try. "Harry are you awake?"

He moans gently, and I try not to look at the bloody gash on his neck.

"Harry, sweetie, I have to get you out of here. It might hurt but only for a minute, okay?"

"Hurry, the car could blow at any time," a man's voice shouts. "We don't have long."

I flip over awkwardly onto my back and unlatch Harry's seat belt. When he comes loose, I slowly and carefully lower him onto my chest. He's heavier than I expected, but my heart quickly takes over. Lost in an ethereal blend of past and present, his weight shifts and Harry feels as light as a six-year-old as I slide back out onto the road. "I've got you," I whisper, as tears slip over my cheeks. "This time I've got you."

I squint from the glare of sunlight, as two men take him from my arms. Behind us, a parade of police, fire, and ambulance vehicles chorus toward the crash site. "The woman I came with and the little girl," I manage, "where are they?"

A teenage girl with flame-red hair points to the side of the motorway where Madelyn-May is sitting cross-legged, Harlow draped across her lap.

"Were you first on scene?" a stern police officer asks, pad in hand.

"We were traveling behind the car that crashed."

"We?"

I point over at Madelyn-May. "Her daughter was in the car. Her son too. I got him out. They were being..."

"...they were being what?"

"Taken..." is the last word I manage before the road rushes up to meet me, and everything goes black.

Chapter Forty-Eight

MADELYN-MAY

S he feels like a lifeless rag doll in my arms. Blood has matted her hair and I can tell from the way her right arm is twisted that it's broken. I feel for a pulse the way they do on television but have no idea if I'm doing it right. For so many years I pushed her away. Now I would do anything to have her back.

"Ma'am, I'm going to need you to slowly and carefully place the little girl down and then step away," a man in uniform tells me. "You need to let us work on her."

I stare at him blankly, my mind recalling the levels of shock. They say there are three, but that's not true. There is a fourth. One that Sophie understands all too well. And now, so do I.

"She's not dead," I tell the paramedic. "She's not. I'd feel it if she was. I'd know." *Wouldn't I?*

"You're her mother?"

"Yes." *Am I?*

I look over to where Sophie is talking to the police and long to ask if she feels it, a loss like a part of her has slipped away. If Harlow is dead, surely Sophie would sense it. They share a biological connection that Harlow and I never can, but maybe it doesn't work that way. Maybe when a part of you dies, all the other pieces knit together to save your heart from literally breaking. I tell myself this must be what happens. How else would Sophie have been able to carry on all these years?

"I'm going to need you to put her down, slowly and carefully," the paramedic tells me again, his voice more forceful this time.

I nod and slowly slide my hands out from under her slender frame. "Is she going to be okay?" I ask him. "I mean... it's not too late?"

More paramedics rush forward, and the man crouched at Harlow's side gives them an almost robotic description of her injuries.

"Patient is an eleven-year-old female involved in MVC. No seat belt and thrown clear. Unconscious, with suspected internal hemorrhage and possible TBI. Right arm has clear humerus and distal radius fracture, possible ulna fracture."

"Let's go, let's go!" a woman, dressed in a navy paramedic uniform, shouts. "Clock's ticking."

Behind us, the lights of a red-and-white paramedic van continue flashing, and I squeeze my eyes open and closed to try and stay focused. "Is she going to be okay?" I ask again.

But they ignore me and continue to work frantically on Harlow.

"BLA and central line, do it now. We'll need an air evac."

"Is she alright? Please, someone, answer me."

I try to see her, but she's swallowed up in a whirlwind of words I don't understand. All I can do is stand helplessly on the motorway, my hands dangling uselessly at my sides. I wonder if this is what it might feel like to be a mother without her child, like living in a world where everyone has their back turned and you no longer know what to do with your hands. I take one last look at the swarm of paramedics buzzing around Harlow, then hurry toward the flurry of ambulance lights. I need to find Sophie. She knows where they took Harry. Then somewhere amid all the flashing lights and shouting, it hits me - I knew my son would be safe with Sophie. I knew she would pull him out and that he would be alright. What I don't know is whether I can bare to finish the sentence... *because she is his real mother.*

"My son?" I ask as a police officer comes into view. "His name is Harry. He's eleven. He was in the car that crashed. Do you know where he is? A woman, my... companion, pulled him out of the car."

"He had a laceration to his neck from the seat belt. They've taken him to the hospital for a few tests just to be sure there's nothing else," the officer tells me. "From the looks of it, he's going to be okay."

A tide of relief swells inside me but I can't let myself feel it, not until I know they are both safe. "And the woman who was with me. Do you know where she went?"

"She lost consciousness a few minutes ago. A road ambulance is taking her in for some tests, but maybe you could help us. Did the car you were traveling in stop abruptly? Was she wearing a seat belt? Did she hit her head? Any details like that would be helpful for the hospital."

"No, nothing like that," I tell him. "And yes, we were both wearing seat belts."

"Does she have any existing medical conditions?"

"I'm not sure."

"Any chance she could be pregnant?"

"Pregnant?"

"Yes, is that a possibility? Could explain the loss of consciousness."

"I... I don't think so."

My knees go to jelly at the suggestion Sophie could be pregnant, but now is not the time. I shake it off and try to refocus as he jots something down on a notepad. "Which hospital are my children being taken to? Could someone take me there?"

Before he can answer, there is a flurry of activity as Harlow is brought toward us. "Is she alright? Is she alive?" I hover over her as best I can, but she is dwarfed by paramedics and IV lines.

"The PenneSTAR1 rescue helicopter is on its way," a woman dressed in navy pants and jacket tells me. "Your daughter has a broken arm, but what we're most concerned about is her head injury and the possibility of internal bleeding. The chopper is the fastest way to get her the help she needs. A road ambulance will take you to the hospital to meet us."

"They said something before... T-something. What is that?"

"TMI. It means Traumatic Brain Injury, but we won't know the extent of her injuries until we get to the hospital. We're doing all we can."

"But she'll make it?"

The woman softens her gaze. "You should try and prepare yourself. Her trauma is signif icant.'"

Above us, the rescue helicopter's rotor thumps like a celestial heartbeat. As it descends, wind whips my hair across my face and for the first time in my life, I bow my head and say a prayer.

Chapter Forty-Nine

SOPHIE

One Month Later

Bastian closes the back of the truck, and I smooth down my hair. "I appreciate your help with all of this," I tell him. "There was a lot more to load up than I thought."

He simply shrugs and smiles. "And you're sure about this?"

I look back at the brownstone James and I bought together, a giant red SOLD sticker plastered across a sign out the front. "Bit late if I'm not".

"Come here…" I step into his embrace, and he holds me tight. "I can't believe you're really leaving, Soph."

I swallow hard and will myself not to cry. This is harder than I thought – then again, doing the right thing usually is. "You know it's for the best, Bastian. For everyone."

His chin moves against my hair, and I can tell that he's nodding. After the accident, Harlow was in intensive care for almost three weeks. She suffered a punctured lung, broken arm, and the impact as she went through the windscreen caused her brain to swell. But according to Bastian, the doctors expect her to make a full recovery.

"This whole thing has been a wake-up call, that's for sure," he says. "Regardless of what Madelyn-May did, I should've been there. I don't know how I can ever forgive myself for not answering her call."

His tears trickle to the edge of my lip, and I taste their bitterness. "You couldn't have known Bastian, and the most important thing is that they're okay. You have a lifetime of opportunities to make it up to them. Don't be too hard on yourself. You're an amazing father. They know how much you love them."

"Right," he nods again. "Now all I have to do is convince myself of that."

I step back and take him in, reminding myself this will be the last time we ever see each other. "You've meant a great deal to me, Bastian. If you hadn't been in my life…"

"I feel the same way. I think in a lot of ways we saved each other."

"I think we did," I smile. "And Madelyn-May? She knows you're here?"

"She does, as weird as that sounds."

I kick at an invisible stone on the sidewalk. "It's probably none of my business, but how are things between the two of you?"

"There's a long way to go. A very long way and I can never forget what she did." He lets out a long breath, and I wonder how he will ever come to terms with all that's happened. "But it's best for the kids if we at least try. And she is trying."

"Well, she let you come today. That's a good thing."

"I think she understands that I had to say goodbye." He steps closer and takes my hand in his. "Sometimes you need the pain of watching someone disappear before you can really let them go. Does that make sense?"

I think of Josh and know exactly what he means. "We always did understand each other, you and I," I tell him. "I've loved that about you."

"And I've loved many things about you too, Soph." It's as close as we can get without saying the words out loud. "And you're sure everything is alright with you? Madelyn-May said you passed out after the accident."

"I'm fine. It was nothing," I tell him. "I was just overwhelmed, I think."

"Because Madelyn-May thought maybe..."

"...maybe what?"

"One of the police officers asked if you might be pregnant."

"Really?"

"I guess because you passed out."

My hand falls over my stomach. "And how did she take that?"

"About how you'd imagine," he grins. "Anyway, so long it was nothing and you're alright."

"I am. I'm alright."

He nods, and we both fall silent, the inevitable drawing nearer. "Do you know where you'll go?"

I glance over at the U-Haul, Miss Molly front and center in the passenger seat. "You know, I have no idea," I smile. "And I can't believe I'm saying that. Me, can you imagine? Driving off into the great unknown, with no idea what might come next." *Or how my life might be about to change.*

"The great unknown maybe, but certainly not alone," he says. "You have your best friend. What more could you need?"

I look at Miss Molly and smile. "Speaking of which, we better get going."

"Well, I'd say let me know where you end up, but... Madelyn-May is stepping away from the business. We're taking that trip, and I do want to try. I hope you don't mind me telling you that, Soph," he says. "It doesn't mean what I felt for you wasn't real."

"I know. Maybe in another life."

He smiles and squeezes my hand. "You know, I never thanked you."

"Thanked me? For what?"

"For them," he smiles. "If it wasn't for you, my children wouldn't exist. They wouldn't be who they are. Don't get me wrong, there's plenty of Madelyn-May in there, especially with Harlow, but they're also you. I can see it in them now, and I guess in some way, even though we're saying goodbye you'll always be with me. Every time I look at them, I'll see a tiny piece of you, Soph. Forever."

He kisses me gently on the forehead and slowly walks back to his car. He wants to wait until we drive away.

I climb up into the U-Haul and scratch Miss Molly on the head. As I push the key into the ignition, I take one last look at the house. It was our place. The place James and I planned to watch Josh grow up, to laugh with friends, mow lawns, cook meals, laugh, love, fight, make up, and grow old together.

My life. My love. My family. James and Josh. My beautiful ghosts, forever young, and forever loved. I will miss them until the last days of my life, but until then it's time for me to learn how to live again.

I turn the key and right on cue Miss Molly barks. "That's right, sweet girl. It's time."

We pull out onto the street, and I wave goodbye to Bastian. He's a good man, maybe even a great one, and I want the best for him. But as we turn the corner, it's not Bastian I watch in the rear-view mirror. The last thing I need to see as we slip away is our home because sometimes you need the pain of watching something disappear before you can really let it go.

Epilogue

LACY

Just so you know, the walls of this prison are not the view I had in mind. We were supposed to be in a trailer on the beach by now, salt in our hair and the warm Mexican sun on our skin. But instead, for the past six months I've been trapped in this cage with its cold hard floor and lack of sunshine.

When I was arrested, I told the lawyer, a stupid bitch who never stops popping Quick-Eze, that Madelyn-May was the one who needed to be locked up, not me. I told her that she was the one who murdered her own father then set a fire and left me to burn.

For a minute I thought I was getting through to her, but then the FBI went and screwed everything up. Apparently, their so-called findings were grounded in a statement made by old Avril Beanie, who insisted it was Melody she saw acting weird and stinking of gasoline the night of the fire. Avril Beanie, who is so damned blind and senile, once saw her walking on down the road wearing two different shoes and biting into an onion. Could only figure she thought it was an apple, but either way, she's not exactly what you might call a credible witness. The thing is, after that, the whole damned trailer park wanted to get in on the action saying they saw Melody that night. Every time someone recounted the story, it got more and more stupid until those FBI idiots took a report from a so-called eyewitness who claimed to see a scuffle happening inside the trailer. Whoever it was swore blind they saw Melody shouting and throwing gasoline on Bobby-Ray, trying to set him alight.

So, as fate would have it, testimony made by residents of the trailer park eventually tried and convicted a girl who had already gone and sentenced herself to death by lethal injection. If you can find the logic in that, then you're a lot smarter than me. Seems pinning the blame on a dead girl might've been a whole lot easier for the FBI than chasing down Madelyn-May - a millionaire who had taken her family and fled the country. But that's just me.

The female guard with mud-brown hair and a nose like she's been punched in the face one too many times bangs on the side of my cell. I tear my eyes away from counting cracks on the floor and raise my brow.

"Lacy, must be your lucky day," she tells me. "You've finally got yourself a visitor. Up and at 'em, let's go."

The walk down through C-block toward the visitation room is better than being in the cell, but I can't say it's much to get excited about either. It might as well be D-Block, B-Block, or a damned ice-block for all the difference it makes. All the cell blocks are freezing cold and look the same. They have the same sounds, the same feel. They're all the same-same and not different.

I push against the door with my shoulder and make my way over to the table. A clear Perspex shield separates us, but I don't need a phone to hear her. "Took you long enough," I huff.

"Really? That's all you have to say for yourself?"

I look her over. She's twenty-one now, with shiny black hair and the same dewy skin I once had. Around her neck hangs a pendant with a bright blue butterfly and along her arm, a flutter of blue wings is tattooed from her wrist to her elbow. She catches me looking down at the brightly colored ink.

"Did you know a group of butterflies is called a kaleidoscope?" She smiles at the tattoo on her arm, then looks back at me. "A kaleidoscope of butterflies. It's a pretty description, isn't it? I was so looking forward to seeing all those beautiful butterflies in Mexico, their delicate wings carrying them along on the breeze."

"What's with you and those blue butterflies anyway?"

She touches her hand to the pendant, then flips it over. On the reverse side, its wings are drab and brown, the color of dog shit.

"The Blue Morpho butterfly is a master of camouflage," she tells me. "The brown underside of its wings blends perfectly with its surroundings, so when it flies the contrast of blue and brown gives the illusion it can appear and disappear all at once. In other words, it can wander through the world without anyone knowing it's there. Unless it wants them to, of course."

I raise my brow and pretend to be impressed. "Valentine, listen—"

"No," she snaps, her face instantly changing. "You listen. You owe me an explanation, and it better be good. What the hell happened out there?"

"They were leaving the country. What choice did I have?"

She leans forward until her face is almost touching the Perspex. "You report back. You tell me so I can make a new plan. You don't go off half-cocked, trying to do God-knows-what in the middle of a motorway. What were you thinking?"

"That I wanted to finish what we started."

She sits back and tosses her long dark hair over her shoulder. "You promised to bring me the girl. I had new passports and papers made for her. Do you have any idea what I had to go through, the kind of people I had to *persuade,* in order to get those?"

"I know, and I'm sorry."

"You wanted your revenge. You said you could handle it. You gave me your word, and now here you are, locked up in prison."

"I don't need reminding about what I said."

"Well, clearly you do because I don't have Harlow."

"What the hell was I supposed to do?" I shout, finally losing my patience at being spoken to like a child.

"Keep your leg on... and lower your damned voice," she says with a hiss. "This is your fault. You messed up because you let your emotions get in the way. Don't forget I'm all you have left. I'd be careful how you speak to me if I was you."

As much as I hate it, I know she's right. My husband is dead, and my daughters are all gone. "I'm sorry, alright? I messed up. So, what do we do now?"

Valentine looks at me, her eyes rich with arrogance and anger. "Now, we escalate. I may not have met Madelyn-May, but I know what pain she caused. How everything unraveled because of what she did."

"You know, Valentine, maybe it's time to just leave it alone," I sigh, suddenly more tired than I've ever been. "I'm not going anyplace soon, and that's how it has to be. Maybe you should let it go and move on before it's too late and you end up right in here with me."

Valentine leans in, her eyes hard, and her lip curled. "First of all, I'm not stupid enough to get caught and put in prison. Second, you can accept whatever you want, but Madelyn—May owes me. It's her fault our entire family ended up the way it did. She beat her pretty wings and it caused a tidal wave none of them could ever survive."

I watch my granddaughter and wonder if the vials of poison that lived inside my beautiful monsters were all poured into her at conception. When that piece of shit husband paid his last visit to Melody and got her pregnant, he never could have imagined what he was creating. His daughter is conniving, clever, vengeful, and despite her beautiful face, she has the uncanny knack of blending in perfectly with her surroundings.

And I guess I don't have to tell you - no one ever sees her coming.

Can you ever really outrun the past?

Find out in the highly anticipated sequel to The Secrets We Keep.

Accused of murder and on the run, would you choose to save yourself or the life of a little girl you've never met?

Five years after being kidnapped and almost killed in a car crash, seventeen-year-old Harlow just wants to live a normal life. But when a controversial video of a drunken night out goes viral, she quickly finds herself exposed to the vicious attacks of online trolls.

What they don't know is that their cowardly online abuse is about to trigger a chain of events that will not only put Harlow's life in danger but will force her to choose between saving herself and the life of a little girl she's never met.

In this intense, edge-of-your-seat thriller, Taylor takes readers on yet another emotional roller coaster as The Secrets We Keep and the fate of Harlow, Sophie, Bastian, and Madelyn-May reaches an unflinching and unforgettable conclusion in The Truth We Tell.

Once again, the book explores the complex and intricate relationships we have with others and ourselves, as Taylor crafts an intense and compelling narrative around the bonds of family and how truth has the power to set us free.

If you love authors like Lisa Jewell, Gillian Flynn, Frieda McFadden, and Nicole Trope and your go-to reads are domestic thrillers with flawed characters, intriguing female protagonists, and twists you never see coming - you will enjoy this book.

THE
TRUTH
WE TELL

NIKKI LEE TAYLOR

THE TRUTH WE TELL
BOOK TWO

HARLOW

There is no heaven. When you die there's no tunnel of bright white light or angels floating around a golden gate. There is nothing. You simply stop existing. End of story.

A lot of people have argued with me about this, mostly because they're scared and sometimes because they think I'm just a dumb seventeen-year-old. Like what do I know, right? But in the end, I always win the debate. And why shouldn't I? I'm the only one who's ever been dead.

I was eleven when it happened. A car accident. Well, a kidnapping and attempted murder if we're being honest, but the medical report called it a car accident. I was officially dead for three minutes before they managed to restart my heart. Apparently, that's the longest your heart can stop pumping blood and oxygen before you begin to suffer irreparable brain damage.

Everyone expected me to be traumatized by what happened, maybe suffer post-traumatic stress disorder having *died* so young and all. But for me, the experience was nothing short of cathartic. When my injuries healed, I left the hospital knowing exactly what I wanted. To be free of my fame-seeking mother, the infamous Madelyn-May Marozzi, parental blogging queen of North America. I wanted, no, I *needed*, to be free of her. I felt as though my second chance at life depended on it.

Not long after I was released from hospital, my parents and brother Harry moved to Australia to start over. Much to my mother's disgust, I stayed here in Philly with my best friend Kempsey and her parents Steve and Rhonda who were more than willing to become my official guardians until I come of age.

For so long, I thought of the day I moved in with them as my rebirth. The day I got to *choose* my family. Since then, I have lived a quiet, reserved life, away from the spotlight forced on me by my mother. For six years it's been a wonderful life in a lovely home surrounded by warm and caring people. If only things could have stayed that way.

SOPHIE

Poppy was born at one minute past two at the University of Maryland Harford Memorial Hospital, and to everyone's surprise, she came out with an extra thumb. According to the doctors it wasn't that uncommon. But lying there in the birthing suite, my hair wet and my skin slick with sweat, I felt as though I failed my daughter before she even took her first breath. In terms of natural childbirth, at age thirty-five I was considered geriatric. I knew without a doubt that it was my aging body that let her down. I hated myself but the doctors were adamant. There were no signs of congenital defects or issues of concern, other than the thumb. To them, she was perfect.

Because Poppy arrived right on my due date, I took it as a sign she might be an easy baby. I hoped it meant she had some in-built understanding that the world of adults was ruled by dates and times. That she would work in with my plans. But she didn't.

As the weeks turned into months and months turned into years, Poppy became a tired and irritable child. I was sure she slept and cried more than any normal baby should. More than Josh had.

By the time she was three, we were regulars at the Westbrook Family Medical Clinic, but no matter how many times I pleaded for him to look harder, Dr Martin Havinack remained adamant that she was fine. She was just *'one of those children who needs a little extra love and attention'*, he would say. But deep in my heart, I knew something was wrong. I just didn't know what it was.

By the time she was four, five separate psychologists had assured me it was normal to be overcautious. To not just think the worst but to expect it. My son Josh died when he was six, not because I missed the signs of an underlying health condition, but because a drunk driver killed him and my husband in a car wreck. They told me again about survivor's guilt, post-traumatic stress disorder, and all the other conditions grief can create. They willed me to believe that it was fear not fact when I told them something was wrong with Poppy. They said my ongoing anxiety, coupled with the fact that I randomly uprooted my life and moved to Havre De Grace, was proof enough that I was the one who needed medicating. I hoped they were right, but I also knew they were wrong. My move to Havre De Grace was not random. It had been very much on purpose.

"Now you be careful," I tell Poppy, my face pressed gently against her tiny button nose. "Some of those kids are bigger than you."

"Come on, Mom," she whines. "I'm up next."

I zip up her hot pink parka and say a silent prayer. She's five. It's March and still cold out. Our school has a team in the local social baseball competition for under-eights. The team is a mix of boys and girls and at the end of the season, the winning team gets to host an all-expenses-paid day at the Fun Factory, a popular kids' game and pizza place just off Main Street. All the teams in the league attend, so no matter how good or bad the kids play, everyone gets a prize at the end of the season.

"Are you sure about this?" I ask again.

"I want to play," she says, her tiny hands clenched into determined fists at her sides. "Please, Mommy, I want to play."

"Alright, okay." I tuck her long ponytail into the back of her parka so none of the other kids accidentally pull on her hair. "Come straight back if you feel puffed out or tired. I'll be right here."

She runs off and I pull myself up, my stomach twisting. Since the day she was born, I feel like I've been waiting, side-stepping the inevitable.

Beside me, my golden retriever Miss Molly doesn't bother to get up. She was a rescue so it's hard to know her exact age but if I had to guess I'd say she's around ten years old. Her bones creak and her gait is slow, but she never leaves my side. It's been that way since the day I brought her home. I give her a smile and a scratch behind the ear then glance out over the field.

Poppy is up on the plate, bat in hand. She swings and the bat connects. She is off, running toward first base, her ponytail already untucked and flapping around like a happy dog's tail. When she trips and falls, I take a nervous step forward, hand on my chest, silently willing her to get up. One. Two. Three...

As I am about to run forward, her giggle carries on the breeze and she gets to her feet.

See, you're being ridiculous. She's fine.

Feeling silly, I sneak a glance at the other parents. Did anyone see me lurch forward, eyes wide with panic? Do they think I'm a helicopter parent? Or worse, do they think I know something is wrong and am letting her play anyway? I'm so concerned with deciding if other people are staring at me that I don't see her fall the second time.

"Sophie," one of the other parents says, an edge of concern pitching her voice higher. "Is Poppy okay?"

I snap my head back and peer out over the field. A tiny shape wrapped in hot pink is lying motionless on the ground. From the edges of the field parents slowly start to move in, their steps hesitant, not wanting to believe that something is wrong. The referee blows his whistle and hurries toward her. I can't feel my legs but I'm already running, the freezing wind slicing my cheeks.

"Poppy! Poppy!" My cries echo and I can't tell if it's me screaming or one of the other parents. "Poppy!" When I reach her, I throw myself down and push the hair back from her face. Two ribbons of bright red blood trickle from her nose and her eyes are closed. "Poppy, wake up! Wake up!" The crowd is closing in on me. The weight of their fear is palpable. "Poppy!"

"I've called 911," A male voice says. "They're coming but - "

"But what?"

"They have to come from another call. They're fifteen minutes out."

I rest my hand on Poppy's forehead because I don't know what else to do. Her skin is slick and too hot for such a cold afternoon. When I finally look up at the sea of faces staring back at me, some are familiar and others I've never seen before but the one thing they share is the look in their eyes— fear.

I scoop her tiny body up into my arms and cradle her against my chest. The bottom half of her face is stained red from the blood running out of her nose. As I wipe at it with my sleeve and hate myself for every minute I've wasted doing anything other than learning how to save my child's life.

If she dies this will be my fault.

"I'll take you to the hospital." A burly man wearing a Havre de Grace Warriors windbreaker is suddenly standing in front of me, keys in hand. "Do you need to call her father?"

"There's... there's no father," I mutter. "It's just me."

"Right. Let's go then."

People jump out of our way as we run single file toward the carpark. Their faces are a blur, and no one speaks as we pass. A woman in jeans and a windbreaker clutches at her chest as we race by. Next to them a man and woman pull their small son between them, closing ranks.

I know they're worried, but I also know a tiny part of them is relieved it's me racing against time and not them.

The dusty carpark is only meters away, but Poppy's lips are blue. She's gone still in my arms.

"I think she's stopped breathing!" I scream. "What do I do?"

The man stops abruptly and turns back, his brow pulled into a tight frown. "Put her down."

"What? No, I don't know CPR... I can't - "

"We need to find someone who knows how to do it while we wait for the ambulance."

"We can't," I shout back, my voice breaking. "We have to go. They won't get here in time!"

An icy wind whips across the back of my neck as I readjust my grip on her tiny body.

He steps in close. "What's your name?"

"Sophie," I sob. "My name is Sophie."

"Sophie, once we get into my truck there's no one to help us. She won't make it without CPR. If we can keep her breathing the ambulance might get here in time. There's still hope."

I stare at him, willing his words back down his throat. She's heavy in my arms, gravity pulling her down and away from me. "Goddamn it!" I scream as loud as I can. "Help me! Anyone! Help me, please!"

Screams scrape against the tightness of my throat. As each second passes, I feel her slipping away as though a light is slowly dimming inside me. If she dies, every spark of joy will be extinguished from my life. If she dies, I will die with her. Maybe not my body, but my soul, my love, my will.

"I'll find someone," he calls, already running back toward the field. "Stay there, Sophie. I'll find someone! I'll find someone!"

I fall to my knees and fold my daughter's lifeless body across my lap. Her skin is translucent, clouds of gray gathering at her temples. A storm about to break.

"Don't you leave me, Poppy," I whisper. "Don't you leave me."

Seconds feel like hours as I gently rock her back and forth in my arms. I knew this. I knew something was wrong and I didn't prepare myself. All I had to do was take a CPR class. One stupid class. That's all I had to do.

"Lay her down on the ground," someone shouts at me from across the carpark. It's a woman's voice, strong but breathless. She's been running. "Quickly dear, there's no time."

When I look up, I register that the woman is older than me, maybe in her sixties. She has a short bob of gray hair and deep lines etched around her eyes. The rest is a blur.

"Roll her onto her back," she tells me, as I slide Poppy gently onto the ground. "What happened?"

"I... I don't know. She was running. I looked away for just a second." I glance desperately at the man who was going to drive us to the hospital. "Did you see what happened? Was there a collision?"

He is down on one knee. His cheeks are scarlet. His chest is heaving. "Beats me. Best I can tell she was just running and then..." he draws another deep breath, "...down she went. I didn't see any other kids near her."

"Does she have a health condition?" the woman asks.

I note she has the efficiency and tone of someone who knows what they're doing. "Are you a doctor?"

"No, but I was a nurse for thirty-two years. She's very pale. Is she anemic?"

"Anemic? No... I... I've taken her to doctors before. They never found anything like that."

The woman crosses her hands over my daughter's tiny chest and begins compression. "But you thought otherwise?"

I nod quickly not wanting to believe I might have been right. "Please," I whisper to the sky as I watch her tiny chest rise and fall, "not again."

"Where's the damned ambulance?" the man curses, getting back to his feet and looking out toward the road.

"We can't wait," the woman says. "We need to go."

"Are you sure?" I have no control over my daughter's life. I don't know how to help her and will have to rely on this woman, this stranger, to make a choice that will decide whether she lives or dies.

"I've got a faint rhythm," she says. "I'll continue chest compressions in the car. But we've got to move. Now!"

I gather Poppy up off the ground and together we run toward the man's truck. With every step and every breath, I beg. I beg the power of the universe. I beg God, even though I have always been one of the faithless. I beg anyone and anything to take my life and give it to Poppy instead. I silently apologize for what I did, for having her without telling Bastian. I apologize for having slept with another woman's husband. I apologize for thinking I deserved a second chance, and for daring to try and be a mother again. I apologize for everything I can think of. But most of all I apologize for once again failing a child whose only flaw was to depend on me.

"Please, you have to get us there in time," I say, as I slide Poppy onto the dirty back seat of the truck. "She's so little... she's..."

He nods and starts the engine. Beside me, the woman immediately starts compression on Poppy's tiny bird-like chest. But as we reverse, the man catches my eye in the rear-view mirror and it's hard to miss his look of panic. As we race toward the hospital the car is silent. No one dares to speak but if we did, we would all say the same thing - *If we make it, it will be a miracle.*

HARLOW

It's the pain that wakes me. A dull, throbbing ache that immediately settles into my bones. Spiderwebs of lingering sleep cling to me and I wonder if I'm back in the hospital. If perhaps the past six years have been nothing more than a dream.

But as I open my eyes, I'm greeted by soft light falling in through cream curtains and the delicate chirp of birds in the tree outside. I'm safe beneath my lemon and white comforter and up on the wall hangs a familiar abstract painting, its warm pastel hues reminding me of a sunrise.

This time I have not been kidnapped or almost killed in a car crash, but as I reach up and touch my lip, there is no doubt in my mind that I'm injured. I can feel it. Split and swollen.

What the hell happened?

My head throbs, and when I push back the comforter, I see deep scratches running from my shoulder to my elbow. I try to pull myself up, but the room swims in and out of focus. A choking rush of bile burns the back of my throat and I battle to swallow so I don't throw up all over the bed.

'You're awake," Rhonda says, striding in without knocking, the usual warmth missing from her voice.

"If you could call it that," I manage.

"Well, you have to get up, Harlow. We need to talk."

I squint as Rhonda tears back the curtains and bright sunlight assaults my eyes. "What time is it?"

"It's just after one o'clock in the afternoon." She doesn't look at me and instead picks my clothes up off the floor and folds them over her arm. There's dried blood on the sleeve of my shirt.

"Is that..." I peer in closer.

"Now, Harlow. I'll meet you downstairs."

She's gone before I have a chance to respond or ask about the stain on my clothes. It also occurs to me she didn't bother to ask if I was okay. Confused, I cast my mind back to last night and feel a sudden jolt of fear when I realize that I can't remember how we got home.

In my ensuite bathroom, I'm horrified at the disheveled girl looking back at me in the mirror. My hair is mattered with lumps of dried blood. The right side of my lip is swollen, an angry split running from top to bottom. On my forehead, is a lump the size of a potato.

"Jesus..." I breathe, forcing myself to lean in and evaluate the damage. "What the hell happened last night?"

Carefully I pull my nightgown up and over my head, mindful not to bump my lip or the lump on my forehead. When the hot water hits my scalp, I close my eyes and let it wash over me. At my feet, the water turns a bloody mix of red and brown as it circles the drain.

When I eventually make my way downstairs, Rhonda is sitting stiff and stern at the formal dining table. Beside her is Kempsey, both their faces are blank and cold, and I shiver despite the warmth of the fire crackling in the hearth.

"Harlow, come and take a seat." Rhonda gestures to a leather chair directly across from her and it strikes me that we've never sat in this room the entire time I've lived here. Beside her Kempsey's head is down and she's pulling at one of her fingernails, something I know she does when she's nervous.

"I'm so confused about last night," I begin. "How did I end up with all these cuts and bruises?"

Finally, Kempsey looks up and when she does, I cannot hide my shock. Her right eye is swollen shut, an angry purple bruise stretching from the rise of her cheekbone up to her eyebrow.

"Kempsey, oh my God, are you alright?" I reach across the table, but she pulls away before my fingers reach her.

"Harlow, what you did last night is beyond words," Rhonda begins. "I don't even know where to start."

"What I *did*?" I repeat. "I can't remember anything about last night."

Kempsey huffs and looks away. "As if."

"No really," I try. "I can't remember anything. What happened to us?"

"To *us*?" Kempsey snaps. "You. You are what happened to us. You freaked out at the club and started acting like a crazy person."

"The club?" I close my eyes and brush through the spiderwebs trying to remember.

"Yes," Rhonda says. Her tone is sharp. Her lips are tight. "You are both seventeen years old. Too young to be out in a nightclub with boys."

"It wasn't a nightclub, Mom," Kempsey says with a sigh. "It was just a beer garden."

"At night with boys."

"I remember sitting with Darcy," I mumble. "He and I were talking and then we came back to the table. I felt dizzy and then - "

"- you climbed up onto a table and flashed your boobs at everyone. You were yelling and shouting like a maniac," Kempsey finishes.

"No," I quickly shake my head. "I would never - "

"Ah, yeah... you would," she assures me. "Then you started making out with some old dudes letting them feel you up and shit. It was, like, so gross."

"Kempsey, no. I wouldn't... I didn't..." I trail off and feel like I'm going to be sick. *I would never do that... would I?*

"Then, after you saw Darcy and me together you went ballistic." She points to her black eye. "Security tried to throw you out, but you made such a scene you ended up falling and smashing your head on the gutter outside."

I push back against the chair desperate to get some distance from the things coming out of Kempsey's mouth. It can't be true. I would never dream of acting like that. But my physical pain is real, and it's clear from Kempsey's bruises and the look in her eye, that hers is too. I glance at Rhonda hoping for some explanation, a solution, anything, but she just stares back stony-faced.

"So, what do you have to say for yourself, Harlow?"

"I... I don't know. I don't remember any of this."

"Did you take something?"

"Did I take something?" I glance at Kempsey, but she quickly swallows and drops her eyes. Through the fog, I begin to remember that she was the person who brought over my final drink. "Kempsey did you - "

"Don't try and blame this on me!" she snaps before I can finish. "You're the one who got wasted and freaked out."

"I only had two drinks. After the second, I... everything is a blur."

Rhonda rests her palms out on the table and glares at me. "Neither of you should have been drinking at a club. But Harlow, you hurt my daughter. I can't have that."

My heart pounds against my ribs and I begin to panic. I'm being accused of things I can't remember. "If I did then I didn't mean it," I begin, my words rambling. "I would never intentionally hurt Kempsey. Please, you must know that."

Rhonda closes her eyes and slowly shakes her head. "I need to think this through."

"Someone must have drugged me." I glance at Kempsey, but she refuses to meet my eye. "They must have. Rhonda, you know me. I would never act like that."

"I can't have drugs here, Harlow."

"But I'm not on drugs!" I get to my feet, my eyes brimming with tears. "I would never take drugs. I don't... I don't want drama in my life... not after everything, you know that. That's why I stayed here. I don't - "

"Then I wouldn't go back to school on Monday," Kempsey tells me with a dramatic roll of her eyes. "Because there's definitely going to be drama."

"Why? Did everyone see what I did?"

"Everyone? Yes, Harlow, *everyone* saw what you did."

"What does that mean?"

"It means your little show went viral. You're all over socials."

I clutch at my chest as the air disappears from the room. "You filmed it?"

"Not me, but pretty much everyone else. I'm surprised you haven't seen it."

I rub my forehead as the room swims around me. "But I... I don't even have socials. You know I hate that stuff."

Kempsey exchanges a look with Rhonda then slides her phone toward me. "Here, but don't say I didn't warn you."

My skin goes cold as I watch the disaster play out on a video posted to Kempsey's social media account. My soft pale breasts are exposed. The fly on my jeans is unzipped. I'm up on a table holding a glass of beer over my head like a trophy. The light is dim but two men I've never seen before, both much older than me, are clearly groping and clutching handfuls of my bare skin. One has a dirty-looking beard and red-rimmed eyes. He squeezes my nipple between his fingers and slurs something to the camera that I can't understand. The other looks just as drunk. He has my left breast cupped in one hand and is taking a selfie with the other. But the most humiliating part of it is that I'm laughing. I look so joyful, so carefree. I swallow hard and close my eyes.

Did I like it? Why didn't I try and stop them?

When I look back at the screen, the camera phone is following me. I climb down from the table and stumble toward two people kissing in a darkened corner of the beer garden.

Through vacant eyes, I glance back at whoever is filming. Dried spittle hangs from my lip and my hair is a mess.

"Whoa... you are wa-sted," a male voice sings from behind the camera. "This is going to be a-ma-zing."

When the two people on screen break apart, to my surprise it's Kempsey and Darcy who were kissing. I glance up from the phone and stare at her in shock. "You kissed him?"

She shrugs and pushes the phone a little closer. "Keep watching."

Suddenly onscreen, I raise a chair up over my head and hurl it at my best friend's face. She screams and Darcy shouts out. The video falls out of focus and disembodied voices yell to call an ambulance. I hear myself sobbing and it's hard to tell whether the sound is coming from the past or present.

"Kempsey, I... I don't know what to say," I tell her, pushing the phone away from me. "Someone put something in my drink. They must have. You know I would never act like that on my own... even though you were kissing Darcy."

But again, Kempsey just shrugs and then pushes the phone back into her pocket. "I don't know why you even care that we were kissing. It's not like you guys were dating. You liked him. No one ever said it was mutual."

"I never said I liked him. "

"Oh, please..."

"Girls," Rhonda says, her arms stretched out toward us. "Forget about the boy. This is serious. We have to meet with the school on Monday. Let's see what they have to say and we'll take it from there."

"I don't use drugs. You both know that," I plead. "You gave me a home when I wanted to stay, and I'll always be grateful for that. I would never try to hurt you Kempsey, not on purpose. I don't know what I would do without you guys."

"Well, you could consider going to live with your *actual* family," Kempsey suggests, her tone making it clear she's still furious.

"Is that really what you want me to do?"

"Just... do whatever you want, Harlow. But I really like Darcy so since you messed that up for yourself, don't go messing it up for me too."

"Sure." I force a smile. "Of course not."

She nods and pushes back from the table. "I'm going over to Laura's. Darcy's coming to meet us. Obviously, you're not invited, Harlow. Sorry not sorry, you know?"

I glance at Rhonda, but she doesn't meet my eye. Instead, she gets to her feet and disappears toward the kitchen leaving me to sit alone at the table.

When they're gone, I rest my head in my hands and try to think. One of the last things I remember is Kempsey bringing two beers over to Darcy and me. But what happened after that?

I think hard, trying to remember every detail but my head is throbbing and the best I can conjure are blurry visions of people moving in slow motion. Did she drug me? The thought seems impossible. She took pity on me after the accident and when the truth about my mother came out, she convinced her parents to be my guardians so I wouldn't have to move overseas. She always liked Darcy and I know deep down it bothered her to think he might be interested in me – her weird little introverted sidekick, but to drug me? I don't want to believe she would be capable of doing something like that, of putting me in danger, especially over a boy. But I also learned a long time ago that the people who love you are usually the ones who end up hurting you the most.

SOPHIE

Flanked by the man and woman who helped get us here, I run as best I can toward the hospital's emergency department, Poppy's lifeless body hanging from my arms like a rag doll.

"Help me!" I scream, my voice almost incomprehensible. "My daughter! Help me!"

Instantly men and women in teal scrubs run at us from every angle. People who were slumped across seats in the waiting area are up on their feet, brows knotted, and a woman tucks her small daughter in closer.

A middle-aged woman with cropped red hair and a stethoscope around her neck takes Poppy from my arms and places her gently onto a gurney. Relinquishing her to a stranger is like taking my heart and willingly placing it in the cupped palms of someone I have never met.

"What happened?" she asks, her eyes trained on Poppy as she takes her vitals.

"I... she fell. I don't..."

She leans over Poppy but looks up and meets my eye. "I need you to take a breath and tell me exactly what happened."

"She was playing Little League Baseball," I manage between sobs. "She fell but it didn't seem like she was hurt. I think she fell because..."

"...because what?"

"Because something is wrong. I've felt it ever since she was born. Something isn't right."

She holds my gaze, clearly assessing my mental state versus the strength of a mother's intuition.

"Prep for an MRI and full bloods," she barks at two of the nurses watching on. "Now!"

As they turn and wheel Poppy toward a set of plastic double doors, I gather my bag and begin to follow but a young female nurse wearing so much mascara it has congealed on her lashes, steps in front of me. "We'll need you to stay here and fill out her insurance and medical details."

"But I -"

"She's in very capable hands."

The woman looks too young to even work at a hospital and I panic at the idea of Poppy being taken somewhere I can't see her. "Are you sure? I mean..."

Can I trust these strangers with my baby?

"Doctor Yates is incredible," she assures me. "Your daughter will get the best care possible."

I watch after them as Poppy's tiny shape is swallowed up by a pair of double doors.

"Can you follow me please?" she asks again.

I turn to the man and woman from the field. "I don't know how to thank you both," I say, as a bewildered fog falls over my brain. "I don't even know your names."

"I'm Martha," the woman smiles, "and there's no need for thanks. I'm just glad we made it."

"Agreed," the man says with a nod. "I'm Barry. Baz."

Around us, people slowly fold themselves back into their chairs and slump their chins against balled-up palms.

"I don't understand what happened," I mumble half to them and half to the air around me. "She just fell and -"

"I really need you to come with me," the mascara nurse tells me again. "We need your daughter's details."

"Alright, Christ!" I snap, stress breaking through the fog and catching me unaware. "Oh shit, I'm sorry," I apologize immediately. "I didn't mean that. It's just..."

She nods and opens one arm ready to guide me toward wherever it is I need to go.

"We'll wait over here," Martha offers, but there is a question mark in her tone. She probably has somewhere else to be.

"No, don't be silly," I tell her. "You've both done everything you can. Go on back. I'll be fine."

"You're sure?" Baz asks, awkwardly rubbing the back of his neck. "I'd stay, it's just my son is back at the field."

"No, I mean it. Please, you've both done everything you can."

Finally, much to Mascara's delight I take a seat in an uncomfortable orange chair and begin to fill out Poppy's details. When I'm done, they direct me to a small white waiting room with sparse furniture and a wooden coffee table adorned with biscuits in small plastic wrappers.

Unable to even think about eating, I pull out my phone and call to check that Miss Molly is safe. She won't understand being left behind and I hate that I couldn't bring her with me. I scan through the school phone tree and find Delilah's mother saved under her actual name, Julia.

"Julia," I sigh when she answers, "it's Sophie. I was hoping you took Miss Molly from the field?"

"She's here at home with us," Julia says, and my shoulders sag with relief. "She's quite happy and snoozing by the fire with our dog Bosco."

"Thank you so much. I'm sorry to burden you."

She dismisses my apology and asks how Poppy is doing. I tell her all that I can, which is nothing, and then hang up and wait.

After a few minutes, a tired-looking man who looks like he hasn't slept in days shuffles in and folds himself into the seat across from me. Our eyes meet, he nods in recognition and then looks down at the ground. He doesn't speak and either do I. Neither of us wants to give life to the only words there are to say. *I hope. If only. Please, no.*

Together we wait in silence, the wall clock ticking down the moments that will determine the rest of our lives. Eventually, the woman with the red hair who took Poppy away appears in the doorway and gestures for me to follow her.

"How is she? Do you know what happened? Is she alright?" I feel like I'm barking at her and purposely lower the volume of my voice. "Can I take her home?"

"She's resting."

"Oh..." My palm comes up to my collar bone and I let out a long breath. "So, she's alright?"

What I want is for her to smile and tell me that of course, she's alright. It was nothing. She tripped and bumped her nose. Don't be silly. You can take her home right now. But she doesn't.

"Ms Miller -"

Oh, God.

"It's Sophie, please."

She nods and swallows, her neck muscles constricting for the most fleeting of seconds. It is a tiny gesture but one that sends a shock wave of panic from the top of my head down and into my toes. Pins and needles sting at my face and for the first time in years, my heart beats out of rhythm. The first sign of a panic attack.

"Sophie - "

"I... I think I'm going to have a panic attack," I manage. "I used to have them, not in years, but I can feel - "

She stops where we are and eases me into one of the chairs along the wall of the corridor. "Just breathe. Slow and deep, Sophie. In through your nose, out through your mouth."

The smell of antiseptic and fear flood my nose as I inhale deeply, searching for a stable breath. Beside me, the doctor pulls out a cell phone and asks someone to bring two milligrams of Valium.

"Keep breathing, Sophie. In and out." She leans in and wraps her fingers around my wrist to check my pulse. "You're doing great."

"What's wrong with my daughter?"

"Let's just get you calm and breathing properly then we can discuss Poppy's condition."

"Condition? What condition?"

A male nurse who looks young enough to still be in school approaches us carrying a small cup of water and a plastic thimble containing a small white tablet.

Valium, Xanex, Prozac. None are strangers to me. After my husband and son were killed it was years before I could function without some form of medication. For years my anxiety and I lived a very small life, not leaving the house, each day spent chained to a pillar of guilt and remorse.

Get it together. This is not like that. Fear, not fact.

I take the tablet and scold myself. Indulging in fear and panic is selfish. Poppy needs me. I have no right to escape into a panic attack. Somewhere in this building, my daughter is scared and alone. I have no right.

"I want to see my daughter," I say, finally finding an even tone for my voice. "I'll be fine. Please, just take me to her and tell me what's going on."

The doctor nods and I pull myself up and follow her. We turn left, then right, take an elevator up one floor, and memories of Josh's accident flood my mind. In a hospital just like this one, my family was identified and autopsied. He looked so tiny lying still and silent on the gurney, like his body had contracted around the empty space his soul once took up.

"We have her here in the pediatric wing," the doctor says, interrupting my memory. "We'll keep her here tonight. I'd like to monitor her and run some more tests."

When the elevator doors open, sterile white walls are replaced with lashings of bright color and cartoon animals. Instead of looking cheerful, they strike me as garish.

"But you know what happened?"

"I think so, yes."

I hold my breath and wait for her to elaborate.

"I can't be one hundred percent certain until we do more tests, but your daughter is displaying signs that align with something called Fanconi Anemia."

Oh, thank God.

"Anemia, yes," I gush, instantly relieved. "The woman who helped me get her here, she was a nurse and mentioned something about anemia."

The word anemia feels so benign compared to the atrocities I had been imagining. Lymphoma. Brain tumor. Leukemia.

"Poppy's been to see our local doctor several times though," I tell her. "He never said anything about anemia. But that's good, right? Anemia? I mean, it's treatable."

"I noticed a small scar on her hand," the doctor says, ignoring my questions. "Did she have a birth defect? An extra digit?"

"Yes, an extra thumb but the doctors said it was nothing to be concerned about."

"Mm-hmm."

"You don't agree?"

"Let me run a few more tests. For now, you can go and see your daughter. I'll be back when I have more information."

"But she's going to be alright?"

"For now, she's alright and she's asking for you. I'll update you as soon as I can. She's down the end in bed seven."

As I make my way through the ward, I try not to look at the other children or worried parents hovering over them. Instead, I try to make sense of what the doctor has told me. All I know about anemia is that it has something to do with red blood cells and feeling fatigued which makes sense because Poppy has always been a tired child. Perhaps she'll need supplements, or we'll have to look at her diet, maybe add more red meat. Something about needing iron also rings a bell.

There is a curtain around her bed, and I pause for a moment before pulling it back. I don't want her to see that I've been crying, especially not when a hamburger and some vitamins might be all she needs to get back on her feet.

I force a smile onto my face and push my fears down as deep as they will go. "Hi sweetheart," I chime, as I pull back the curtain and walk toward her tiny shape tucked up in the hospital bed. "How are you feeling?"

She shrugs and yawns, pulling a teddy I've never seen before tighter into her chest.

"Who's your new friend?"

"He's from here," she tells me. "I don't know his name."

I smile and smooth an invisible crease from the sheet that's covering her. "Well, you know what? I bet he'd love it if you gave him a name."

She glances down at the teddy but again just shrugs and looks disinterested. I remind myself they think it's anemia, something that is treatable. Poppy will be okay.

Fear, not fact.

"What's wrong with me, Mommy?"

Her voice is fragile and tiny and yet the impact is powerful enough to tear apart even the hardest of hearts. I swallow and command myself to find a voice that will calm her.

"You, my sweet girl, haven't been taking your vitamins." I give her my best smile and hide my trembling hands where she cannot see them. "And, I think that when the doctor is finished checking on you the first thing we have to do is get you a big hamburger. How does that sound?"

"Can Miss Molly have one too?"

"She sure can," I tell her. "She'll be so happy to see you."

Poppy finally smiles and I tell myself that as soon as they're done I'll take her home and we can fix this. That everything will be alright - because it has to be.

Can't Wait To Find Out What Happens Next?

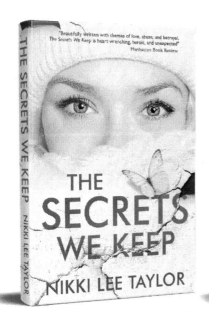 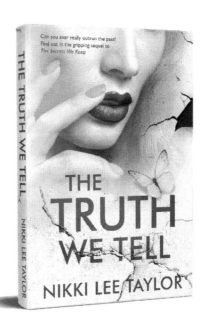

The Truth We Tell is the gripping sequel to
The Secrets We Keep.

Available now from amazon.com

Get your copy now and let the journey continue...

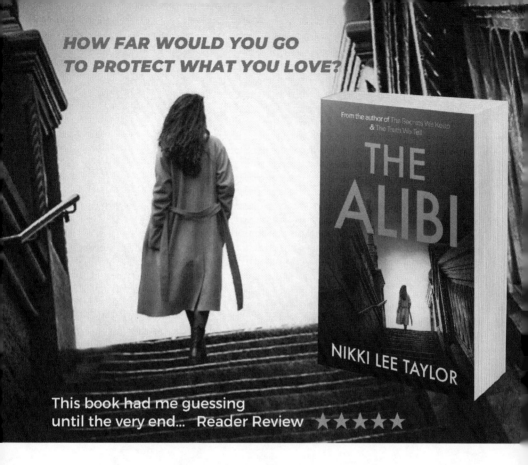

HOW FAR WOULD YOU GO TO PROTECT WHAT YOU LOVE?

From the author of The Secrets We Keep & The Truth We Tell

THE ALIBI

NIKKI LEE TAYLOR

This book had me guessing until the very end... Reader Review ★★★★★

How far would you go to protect what you love?

He's handsome, charming, and the city's beloved Mayor. He's also a cheating husband. But is he a killer?

When a surfer discovers the gruesome remains of council staffer Lauren Ellis in sand dunes just meters from Lord Mayor Andrew Ashley's beach-side home, rumours of his close relationship with the victim quickly begin to circulate.

Andrew's secret affair with local newspaper reporter Elle Nolan is proof he can be an unfaithful husband – but is he also guilty of murder?

As the search for answers continues, Andrew refuses to tell police where he was the night of Lauren's death.

When Andrew reaches out to Elle from police lock-up begging her to provide an alibi for the night in question, she quickly realises that instead of just reporting the story, she's about to become irrevocably entangled in it.

A thought-provoking and page-turning thriller from the author of domestic thriller series The Secrets We Keep and The Truth We Tell that will make you question – how far would I go to save what I love?

Get your FREE BOOK at nikkileetaylor.com

Tell The World!

Loved The Secrets We Keep?

Your opinion matters! Without readers like you, authors like me would never have the privilege of doing the one thing we love most - writing.

If you enjoyed the book please leave a review on **amazon.com** to let other readers know that they might enjoy it too.

It only takes a minute and would mean the world to me.

Thank you!

About the Author

Nikki Lee Taylor is a long-time newspaper journalist turned fiction writer.

She is also a dreamer, a doer, a storyteller, coffee lover, and fur-mum to two golden retrievers Max and Sam.

She loves to write stories about women finding their inner strength and reminds herself every day that what we see as flaws, are really just the cracks that allow our light to shine even brighter.

Let's Stay In Touch

I love to hear from my readers and endeavor to answer all emails personally.

You can reach me at **nikki@nikkileetaylor.com**

- **Website**: nikkileetaylor.com

- **Insta**: @nikki.leetaylor

- **FB:** Nikki Lee Taylor

- **Goodreads**: Nikki Lee Taylor

Nikki Lee Taylor

Made in United States
Orlando, FL
30 August 2023

36527704R00150